KILL TOWN

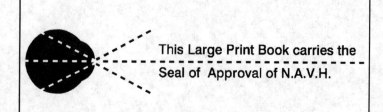

This Large Print Book carries the
Seal of Approval of N.A.V.H.

A CORRIGAN BROTHERS WESTERN

KILL TOWN

COTTON SMITH

THORNDIKE PRESS
A part of Gale, Cengage Learning

GALE
CENGAGE Learning·

ncisco • New York • Waterville, Maine
Mason, Ohio • Chicago

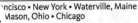

GALE
CENGAGE Learning®

LIBRARY OF CONGRESS CATALOGING-IN-PUBLICATION DATA

Names: Smith, Cotton, author.
Title: Kill town : a Corrigan brothers western / by Cotton Smith.
Description: Large print edition. | Waterville, Maine : Thorndike Press, 2017. |
    Series: Thorndike Press large print western
Identifiers: LCCN 2016049908| ISBN 9781410497093 (hardcover) | ISBN 1410497097
    (hardcover)
Subjects: LCSH: Large type books. | GSAFD: Western stories.
Classification: LCC PS3569.M5167 K55 2017 | DDC 813/.54—dc23
LC record available at https://lccn.loc.gov/2016049908

Published in 2017 by arrangement with Pinnacle Books, an imprint of
Kensington Publishing Corp.

Printed in the United States of America
1 2 3 4 5 6 7 21 20 19 18 17

To Scott F. Smith

ACKNOWLEDGMENTS

Thank you to Sonya, my North Star and my wife. She has kept me on the red road of life. Thank you, too, to my agent, Cherry Weiner, for her fierce and professional attention to detail. And thanks to Gary Goldstein, my editor, for his belief in what I had to say.

CHAPTER ONE

Cassidy County, Texas, sheriff Holt Corrigan adjusted his black string tie in the lopsided mirror that hung over a scratched dresser. He had no idea the Wilkon Bank, the town marshal, and he were about to be attacked while the three Bordner prisoners escaped.

A month ago, the three Corrigan brothers were the only force that stood between the evil Agon Bordner becoming the emperor of Northwest Texas. That seemed like enough. Then.

Holt's hand served as a comb to straighten brown hair laying over his ears. He rubbed his just-shaved chin and brushed his trim mustache. It was important for a peace officer in the county to look right, he felt. The long scar on his right cheek, a reminder of a cavalry battle, had faded into a mark that some said made him more handsome, more mysterious. He was going to wear a black broadcloth suit, new. A gift from his brothers to celebrate his amnesty.

He had been staying in the small sheriff's office-apartment, next to the jail, since federal judge Oscar Pence appointed him Cassidy County's top lawman. It was part of his belated amnesty from the Confederate fighting and alleged crimes afterward. That was just two weeks ago and the whole thing was still a dream.

One minute, he was an outlaw; the next, a lawman.

The judge, like many in the area, was pleased to reward Holt for his help in bringing Agon Bordner and his henchmen to justice, stopping them from taking over Northeast Texas. Not to mention his known heroics during the war itself.

Slipping on his twin shoulder holsters, he checked the loads in each revolver, two Russian Smith & Wesson .44s, laying on the scarred desk. An ivory panther silhouette was inlaid in each black grip, a tribute to his belief in reincarnation and the idea that in one of his lives, he had been a jaguar in South America. The revolvers reminded him of the interview with the Dallas reporter yesterday.

It wasn't the first such story as, seemingly, all of Texas was talking about the outlaw

10

turned lawman. This interview, like the others so far, had been aided considerably by the judge's stern declaration of Holt's innocence and gallantry. Judge Pence linked the accusations to Bordner's gang attempting to frame him and yellow newspaper headlines not checking facts.

To the reporter, Holt had simply said, "I'm very thankful to Judge Pence . . . and honored to serve the county where I grew up."

The reporter wanted to know about Holt's revolvers and he politely showed them, but he didn't explain the symbolism of the handles. Shaking his head, he slid each weapon into place and glanced out the window. The lower right panel was cracked, a long-ago incident. The day was overcast and autumn cool. Up and down the street, false-fronted storefronts looked dark, in spite of people coming and going. Wilkon, the county seat, was welcoming the gray day.

"Going to rain. Too early to snow," he muttered. "Good. That'll knock down the dust. Help the farmers, too."

A few years ago, the county had turned a former tailor shop into the sheriff's office and sleeping quarters. The room contained a bed, a dresser, a desk covered with wanted bulletins and telegrams, and a struggling wood stove. A small closet still contained clothes worn by the late former sheriff. Holt intended to give them away when he got around to it. Bordner and his key henchmen were downed in a fierce fight with the Corrigan brothers, their great friend and mentor, Silka, the former samurai, and help from the Sanchez men.

Three outlaws were arrested, tried, and convicted of murder, coercion, and fraud. They were being held in the town jail for escort to the Huntsville state prison by Rangers who were expected any day.

He heard a freighter rumble down the main street, its trace chains rattling, followed by someone yelling for someone else to get out of the way, then swearing. Holt chuckled.

Unnoticed, Degory Black reined up at the hitching rack outside the bank near the end of the street. A killer of men, women, and children without remorse, he wore a long duster and a wide-brimmed hat. Under his coat were crossed belts holding handguns. With a quick look around, he went into the bank. A minute later, the crazy twins, Dek and Lennie Kinney, rode up to the adjacent hitch rack and swung down. Like Black, they were among the last of Agon Bordner's gang, managing to escape the Rangers' follow-up pursuit. Nonchalantly, they entered the bank.

The townspeople were happy after the removal of the would-be "king" of the region and his reign of evil acquisition of area ranches. However, many were also unsettled by a Confederate outlaw, known to them only from yellow newspaper headlines and saloon talk, becoming the county's top lawman.

Holt eased into his coat. Looking around, he spotted his narrow-brimmed hat laying on the unmade bed and walked over. After running his fingers over the cardinal feather in its band for luck, he put on the hat and tugged on the brim. He planned to check on the new town marshal and his deputy, who were guarding the Bordner men.

Along the crowded main street, two additional armed men of the Bordner gang dismounted on the far side of the thoroughfare. A third rider, blond-haired Chetan Jenson, nonchalantly pulled up to a hitch rack outside the Hammon General Merchandise Store. Two more armed riders rode down the street and dismounted; both were noted for their assassination skills and wanted in Texas and Kansas.

Just before stepping outside, Holt remembered something. Glancing back, he saw the sheriff's badge on the dresser and returned to pin it on his vest. Outside, German Hedrick pulled up alongside Degory Black's horse. A half-breed known only as Pickles, because of his love of them, trotted toward the middle of town and disappeared down an alley. Hedrick quietly waited. Four more former Bordner gang members rode into town from the south and went into the livery.

Unaware of the pending trouble, Sheriff Holt Corrigan stepped from his small office next to the jail and onto the planked sidewalk. Hot coffee would be waiting as usual. Sounds of the day greeted him. An unseen dog barked at something it didn't like. A water pump creaked and groaned before releasing its liquid. A door slammed. Somewhere a woman laughed and a tinny piano tried to brighten the day. A few buildings away, two businessmen were arguing loudly about a delivery of goods.

Seeing a button on the sidewalk, Holt leaned over and picked it up as he continued along. Good luck. He slid the tiny piece into his coat pocket. Only his two brothers, and Silka, knew of Holt's superstitious nature. Hard-faced with light blue eyes and high cheekbones of bronze, the young lawman was an imposing figure, even though he was only average height. In the short-brimmed black hat, Holt was the shortest and second oldest of his brothers, Deed and Blue. Most men who saw him sensed the warrior within, even though he was a rawboned gunfighter, and were intimidated whether they admitted it or not. Many women were drawn to the hidden gentleness.

He passed an older couple obviously uncomfortable being near him. Regardless, his smile was as warm as his greeting, coming with a slight bow as he walked on.

Touching his hat brim as Miss Behesba Miller smiled and stopped to speak with him as they passed, Holt felt his face turning red with her attention.

"Oh, aren't you just excited about next Saturday's big day?" she purred. "All kinds of fun things are planned, you know." Her smile was inviting.

She went on to explain that there was going to be a horse race, a footrace, a dance, a cake contest, a box supper auction, and a much anticipated baseball game between the town's menfolk. There was also the possibility of a spelling bee for young and old. She was particularly interested in the dance and whether or not he was planning on attending.

His response to her engaging questions

were mostly a series of "mmms," "uhs," and "maybes" as he shoved his hands into his coat pockets and alternately stared at the ground and looked into her brown eyes. A boyish grin followed. For a man who had faced all kinds of death, in war and afterward, it was unexpected that he would act so uncomfortable around women. It had always been so, even with Allison Johnson; she had been the aggressor.

Coyly, Behesba dropped her handkerchief and he bent over to retrieve it.

Three shots blistered past where his head had been. The movement saved his life. Behesba screamed and spun to the ground as her blue, wide-brimmed hat fluttered from her head. Instinctively, Holt dove and drew his Smith & Wesson revolver from one of the two shoulder holsters.

His dive carried him behind the support beam holding up the jail front's overhang. It was the only thing keeping him alive at the moment. Cocking the big gun, he fired at the blossoming orange gun blast coming from behind a parked freight wagon across the street. Neither shot was effective.

"Stay down, Miss Miller," he managed to say before more bullets clipped the beam inches above his head.

He thought she was wounded and had

fainted, but couldn't tell for certain. The wood planks under her showed streaks of crimson. There wasn't anything he could do for her at the moment. A light rain began to take over the town as the street emptied quickly; people scattered when the first shots exploded into the quiet morning. The firing was coming from men with rifles, spread out across the street.

Town marshal Micah Foster burst from the jail, shotgun in hand. His deputy, Billy Jorgenson, was a stride behind, levering a Henry.

"Get back, Micah!" Holt yelled.

Bullets slammed the farmer-marshal against the wall. He shuddered and slid down the unpainted surface into a strange heap. The deputy spun sideways, knocked off balance by the marshal's collapse. A bullet caught the deputy's shoulder, but he managed to scramble behind the doorway.

Holt's hat brim wasn't helping stave off the wetness as he squinted for targets. Four more shots spit at him; one creased his lower right leg; another clipped the beam, sending splinters into his cheek. Forcing himself to ignore both, he drew a bead on the legs visible under the wagon and squeezed the trigger. His assailant screamed and stumbled sideways, grabbing for his

17

wounded leg. Holt's second shot spun him around; his third jolted the outlaw backward into an unmoving heap.

He knew who these men were, even though he'd never met them. They had to be part of the old Bordner gang, and they were trying to break out their fellow outlaws. The thought slid through him: where were his brothers? Both were in town. So was Silka.

Firing quickly twice more, he missed the heavyset man firing with a rifle from behind a barrel next to the Blue Dog Saloon. The return fire was intense, but so far the beam was protecting him as he shoved new loads into his gun. The remaining outlaws continued their firing and he kept his head down. If he attempted to dash for the jail door behind him, their gunfire would stop him before he went two steps.

"Let us go, law dog! They'll quit shootin' if'n you drop your gun an' hold up your hands." The suggestion came from one of the jailed outlaws, Rhey Selmon, able to see through the half-opened door from his cell.

"Go to hell. Before they get me, I'll kill all of you bastards."

"So will I," Deputy Jorgenson added.

That quieted the prisoners.

"Blue, Deed, Silka, where the hell are

you?" he mumbled.

As fast as it had come again, the rain decided to go elsewhere, leaving only a gray mist and equally gray day.

Sneaking toward Holt from his left was Pickle, the half-breed in a brand-new Stetson hat with a cocked Henry. He moved silently from alley to alley with the goal of getting close enough to kill Holt.

CHAPTER TWO

Across the street, Deed Corrigan, Holt's younger brother, and Nakashima Silka, who was like a stepfather to all three brothers, were in the general store, buying supplies for the ranch. A former samurai who had emigrated from Japan, Silka had raised Deed, in particular, to fight effectively with any weapon as well as with his hands and feet in classic Japanese style, to understand the importance of timing and leverage. Deed's reputation was at least as great as Holt's.

Deed and Silka reacted in unison as soon as they realized the shots weren't the sounds of a cowboy letting off steam.

"Where you heading?" the storekeeper asked. "What about your supplies? There's a gunfight going on out there, you know."

"We'll be back," Deed said.

He saw the fat outlaw, hiding behind the barrel next to the saloon, as soon as he left the store and headed for him. Two strides away, he yelled and the outlaw turned toward the sound. His eyes opened wide and he swung his rifle toward Deed. The youngest Corrigan flew into the air, cocked his legs, then straightened them, driving his boots into the man's face and throat. The outlaw's head snapped back, and he groaned and fell to the ground. His rifle rattled onto the sidewalk.

Landing on his feet, Deed spun, drew his .44 Remington, and leveled three quick shots at blond-haired Chetan Jenson, who was concentrating his firing at the wounded deputy. Deed's first shot sent splinters from the stack of building materials where Jenson hid. He turned and Deed's second and third shots caught him belly-high. Jenson half-stood, reacting to the impact, and Holt's shot from across the street struck him again. The blond outlaw staggered and fell into the water tank.

From inside the store, hiding behind a shelf of canned goods, a bearded man with big ears and long hair took the corncob pipe from his mouth and growled to no one in particular, "Ain't never seed nothin' like that a'fer." He turned around to a nodding farmer and his wife.

Silka was close behind Deed, drawing a

classic samurai sword carried in a sheath across his back. The short, stocky Japanese man was many years older than the Corrigan boys; he had a graying mustache and hair pulled tight to a tail in back. His clothes were definitely those of a cowboy. Around his waist a wide belt held three sheathed throwing knives. His broad-brimmed hat flew from his head as he ran at the other outlaw concentrating on Holt across the street.

The gravel-faced outlaw heard the rush and turned to meet Silka's charge.

"Aiiie!" Silka yelled, and drove his sword into the outlaw's stomach. The outlaw fired his rifle into the sidewalk and dropped. Silka withdrew his bloody sword and wiped it clean on the dead man's shirt, returned it to its sheath, and picked up the dead man's rifle.

From the store, the grizzled man shook his head. "Damn. Sakes alive. It don't pay to mess with those boys."

Inside the hotel on the same side of the street as the jail, customers in the lobby had ducked under tables and behind chairs to wait out the fight; a few were brave enough to peek through the main window.

Striding from the adjoining restaurant was Blue Corrigan. Holt's older brother by two years stepped into the lobby from a meeting in the restaurant. Blue's coat and chaps showed signs of trail dust. The sleeve of his left arm was pinned against his coat. Yankee artillery fire had blown it off; he was lucky to have survived. His right pocket was jammed with extra cartridges but had room for the small Bible his mother had given him. He always carried it, even during the war, and credited the Scripture with saving his life.

At his hip was a holstered Walch Navy 12-shot revolver with two triggers and two hammers. Weighing two pounds, it was twelve inches long. It was a gun rarely seen in this part of Texas. Blue had taken it from a dead Union officer during the war and decided he liked it, especially since reloading a standard six-shooter wasn't easy one-handed.

Three steps behind Blue came Judge Oscar Pence, the circuit judge for this federal district.

The two were meeting and going over final details of how Bordner's ill-gained ranch holdings and town business would be distributed or sold. In his hand was his usual can for holding tobacco juice. Judge Pence stepped in after the death of Bordner and put up his ill-gained ranch holdings and businesses for return to their proper owners or auction. Taol Sanchez, the oldest son of the patriarch of the Lazy S Ranch, bought two of the smaller ranches Bordner had absconded with. Bordner's largest illegal gain, the Bar 3, was divided between the Corrigan brothers and Jeremy Regan, since it was the boy's family who had owned it originally and been murdered by Bordner's gang. Jeremy was now an adopted member of Blue Corrigan's family. The three Corrigan brothers would run the Bar 3, as well as their own Rafter C spread, until Jeremy was old enough to officially become a co-owner.

The bank, taken by Bordner, was purchased by a combination of the Sanchezes, Corrigans, and Judge Pence. The general store, his other grab, was bought by a family well known in Wilkon. Bordner's mansion in El Paso was put up for auction and a local businessman had bought it.

"What's going on?" Blue asked no one in particular.

A baldheaded businessman with scrawny sideburns, watching from the corner of the window, turned away and said, "Gunfight. A bunch of gunmen are trying to break out those fellas in jail. They've got the sheriff pinned down. Looks like they killed the marshal." It was as if he were describing a town baseball game.

Blue's move to the window was so swift the businessman didn't have time to get out of his way. The baldheaded man stumbled and fell.

"Anybody gonna help your lawman?" Blue barked.

"Not my town. He was an outlaw before anyway."

Blue spun and pushed back past the same man.

"Sir! I demand an apology," the red-faced man said, slamming his fist against the floor.

Blue stopped and looked puzzled, "For what? Calling you a coward?"

"No, you didn't call me a coward, you . . ."

"Guess I just thought it." Blue hurried toward the main door, drawing his massive handgun.

"I hope he makes it," a thin-faced man with sad-dog eyes behind thick glasses uttered as he stared at the street through the lobby window. Wearing an ink-stained coat and shirt, he held a pad of paper in his hand.

"I'm doing a story on him, for the *Wilkon Epitaph,*" Leroy Gillespie announced proudly. The *Epitaph* was the name of the town's new newspaper. Gillespie had come to town two weeks ago with a printing press and was aggressively trying to build interest in his paper.

The newspaper owner and editor glanced at Blue. "The president of the Amarillo Bank said Holt Corrigan wasn't a bank robber. Isn't that something? I read that in the *Amarillo Post.*"

As he left, the man huddled under the next table leaned forward and whispered to the baldheaded businessman. "Don't you know that was Blue Corrigan? He's the sheriff's brother. That fellow across the street, the one who just hammered a man with a flying kick and shot another, that's Deed Corrigan, his other brother. That Oriental with the sword, he's their partner."

"Is that the Deed Corrigan who stopped three bank robbers? With only his hands? In Austin it was. A few years ago?" The reporter asked.

"Yeah, that's him."

The businessman looked like he was going to be sick. Gillespie, the editor, wrote a quick note on his pad, then resumed watching through the window.

Outside, Blue studied the street. The jail was down the way. A rider in a wet slicker rode past, but he was interested only in getting out of the way. Blue's gaze took in the half-breed sneaking toward Holt.

Blue's first shot slammed against the sidewalk in front of the creeping outlaw. It was like him to shoot to stop the action, not kill. Pickles froze, uncertain of where the shot had come from.

Running toward him, Blue growled, "Drop your gun and raise your hands. Or the next bullet hurts. Bad."

The half-breed dropped his rifle as if it were hot, raised his hands, and turned toward Blue.

"I go to help sheriff," Pickles blurted. "He need help."

"Not your kind."

From the bank doorway, Degory Black watched the destruction of most of their plan. German Hedrick, already mounted, held Black's horse for him as the Kinney twins jumped on their horses holding the bank's money. The four men eased around the back of the bank, out of town, smiling. They looked at the sky and hoped it foretold of a downpour coming soon and wiping out their tracks.

Unsure of what had happened, Holt took a deep breath, held it, and looked for an outlaw. He saw none. Only his brothers and Silka. Slowly he stood, holding his revolver at his side. Grinning, he yelled, "Wondered when you boys might join in. Is that the end of it?"

From across the street, Deed yelled back, "Think it is. Are you hurt?"

"No, just wet." Holt ignored the burning crease along his lower leg and wiped his forehead.

Of medium height and build, all three brothers looked much alike, resembling their late mother and father, even down to their once-broken noses, courtesy of each other. Deed was eight years younger than Blue, an inch taller, fifteen pounds heavier, and definitely wilder; he and Holt resembled each other the most in looks and temperament.

Distinctly, the three brothers had elements of their mother's approach to life within them. Deed cared about all things of nature, from snakes to birds to deer, much like that of an Indian. Holt had picked up their mother's fascination with superstition and reincarnation. His first experience in believing he had lived before had occurred during the war. Blue's beliefs were more traditional. In fact, he served the Wilkon church as a part-time minister, along with a townsman, whenever the circuit rider wasn't available.

"Wait! If they were trying to bust out their friends, somebody's probably at the livery, getting extra horses," Blue yelled back.

"You're right, Blue. Watch these bastards, and Silka and I will check it out," Deed hollered, and ran toward the end of town, not waiting for a response.

"What's to watch? Nobody's moving but this fellow," Blue said, pointing to the Indian.

"Put him in the empty cell," Holt said. "Keys are probably in the marshal's pocket. He's dead. Jorgenson's hit. This nice lady was shot, too."

From the doorway, the deputy stammered, "I-I'm gonna be all right. I-I got the keys."

"Miss Miller, are you all right?" Holt went over to Miss Miller and knelt beside her. It didn't look like her wound was serious, but she had lost some blood and had fainted.

She looked up at Holt and stammered, "W-what happened?"

"You were shot, ma'am. Lie still. You've lost some blood." He removed a handkerchief from his pocket and pressed it against the wound on her upper left shoulder. He guessed it was more of a crease than any penetration. There was no way to know without unbuttoning her dress. He wasn't about to do that and said to a townsman venturing from a store, "Get the doctor. There's a lady down."

The townsman frowned and hurried away.

Blue returned from the jail after shoving Pickles into the lone empty cell. "Catch up with Deed and Silka. I'll stay with this woman until Doc comes."

The reporter emerged from the hotel and bounced along the sidewalk, poised beside Holt, and unleashed a barrage of questions, "Mr. Corrigan, were you scared? Was this like the war? Do you know these men? Why do they want to kill you and the town marshal?"

"I'm guessing it's some of Agon Bordner's men." Holt stared at the man, then looked at Blue. "Thanks, little brother." He started after them, limping slightly from the earlier crease on his leg.

Frowning, the reporter started after him. "How does it feel to be a lawman instead of an outlaw?"

Without pausing, Holt snapped, "If I were you, I'd get back inside. Bullets don't care what they hit. This isn't over."

The *Epitaph* editor stopped, pursed his lips, and adjusted his glasses, then walked quickly back inside the hotel.

Holt caught up with Deed and Silka at the building next to the livery with guns readied. They were waiting to see who emerged.

Deed watched him approach. "You're limping. Thought you said you weren't hurt."

"Just a scratch. It's nothing," Holt said, and changed the subject. "Livery door's closed. Jesse would have it wide open by now."

"Looks like we guessed right."

Holt spat on the barrel of his handgun. "For luck."

Deed checked the loads in his Remington .44 revolver. "How many of Bordner's men will be waiting for us?"

"I'd say no more than four," Holt replied. "It could be eight or more, I suppose, but I think if that were the case they would've sent more at the marshal and me." He motioned toward Deed's gun. "Better spit on it, for luck."

The youngest Corrigan hesitated, then spat on the long barrel of his handgun. "Sure. Why not?"

Silka nodded and did the same on the recovered Winchester.

"How many horses would Jesse keep saddled during the day?" Deed asked.

"Oh, no more than four, plus mine and Micah's. They're always saddled and ready."

"They'll need only four," Deed said, "so they're ready and probably waiting for a signal to come out. Let's go in instead."

Pointing with his right-hand gun, Holt said, "Makes sense to me. I'll go around and come in the back door. Give me a minute to get there, if you can."

A brown-and-gray dog with large, floppy ears bounded around the corner, preparing to bark. Holt leaned over and held out his hand for the animal to inspect, then scratched its ears. Deed was surprised at his brother's attention to the animal, but it made sense to keep from warning those inside. Likely, no one paid attention to the dog and it was pleased and surprised to be given that consideration.

"You know that dog?" Deed said in a low voice.

"Seen him around. A stray. Kinda like me, I guess."

"Good boy, be quiet now and stay out of the way," Holt said, and headed for the back of the livery. The dog followed, wagging its tail.

Deed watched his brother and the stray dog, then eased beside the closed livery door, listening for noise inside. Muffled conversation was indistinguishable. He turned to Silka. "Shall we let them know it isn't going to work?"

"Aiie, let us do so."

32

Silka touched a small, Oriental-looking brass circle on a rawhide thong worn around his neck. The Japanese word *Bushido* was engraved on the disk. Deed wore the same disk, only his was connected to a sheathed throwing knife carried under his shirt and down his back. It was a gift from Silka years before.

Leaving Japan when the samurai were forced out, Silka had traveled to Texas, learning English as he went. It was the classic samurai "way of the warrior," *Bushido,* built on honor, inner strength, determination, freedom from the fear of death, and directed action. Now his blades were the only physical remains of his previous way of life.

"Touch *Bushido* . . . for better luck," Silka said. Under his careful training, Deed had become a fierce warrior.

Deed touched the brass circle at his neck, then grabbed the handle of the livery door and yanked one side wide open. After leaving the rifle propped against the building, Silka slipped inside, stepped to the right, and drew his sword. A stray beam of light glanced off the sharp steel. Deed followed, moving to the left. The enclosed building smelled of horses, manure, and hay. There were four outlaws in the livery, each mounted and holding the reins of another readied horse. All of the horses held rifles in scabbards and two canteens.

"That you, Jethrum? Thought you was supposed to holler at us when it was done," a tall outlaw responded, looking into the opened doorway and squinting. "We could've . . ." The closest outlaw half-raised his rifle in response to the sudden door opening.

Silka took a quick step beside the mounted man, slammed the sword down on the man's forearms, then drove the blade into his stomach, ending the outlaw's scream as his arms spurted blood. He collapsed, sliding from the saddle into a strange bloody heap.

"Change of plans, boys. Your friends weren't good enough," Deed snarled. "Unbuckle your iron and climb down."

The redheaded outlaw began to swing down, drawing his holstered gun as he moved. Deed fired twice and the redhead groaned and stumbled onto the livery floor. A lanky outlaw with a narrow, tight face and an eye patch over his left eye reached for the rifle across his saddle.

Holt stopped him with a second challenge. "Want to make it three?"

Beside him, the dog growled.

The man shivered and raised his hands. "Jes' keep that crazy Oriental away from me."

Silka swung his sword above his head and Holt growled, "He's a former samurai. Be careful what you say around him."

"Yes, suh."

"Your turn, boys. How do you want this to go down?" Deed pointed his gun at the lanky outlaw and the other man, a short, fat-bellied man wearing two belted guns.

The two men unbuckled their gun belts and let them slide from their waists to the ground; their rifles followed.

"Who are you?" the outlaw with the eye patch asked.

"We're the ones you came to kill."

Holt looked around. "Where's Jesse? The livery operator."

"Uh, he's in there. Tied up. We didn't hurt him. Honest." He pointed toward the closed tack room.

"We'll be the judge of that."

The dog rejoined Holt, seeking more attention, which he got.

CHAPTER THREE

Minutes later, Jesse Littleson was untied and the Corrigans led the outlaws outside. The two killed outlaws were left where they lay. Wilkon was beginning to believe the shooting was over, and people were appearing all over the main street. Deed, Holt, and Silka directed the two outlaws toward the jail. The dog trotted beside them.

"Think you're going to have to give that dog a name," Deed teased.

"Yeah, maybe so. How about 'Tag-along'? I'll call him 'Tag.' " Holt looked down at the animal. "Tag, what do you say, boy? Do you like Tag?"

The dog wagged its tail.

"There you go." Holt chuckled and scratched the dog's ears.

From down the street came a fat man with a rumpled shirt and wrinkled vest. It was Claude Gausage, the town's undertaker, dentist, and furniture maker. Without slow-ing down, Holt yelled, "There's two more in the livery, Claude. The county'll pay."

"Sure. Is it over?" Gausage asked, pausing.

"Let's hope so," Holt said.

The tall outlaw with the eye patch turned toward him as if to say something, then shook his head and kept walking.

As they crossed the street, two boys ran toward them. "Hi, are you Holt Corrigan . . . and Deed Corrigan?"

Holt smiled. "Guilty. What's up?" He pointed to the dog. "And this is Tag."

"Heard you were once an outlaw . . . an' now you're the sheriff," said the boy with a string of freckles across the bridge of his nose.

"Yes, that's true." Holt glanced at Deed.

Deed pushed the outlaws along and said, "Boys, Holt Corrigan was a hero of the war. He brought in Rhey Selmon . . . alone, too."

"Gosh! My pa says both of you are gunfighters," the dark-haired boy said, shoving his hands into worn pockets.

Holt glanced around the street. "Not us, son. Your father's thinking of someone else, I'm sure. Maybe the James brothers up north. Boys, we've got some work to do. These are bad men. They're going to jail." He smiled. "Say, how come you aren't in school?"

After looking at each other, the taller boy said they were on the way to school when they heard the shooting and came to see what was happening. Deed suggested they should head to school now. The two boys agreed and ran off.

"Think they're going to school?" Holt asked.

"Not a chance."

Silka added something in Japanese. Both outlaws jumped at the sound of his voice.

Inside the jail, Rhey Selmon in his bear-skin coat yelled out as they entered. Holt told the dog to wait outside.

"Looks like you Corrigans had your hands full."

Forced laughter from the other outlaws filled the room. A curse punctuated the response.

Deed stepped next to the cell. "How about I let you out, Selmon? Let's see how tough you really are. I'll even give you the first punch."

From the back of the cell, a badly bruised Sear Georgian warned, "Don't try it, Rhey. He'll tear you apart. I know. Don't."

Selmon backed away from the bars, waving his hands. "Hey, not me, Corrigan. I saw what you did to Georgian."

"Then shut up. I won't ask again."

Selmon eyed him suspiciously. "What are you saying?"

"I'll shoot you. Right where you stand. You bastards have caused too much trouble."

The bear-coated outlaw turned away and sat down on a bunk.

Holt and Silka jammed the two newest outlaws into the cell with Pickles, locked it, and Holt shoved the key into his pocket. Both outlaws avoided looking at Silka.

"Let's check out the town, Deed. I don't see Blue or the judge."

Holt leaned over to pet the stray dog that had followed him from the livery. Deed grinned. Usually it was he who befriended animals. Silka said the animal had become Holt's friend. From down the street, Blue and Judge Pence came running toward them.

"The bastards robbed the bank!" Judge Pence yelled, almost dropping his spit can. He stopped, caught his breath, and spat a thick brown stream into the tin.

"When?" Holt asked, his eyes giving away the weariness of battle.

"While you boys was a'fightin'," Pence growled. "Reckon they got a good head start on ya. Jes' found out a few minutes ago."

Calm as ever, Blue said, "They locked everyone in Lester's office. The judge heard those folks yelling."

The Corrigans knew "Lester" was Lester Shruggs, the new bank president installed by the new ownership. An honest man who had come to Wilkon as part of a railroad surveying team, he had stayed to marry a local farm girl.

All were surprised that Holt's next question was about the wounded woman. "How is . . . Miss Miller?"

Blue smiled. "Uh, Miss Miller is doing well, in spite of her traumatic day." He glanced at Deed, then back to Holt. "She's at the doc's now, resting."

After spitting for emphasis to reinforce his irritation at Holt changing the subject, Pence declared, "They coldcocked Lester jes' to make sure nobody tried gettin' out."

"Is he going to make it?" Deed asked.

Pence rubbed his chin. "Reckon so. Doc says it'll be a while though. Damn sorry, boys. None o' us saw this a'comin'."

Holt returned one of his guns to a shoulder holster. "How many?"

"Four. One stayed outside holding their horses. Rode south," Pence reported.

"Looks like I'm going to have to earn my pay, Judge," Holt said, and shoved his hand into his coat pocket and touched the panther claw there, something he had carried for years. His hand left his pocket and touched something in his right shirt pocket.

"I'll be riding with you, big brother," Deed replied.

"Counted on it."

"There's horses ready in the livery."

"Let's go."

Waving his right arm, Pence declared, "Holt, I've got to insist on havin' Blue . . . an' Silka . . . stay hyar. They'll be the actin' law."

"I'd sure like them with us," Holt said.

"I know'd that. But we don' know if thar's more o' Bordner's gang out thar." Pence waved his hands. "Jes' a'waitin' for you Corrigans to leave." He spat into his can. "Deputy Jorgenson's down. Restin' in the doc's office. I ain't got no choice."

"Sure."

"*Koketsu ni irazunba koji wo ezu,*" Silka spat, hearing Pence's declaration.

The Corrigans knew the samurai's Japanese expression well. Literally, it meant if you don't enter the tiger's cave, you won't catch its cub. Basically, it meant nothing can be achieved without risk.

"I don't like it, either, Silka," Blue said, "but it makes sense. We don't know if there

41

are more of Bordner's men. I'd rather be riding with my brothers, but we can't leave the town unprotected."

Silka's response was another Japanese curse.

"I'll get the horses, Holt. Get some grub . . . and a coffeepot," Deed said, and started down the sidewalk toward the livery.

"Make sure you bring Buck." Holt referred to his favorite horse, a buckskin that could travel day and night without tiring. "And plenty of grain and canteens." He turned to Pence. "Judge, better wire all the surrounding towns. We might get lucky. Anyway, we don't want our neighbors surprised."

"Consider 'er dun."

Men came running from all parts of town as news of the bank robbery flew through Wilkon. Two businessmen told Holt that he had to get the money back, that it was all they had. He reminded them that the Corrigans, Judge Pence, and the Sanchezes owned the bank and that their money had been stolen as well.

"We'll get our money back, all of it," Holt snapped. "Anybody who wants to ride with us is welcome. But it'll be hard. Plan on being gone several days. They've got a good lead on us."

"You can take anybody else with ya that ya want," Judge Pence declared, then spat a long stream of tobacco. "Gotta tell ya sumthin' else. Achak is a-raidin' through thar. He's leadin' a mean bunch o' Comanche. Jes' came over the wire from the army. They're after him now."

Achak, or Spirit, was a well-known and feared Comanche war chief. Fierce and mean, he was known for cutting out the tongues of the men he murdered and making a necklace of them. He had escaped from the reservation with a band of twenty-five or so warriors. The very mention of his name stopped most of the interest in joining the posse.

The judge spat into his can and declared that Saturday's big day would be postponed until the posse returned with the bank money, giving the town something extra to celebrate. No one argued.

From the hotel came a familiar sight. James Hannah strode toward them, wobbling slightly. His shoulder was tightly bandaged and his Victorian black suit coat was draped over that shoulder. In his hand was his silver-plated revolver. His bowler hat was askew. He was pale and had lost weight, but there was a determination in his walk.

"How come you boys didn't tell me there was a gunfight going on?" Hannah said.

"You shouldn't be out of bed, James," Holt said.

Blue headed toward the known gunman who had befriended them during the battle with Agon Bordner and his men and been seriously wounded.

"Don't tell me what I can and can't do," Hannah snapped, shoving his gun into his waistband and pushing his glasses back on his nose.

"Please, James, you've done plenty." Blue took Hannah by his good arm. "Where's Rebecca?"

"She's asleep. I heard the shooting and figured you might need another gun."

Hannah looked around at the small gathering. Not far away was Silka, obviously sulking. "Where's Deed? What's with Silka?"

Blue told him.

"Look. Let Silka ride with Deed and Holt. I'll stay with you," Hannah said. "I can't ride yet . . . but I can sure shoot. How about it, me for Silka?"

Turning to the judge, who was spitting into his can, Blue shrugged his shoulders. "Hannah gives us another gun. A damn good one, even if he is hurt. What do you think?"

"Wal, yah. Sure." Pence spat for emphasis.

Silka was already hurrying for the livery. The judge chuckled. Hannah headed for the jail, not wanting to let anyone know how weak he was.

From the general store, the grizzled old-timer who had commented on the brothers' shooting earlier came up and insisted on going. He said he was Mason Mereford and the brother of Alexander Mereford, dead owner of the small M-5 ranch, another of Bordner's victims. He lived in El Paso so no one knew him in Wilkon.

"When I did come to town, I stayed out at the ranch with my brother. Didn't see anybody. Didn't need to," Mason said. "I just come to town now to see justice done. I wanna go with you all."

The *Wilkon Epitaph* editor asked to ride with them, but when he was told where the ride would go and that Achak was killing in the area, he decided to wait for a report.

Two other townsmen volunteered to go along, in spite of the warning about the Comanche war chief. Judge Pence advised Jesse that the livery would be compensated for their rental or loss. Wearing a belt gun over his coat, Malcolm Rose owned the dry goods and clothing store and had served with the Union during the war. No one saw

45

him pack two whiskey bottles into his saddlebags and slip a full flask inside his coat.

The other townsman, Ira McDugal, was a clerk at the general store and had a tendency to sneeze when he was outside for any length of time. He was stocky with a pronounced belly. His fat jowls jiggled when he was in the saddle and he hated the whole idea of this pursuit, but he felt it was his duty. The buttons on his vest looked like they could give up their task at any time, especially when he sneezed, which was often. Across his saddle was a Colt revolving shotgun, a nasty weapon at close range but inclined to jam.

Each man carried a sack of food for a week and two canteens; in addition, the posse would take two packhorses. The two townsmen were given the responsibility of leading the packhorses. Deed Corrigan's buckboard was driven to the livery and left for their return. The dog Holt had befriended came up to him as he was preparing to leave and Holt gave him a piece of jerky from his food sack.

As they were moving out, Blue came over to his brothers. "Grant me this favor, my brothers. Bow your heads a moment as we, together, ask God to watch over you and bring you back safely."

"Amen," Holt and Deed said together, and Holt added, "And with the money."

After Blue's benediction, they shook hands, Holt told the dog to stay with Blue, and the posse galloped out of town. The trail of the bank robbers was clear. They were definitely more interested in distance than misdirection. Overhead, the sky was bubbling with ominous clouds that threatened more rain. A heavy downpour would wipe out their trail, and Holt wondered if the outlaws were counting on it.

The land lay wide and open before them. They rode without talking, rifles across their saddles. Trees began to thin out as the ground turned to mostly sand, and the birds in them chattered angrily at the interruption. Shallow inclines looked empty until they rode close. A band of outlaws, or a war party of Comanche or Apache, could hide in any one of them. All of the men rode tensely after that, looking for something that moved.

They rode alongside an uneven, but determined, creek that curved around bunched hills and kept a small grassy meadow from stretching too far. Three steers grazed; one raised its head to the riders as they passed. The only sounds were the occasional rattle of a spur, the crack of a saddle, or a sneeze. The outlaw horses had skirted the stream and kept moving fast. Deed looked at Holt somewhat surprised; Holt shrugged his shoulders.

Puffing on his pipe, the grizzled man, who answered to Mason, looked up at the sky and said, "I reckon that rain's gonna slide ri't over us. Probably hit north o' hyar."

Deed agreed. "Maybe it'll get to our place. We could use it."

"Yeah, the sky's clearing. See?" The square-jawed and rail-thin Malcolm Rose pointed. His large Adam's apple bobbed with the declaration.

"Yeah. That's good for us. Bad for those boys ahead of us," Deed said without looking at Rose.

"Yeah. Makes sense," Rose responded. "How far ahead do you think they are?"

"Hard to say. These tracks are fresh. They couldn't be more than an hour before us."

"You think we'll be home by tomorrow?" McDugal asked, trying to act nonchalant about his question. He stifled a sneeze by pinching his nose.

"No, unless they turn back to try to ambush us," Holt replied, and shifted in his saddle. His leg wound was bothering him, but he refused to acknowledge the pain.

"By the looks o' them tracks, they's more interested in gettin' away. May not ketch 'em," Mason growled. He hit his pipe against his leg, refilled, and lit it again.

McDugal sneezed and Rose blessed him.

CHAPTER FOUR

At Holt's insistence, the posse kept to low ground as much as possible. No one expected the outlaws to stop, but assumption could get them killed.

A jackrabbit popped out of a thin brush and all six men grabbed their rifles.

Deed smiled. "We'd have nailed that boy."

"Or scared the hell out of him." Holt touched the cardinal feather in his hatband. "I think Achak's a bit bigger than that." He chuckled, but no one else did.

A long hour passed, riding through clumps of yucca, mesquite, ocotillo, and prickly pear, among sparse clumps of grass. It was land no one wanted or lived on, except Comanche or Apache. They passed a thicket of juniper bordering a long wash, alert for a possible ambush.

"Let's water our horses up ahead. This creek runs out somewhere along here. Swells into a pond, sort of," Deed said, motioning to the south.

"Good idea," Holt said.

Silka answered in Japanese and smiled a lopsided sort of smile. *"Neko ni katsuobushi."*

Both Corrigan brothers knew the expression meant a cat can't resist stealing your fish, but the bigger meaning was that this was a situation where one cannot let his guard down.

"Agreed, Silka. We'll take turns watering," Holt said.

"That is most good."

"Sounds good to me, too," Mason said. "Whar do you boys think they're headed?"

Holt frowned. "Been thinking about that. They could cut east for the fort. Or head south to Amarillo. Or they could even head for Hammonds, I guess."

"They might spin west and head for New Mexico," Deed added. "That's where Bordner and most of his men came from."

"So, bottom line, we don't know. We'll know when their trail tells us," Holt said.

McDugal sneezed and wiped his nose.

Conversation died as each man contemplated the robbers' options. The end of the creek would provide a solid place to rest their horses. It appeared the outlaws had stopped there earlier.

Deed turned in his saddle. "There's some-

51

thing trailing us. Been following us since town, I think." He laughed. "Well, I'll be damned. It's Tag. It's your dog from the livery, Holt." He took off his hat and held it over his forehead to block out the sun. "Looks like he's adopted you."

"That's crazy," Holt said. "There's no way he can make it out here."

"Coyotes do pretty well." Deed was smiling. "It's all right, Holt. You can figure it's good luck."

"Let's kept riding," Holt said. "Maybe he'll turn back."

"Your decision, Holt. But I think he's planning on joining you."

The dog caught up with them at the creek's bend, his tail wagging and his tongue hanging out. The pond was definitely the end of the creek, at least above ground. A few scraggly cottonwood, ash, willow, and buckthorn were doing their best to surround the water. A Joshua tree stood alone on the south side. An overhanging rock was tilted just enough to let gravel slide into the otherwise clear pool. It wasn't deep.

"What am I going to do with you, Tag?" Holt said, and went over to the panting animal.

Happily, the dog greeted Holt and he sat beside the small animal, ignoring the men.

He rubbed the dog's back and checked its paws for problems. Behind the two, the horses were led to the stream, two at a time. Silka and Deed took turns watching the empty prairie around them. After the horses drank, the six men and the dog also took turns and drank the pool almost dry. McDugal wiped his eyes with his handkerchief and sneezed several times. Rose blessed him each time, then took a long drink from his flask and quickly put it away inside his coat.

Deed mounted first and walked his horse away from the creek bed and over a slight rise. He reined up and studied the broken land ahead of them. It was mostly prairie, marked only with a few tumbleweeds interested in going somewhere else, rocks, and strong-willed plants. He hoped to see dust in the distance that would indicate riders, in spite of the earlier light rain, but saw nothing.

"Wonder where they're headed," he said to himself, and pulled field glasses from his saddlebags. "There isn't any water until . . . Turkey Wing. That's got to be it."

Riding up beside him, Holt looked out across the same desolate terrain. The dog rested on Holt's saddle in front of him.

"It'll be just about nightfall before we reach Turkey Wing. No water before then that I know of," Deed said. "Figure they're headed there. Agree?"

"Makes sense to me. We'd better keep a sharp eye out, though. Plenty of places to hide and ambush us. Outlaw or Comanche."

"Yeah. Picked up a passenger, I see," Deed said.

"Couldn't just leave him."

"I know you couldn't."

"Would you have?"

"You know I wouldn't. Carrying him is smart. Won't slow us down, waiting for him to catch up." Deed grinned and loped away.

They passed a dry lake that once had been the goal of the earlier stream. The outlaws had crossed it, but one rider had peeled back as if to scout their back trail, then rejoined the gang. A few feet from the lake's now dry shore were two long spoon-like indentations that had once been buffalo wallows.

"Think he spotted us?" Deed asked, assuming the others read the sign as well as he had.

"Naw," Mason answered. "Too far."

"Better figure he did," Holt countered. "There's no way we can't be sending up some dust."

Mason clamped down on his pipe but said nothing more. McDugal sneezed; his eyes were red. Overhead, a buzzard flew looping circles in the graying sky, looking for supper. They crossed over a low hill and startled two small deer.

"How 'bout we get ourselves some supper?" Mason said, and raised his rifle.

"Can't risk it." Holt waved his hand. "A gunshot'll carry a long way out here."

"I think yur a mite jumpy, Sheriff," Mason said, lowering his rifle. "They ain't nowhar close."

"Maybe. But still no shooting."

They rode past a shoulder-high fish-shaped stone surrounded by mesquite and long grass. There weren't any other huge stones in the area. The stone was larger than a man on horseback, and it looked like God had decided he didn't want to mess with it any longer. Holt studied the formation as they went by and decided it was a sign of good luck. The fish shape was the sign that the early Christians used. He looked over at Deed, but his brother was watching the fading landscape.

Holt patted the dog in front of him and Tag licked his hand. His Winchester was propped between his thighs and the dog. He wouldn't be able to bring it up as quickly as the others, but he wasn't about to make Tag walk. The dog was clearly worn out from catching up. Holt didn't want to admit he was pleased to have the animal along, but he didn't intend it to slow them down, either.

The clouds pushed on without relieving themselves of rain, and only a bitterly hot sky remained. The afternoon dragged with only the sign of horses' hooves to guide them and the only sounds, saddles creaking and McDugal's sneezing.

The last streaks of a dying red sun were upon them as they closed in on the rocky area known as Turkey Wing. It was another odd-shaped sandstone configuration that someone years ago thought looked like a turkey wing, only huge, and the name had stuck. Below the signature boulder was a deep crease that cut through the entire rock structure, creating a jagged opening at its base.

In front of the crack was a large rock basin that usually held water trickling from an underground spring. Around the basin itself were several other pockets in the rocks that often held rainwater. Turkey Wing was known to savvy travelers and used by them, except for Indians. They believed the area was haunted and didn't come near. That idea was strangely comforting, at least at the thought no Indian would be around.

Not far from the rock formation was a painted buffalo skull with a tied eagle feather blowing in the wind. Brush and tumbleweeds surrounded the skull, and two stunted oaks and a lone cottonwood stood on its south side. Holt guessed it was a tribute to the spirits that the Indians thought lived there. A huge cottonwood had fallen years before; its roots praying toward the sky.

Both horses and men were weary, thirsty, and hungry; the horses smelled water and wanted to advance. It was possible the outlaws could still be at the watering hole, waiting for the posse, and Deed told them to hold back.

"Likely spot for an ambush," Holt said, and eased his rifle from beside the dog.

"You boys stay here," Deed said. "I'll ride close and see what's going on."

"I'll go wi' ya," Mason declared.

McDugal sneezed and the men stared at him. Rose blessed him.

"Sorry, I can't help it," the stout clerk said.

"Well, keep your handkerchief handy," Deed advised.

Deed and Mason pushed their tired horses into a gallop.

Fifteen minutes later, Deed returned. "They've been here and rode on. No one's around now."

"Where's Mason?" Holt asked.

"He stayed behind to start a fire."

"A fire? You think that's a good idea?"

The clothing store owner rode beside them. "Coffee would sure taste good."

"Mason said he was going to build it down in a gully. Wouldn't be seen," Deed added. "It'll be all right. We're going to have to stop for the night. Can't see much even now."

"Can you tell where they're headed?" Holt asked.

"It looks like they split up. Two headed south and two west. We'll know for sure in the morning," Deed said. "I can't track at night, can you?"

"Not worth a damn," Holt answered, and looked at the former samurai. "Silka, can you track at night?"

"Only with very bright moon. Not so this night."

"All right. We'll camp here," Holt said, remembering he hadn't eaten all day.

They rode into the Turkey Wing area, keeping their horses away from the water until they cooled down. Shadows lying across the rocks created all kinds of strange-looking shapes. A batch of windblown willows struggled to keep watch in a narrow hollow that offered some grass. A few hardy catclaw, Spanish dagger, and Apache plume grew among the cracks in the rock.

Mason's fire was burning higher than either Corrigan thought was smart, but the old-timer said some of the dry wood surprised him at how hot it was burning.

Gradually, the horses were unsaddled, rubbed down, and watered, then tied to a rope stretched between the cottonwoods. Each horse was tied to the main rope with a lead line that allowed grazing. Deed and Silka checked the horses' hooves to make certain none were carrying lodged rocks.

From the tracks around the rocks, it was clear many animals depended on the source for the precious water. Deed and Holt walked the outlaws' trail leading away from Turkey Wing. Tag jogged along, refreshed by the water. It was getting dark quickly and the posse could soon only see a few feet ahead.

"See? They split up. At least that's what it looks like," Deed said, pointing at the ground.

"Yeah. We'll do the same in the morning. Three and three."

"Have to," Deed responded, staring off into the black. A timid star had climbed into the night sky, leading the way for others.

Holt leaned over to pet the dog. "How far

ahead are they?"

"If they kept running, I'd say we haven't gained any on them. Haven't lost any, either."

"You think they know somebody's after them?"

"I wouldn't bet against it."

They heard McDugal sneeze and chuckled. Rose's blessing was a hiccup behind.

"Give him credit. He's not used to this. Probably has some kind of reaction to the desert," Holt said.

"He's a good, steady hand. So is Rose."

"Yeah, good men."

Deed stood looking toward their camp. "Wind's coming up. Feels good."

"Yeah, nothing's close that shouldn't be. Night sounds are all around us."

They strolled back to camp; walking was hard on Holt's leg but he managed. Coffee smelled good, so did the frying bacon. It had been a long, hard day for all of them. Holt noticed the fire was crackling with occasional blue flames. To him, that meant spirits were near. He wondered why the Indians thought the area was haunted. The idea bothered him, but he said nothing.

After they finished eating, Deed suggested they pull away from the fire to sleep and keep spread out. The fire would be allowed to die. He would take the first watch, Silka the second, and Holt the third.

"You think they'll jump us . . . tonight?" Rose asked.

Mason snorted and continued cleaning the dishes with sand. McDugal washed his face and eyes and kept his handkerchief close at hand.

"It's a smart idea to think so," Holt said, and moved toward a dark place away from the others. He heard McDugal's muffled sneeze and Rose's quiet blessing. It had become an almost comical routine.

A light wind continued to push across the land as the men settled into their blankets. Deed took a position near where the horses were tied. He liked the smell of the land and truly felt alive when he was out like this. Mother Earth was relaxed and, everywhere, the night sounds were comforting. From here, he could see in all directions. All of the horses were munching grain from their bags.

Suddenly, a shrill moan cut through the darkness and all six men were startled by the haunting cry. Tag growled but stayed near Holt.

"What the hell was that?" Mason was on his feet, still dressed, with his Sharps carbine in hand.

"It's coming from over there." Deed pointed toward the crease. "Must be the way the wind cuts through."

"A-are you sure?" Ira McDugal said, sitting up and holding his blanket against his chest. "Maybe it's Achak. Doesn't his name mean 'spirit'?"

Silka walked over to the opening and listened. He looked up. "Aiie, wind talks through here. Is nothing." He returned to his blanket and pulled a shirt from his saddlebags. After rolling up the shirt, he walked over and stuffed it inside the crease, covering most of the opening, and said something in Japanese. He returned to his blanket and was asleep in minutes. From his bedroll, Rose took a drink, then another, from his flask.

Holt went to sleep, too, comforted by knowing why Indians thought Turkey Wing was haunted. He kept his guns close under his blanket. His dreams were wild, glimpses of his previous lives, he thought. Before being asked, he woke up and saw Silka standing guard by their horses. Holt stood, strapped on his shoulder holster rig, picked up his rifle, and went over to the former samurai.

"Is quiet," Silka said. "No more wind talking." His grin was unexpected.

"Get some sleep."

Silka said, *"Dou itashi mashite."* It was Japanese for "You're welcome."

False dawn was an hour away, but all six men were up. The moaning had stopped, but worry about what lay ahead keep them from sleeping well. Mason had already rebuilt the fire. Too high again.

This time, Deed challenged him. "Mason, are you trying to warn them? What the hell are you doing with a fire like that?"

Mason frowned, shrugged his shoulders. "Sorry. I was cold. Didn't figure it'd matter." He avoided looking at Deed.

"You're going to get us all killed with stunts like that," Deed growled, and walked away. "Comanche can see a big fire forever."

Holt strolled over from the horses, wiping clean one of his shoulder-holstered guns. When he looked up, there was a hole in the middle of the fire. A sign of death. He shivered and kicked at the wood to eliminate the gap and walked on, ignoring Mason.

After a quick breakfast of cold biscuits, jerky, and coffee, they saddled up. Holt rode out first with Tag trotting beside him. If any of the posse were uncomfortable having a dog along, no one said anything. Just outside of Turkey Wing, the outlaw tracks separated as the Corrigan brothers had thought. Even

63

in the faint light of early dawn, the separation was clear. Deed, Silka, and Rose took the trail of two men leading south; Holt, Mason, and McDugal followed the other two riding west. Separating made all of them uneasy, but it was the only thing that made sense.

Quick good-byes and the two groups loped away, each with a packhorse. The outlaw tracks were easy enough to read even at first light. The bank robbers were keeping to a fast pace. The day promised a fierce, yellow sky. It would be hot, very hot, in spite of being late autumn.

Holt drew one of his shoulder-holstered revolvers and shoved it into his waistband for quicker access. His rifle was draped over his saddle as usual. He, Mason, and McDugal rode steadily for a mile, then eased their horses into a walk. Tag moved along without a problem. The other set of posse-men were long out of sight.

"We'll stop by those rocks and give our horses some of our canteen water," Holt said. It wasn't a suggestion.

McDugal sneezed into his handkerchief. "Is there any water close by?" he asked, wiping his nose.

"Not till we're into those hills." Holt pointed. "We'll be there tonight."

"When do you think we'll catch up with them?" McDugal asked, looking around at the desolate land.

Mason squinted. "They'll be ridin' for Hammonds. Hell bent. Sure 'nuff. They ain't worryin' 'bout us none."

Holt didn't respond and changed the subject. He asked Mason how his brother got so good with a rope, one of the quickest he'd ever seen. The older man chuckled and said Alexander was always a good roper, best in the family. Holt smiled and nodded.

They reined up at the cluster of rocks. Mason pulled his horse about ten feet to the left of Holt. The fat clerk was about the same distance on Mason's left.

"Reckon this is as far as ya go, Corrigan." Mason's voice was hard. In his hands was his Sharps carbine. He didn't expect what happened next.

Instead of turning to talk or ask why, Holt stretched along the side of his horse, away from Mason. He drew his revolver from his waistband as he moved and fired under his horse's neck in one smooth motion.

Mason's Sharps roared where Holt had been, but the sheriff's first shot hit Mason in the stomach and his second ripped into the man's throat. Mason's carbine banged against his horse and clattered on the ground. Mason was shoved sideways by the blasts and fell off his horse. He groaned and was still.

Holt straightened in the saddle and studied the unmoving body.

"What was that?" McDugal said, gripping his Colt revolving shotgun with both hands.

"That was a Bordner man set up to kill us if we got too close." Holt shoved new cartridges from his coat pocket into his gun and returned it to his waistband. "I was worried about his big fires and telling us not to worry about the gang being close by."

"I didn't realize Alexander Mereford was good with a rope," McDugal said, still staring at the body.

"He wasn't. Worst I've ever known. My brothers and I used to wonder how he ever caught any of his cattle for branding."

"So you knew."

"I did then. For sure, he was not Mereford's brother," Holt said. "Let's water our horses and get out of here. Got a feeling we're getting close."

McDugal sneezed.

They left Mason's body where it was, stripping it of his guns and ammunition. McDugal led his horse and they rode on. The sun was halfway to noon and everywhere the land looked flat.

Crack! Crack! Crack! Crack!

Gunfire bloomed from an area ahead of them. McDugal stiffened and fell. Holt dove from his horse, drawing his revolver.

CHAPTER FIVE

A cruel sun sucked at Holt Corrigan. Not far was the unmoving corpse of Ira McDugal and the dead horses.

The barrel of Holt's Winchester was too hot to touch as he wiped the bleariness from his eyes and stood. He was convinced the outlaws had left after their attempted ambush had failed. At least, with him.

"Guess they figure I'm a dead man too," Holt muttered to himself. His voice was gritty with sadness as he squinted at the dead horses against the harsh glare of the day. "Too bad my rock medicine wasn't protecting you, too, Ira."

Only the wind answered.

He moved easily, belying the weariness that ate at his soul. His tired face, accented by a trim mustache, showed signs of lack of sleep. Holt's vest pockets were jammed with bullets, an old silver watch and chain, his panther claw, and an uneaten piece of hard candy. In his shirt pocket was his sheriff's badge, which he rarely wore except in town for official matters.

Also there, in his other shirt pocket, was his personal sacred medicine, a small red rock with a white star-like spot in its center. The rock, as a spiritual support, was one he adopted from the very Indians he had fought. He credited its special medicine with getting him through some tough times. No one knew that, though. Not even his two brothers. He was certain the stone was actually something that belonged to him in another life when he, too, was an Indian. The stone had waited for him to find it again.

Holt took another step away from the three dead horses, not wanting to see the oozing bullet holes in the once sturdy buckskin or the dead townsman. One bullet had torn through one of his two canteens; the other canteen had been saved. Instinctively, he reached into his pocket and touched the medicine stone. From his saddlebags, he took a long strip of rawhide and tied it on his carbine as a sling. After lifting his saddlebags, both canteens, and his carbine, he walked away. He had been lucky; only his hat had been hit. The bullet hole through the now misshapen crown was pronounced.

There was no need for his long coat, tied to the back of his saddle, and he didn't want to carry the wool blanket tied there, either. He took off his suit coat and tied it around his waist, not willing to leave the new garment behind. His shoulder-holstered revolvers were heavy but comfortable from wearing the rig for several years.

The sun was pounding against his tired shoulders as he walked toward the broken rock bench, laced with wild cactus and mesquite. Gray sage dotted the cruel land along with an occasional juniper. The outlaws had laid in wait for them a long time. He cursed himself for not being more careful, but it wasn't a likely place for an ambush. Or he hadn't thought so. A man could see for miles across the hot, barren land. Or so he thought.

After another step from the rocks, his anger took hold. He spun back toward his dead horse and fired his revolver four times, shooting from his hip. Three vultures, resting on McDugal's lifeless body and the dead animals, flopped and fell over. The fourth flew away, screaming.

"Not today, you bastards. Not while I'm here."

It wouldn't keep vultures and coyotes

away long, but the shooting made him feel a little better, a little less guilty. After reloading his revolver and returning it to his waistband, Holt continued to climb over the uneven ridge and found one of the outlaws spread, facedown, against the rocks. His earlier shooting in response to the ambush had killed him. Blood on the rocks had dried and turned an odd shade of brown on the stony surface. Not far away were more spots of dried blood. Maybe he had wounded the other man as well, but not enough to keep the outlaw from stripping the dead man of his weapons and escaping with the extra horse.

It appeared the outlaw had changed directions and was now headed south, toward the nearest town. Hammonds, Texas, was a sturdy settlement of farmers, miners, and small ranchers. It probably meant he intended to catch up with the other two there.

Holt was in trouble and knew it. That's why stealing a man's horse was a hanging offense in most of the West. To leave a man afoot usually meant he would perish in the vast lands. He resettled the saddlebags over his shoulder as well as the two canteens, even the one with the hole in it — though luckily toward the top so it still held some water. He slid his rifle sling on the other shoulder and headed south. After a few strides, he paused beside an old mesquite tree that looked like it could tell many stories. He put two fingers in his mouth and whistled shrilly.

As if appearing from within the gray land, a gray-and-brown dog trotted into view.

"How are you, boy? Did they hit you, Tag?" He knelt, laying his carried items on the ground, and petted the ugly dog, checking the animal's body for any wounds. Half the time, the dog had ridden in the saddle in front of him. Now the animal would have to walk.

"They got Buck, you know. So we're going to have to walk. Want some water?"

Taking the bullet-holed canteen, Holt pulled a tin pan from his saddlebags and poured a small amount of the tepid liquid still remaining, using one of the holes for the pouring. Tag lapped up the water gratefully. When the ambush began, he had ordered the dog to run. Staying close to him would have only brought stray bullets.

"We'll have to watch our water close. Got a long way to go."

He stood and adjusted his gear, then touched the cardinal feather in his hat again for luck. The only thing he had going for him right now, besides a strong constitution, was his knowledge of the land. He and his brothers had covered this part of Texas often. Riding through here certainly wasn't his choosing, but it was the fastest way between towns, if a man had a good horse, a full canteen, and knew where he was going. Now he was afoot and in a parched land, inhabited by scorpions, rattlesnakes — and Achak's band. Scattered war parties of Kiowa were also known to ride through here, too. Most of the Indians were on reservations now, or were supposed to be. It was the bad ones that weren't.

Water was the key. As it always was. Certain water holes were well known and well used, like Turkey Wing. Others were rarely used, except by animals, birds — and, of course, Indians. For a moment, he considered hiking back to Turkey Wing, but it would be a false security without a horse. He was better off headed south. That's where the outlaws went. And the bank's money.

"Come on, Tag. We've got to get to that little spring up ahead. It's in a box canyon, but you'll like it there."

He tried to smile, then touched the sacred stone in his pocket and asked the spirits of the land to help him. His own way of praying.

Adjusting his rifle sling, canteens, and saddlebags over his shoulders, he started out with Tag trotting beside him. If they could get to the tiny spring by nightfall, they could eat, rest a little, and then move on. From there, he planned to walk at night, when it was cooler, and sleep during the day when it was too hot to go anywhere. Finding a resting place that was defendable was crucial. If there were any Comanche in the area, they would soon pick up his trail and try to run him down. Just for fun. But there was nothing he could do about that.

Off in the distance were grayish cliffs; they must get there by nightfall. Water was there and, hopefully, no war party.

CHAPTER SIX

Before long, his leg wound began reminding him of its presence. His large Mexican spurs dragged in the soft, hot earth; there was no reason to attempt hiding his trail. It couldn't be done. Not enough to fool an Indian anyway. If Comanche came before he reached the spring, he would die, but die fighting.

Maybe that was the best way for a man like him to go. If he died, Judge Pence would miss him for a while, until he found someone else stupid enough to take the job of sheriff.

Of course, Silka would mourn and so would his brothers. But there was no wife. No children. Not yet anyway.

His eyes took in the searing horizon. There was no sign of a ride in any direction. Obviously the outlaws figured he would die trying to walk out. Or thought he was badly wounded and couldn't. He hadn't tried shooting back for at least an hour after they rode away. They might have taken that as an indication of his inability to move.

After an hour of walking, he sat down, cross-legged. Tag came over to nuzzle his unshaved face. They shared several pieces of jerky from Holt's saddlebags and water from the good canteen. He took a look through his saddlebags to see what they still contained. Overhead a buzzard patrolled the yellow sky.

"Maybe I've got a horse hidden in here, Tag," Holt said with a wolfish grin.

More jerky was kept in a wrapped cloth. There was a potato, an extra shirt, a small sack of coffee, a tin cup and plate, a small skillet, a handful of wild onions, and another of Indian root. A few corn dodgers were gathered among the onions. A jar of medicine salve, secured from a Navajo shaman, sat at the bottom of one bag.

A book of Tennyson's poems with several pages loose nestled beside the jar. His old war field glasses were there, along with a small fire-starting kit of tinder and matches. And a sack of grain for his horse and a can of peaches. So was a thick roll of buckskin and rawhide strings. And a small sack of shredded tobacco for leaving tributes to the spirits. Something else he had picked up from Indians.

There was enough food for three days. Four, if he was extra careful. Water was the key. It always was out here.

Taking off his hat, Holt wiped his sweating brow with his shirtsleeve, ran his finger through the bullet hole, and returned his hat to his head. His lips were parched and cracking; his tongue across them brought only momentary relief.

"Better get going again, Tag. You game?" He started and looked down again. "I'm sorry, little friend. You didn't bargain on this."

Tag responded silently and began to walk beside the young lawman. A rattlesnake slithered across their trail four feet ahead. Holt's decision was as quick as his gun. His revolver fired and the snake's head blew into pieces. Tag was too tired to check it out.

"Dinner for us tonight, my friend."

He shoved the reptile's body into his saddlebags and continued. The shot would be heard a long way, but he felt the risk was worth it. After two hours, he realized the dog was lagging far behind. Turning around, he retreated until he reached the unmoving Tag and lifted the worn-out animal into his arms. It wasn't easy handling the saddlebags, rifle and two canteens, and the sturdy dog, but he knew this had to be done. He'd lost two friends this day in Ira McDugal and his horse, Buck, and he didn't intend to lose another. He trudged on, unthinking, unfeeling, and uncaring.

Where were Deed and Silka? Did they run into an ambush, too? It was foolish to think they might come looking for him. They would assume he and the others were all right, if they thought of him and the others at all. Maybe they would be rejoined in Hammonds, if he could get there.

The gray seep of heavy dusk was taking over as he half stumbled into a narrow box canyon and toward a rock-rimmed spring. He was dizzy and weak; the rawhide strings holding his carbine and his shoulder holsters felt like they were cutting into his shoulders. The box canyon and its water were not well known. He was thankful the recent tracks were of small animals. A sentinel of scraggly shrubs and prickly pear cactus guarded the cracked lava basin. After cutting away a bush, he laid Tag in the opening, next to the seeping water. Gratefully, the dog began to lick up its life-giving wetness.

Every movement Holt made seemed in slow motion. His eyes were glazed from the heat, and his body was so drained he could barely keep moving. When Tag finished drinking, the young sheriff lay down his gear and rifle, half fell on the cracked rocks, and drank the cooling liquid. It was a deep spring, he thought, but far enough from any trail that few knew of its existence. Why would anyone come into a box canyon anyway? The entire area was laced with canyons, arroyos, and washes; there was no reason to pick out this particular canyon.

The water within this spring ran most of the year, he thought, but sometimes it was little more than a brownish ooze. Of course, the desert ridges held so-called water tanks, many of them pits hollowed out by time. They held rainwater for months. He knew such tanks would be waiting, if he could get there.

For now, though, he and Tag were fine and he forced himself to think only of the moment. That was Silka's training. Meet the problem head-on, the former samurai would always say, deal with it with all your energy and all your skill, and move on. Silka would know how to take care of himself, if any man could. And Deed wasn't far behind.

Using twigs, a few dry leaves, and a little dry mesquite, he soon had a small fire going, propped against waist-high rocks. The glow would barely exceed the stone blockage, and it delivered little, if any, smoke.

Brass cartridges in his belt reflected the small flame. Rattlesnake meat, along with some wild onion, broiled in the small skillet, tasted like a grand meal. He had found some squaw cabbage and added a few stalks. A cup of coffee brewed in the tin cup completed supper.

"Well, Tag, that wasn't half-bad, was it?" he said, sipping his coffee and watching the dog finish the meat. "We'll move up there and rest a while. I want to cover some miles tonight, before it gets hot again, you know."

He sounded more confident than he felt. At least forty miles remained to reach town, moving through sparse and broken country. The next water was about fifteen miles north. A sometime pond used by a small rancher. Or if it were dry, one of the water tanks on a ridge would be the next possibility. Tomorrow, he would need to pay close attention to any birds he saw. They might lead him to the closest water.

Glancing at his small fire, he saw two blue sparks. Signs of nearby spirits, he thought. Taking a handful of shredded tobacco from his pouch, he sprinkled the offering in all directions.

"Spirits of the land . . . watch over Tag and me. Help us," Holt muttered, then said what he could recall of the Lord's Prayer from his youth and Blue's urging.

The canteen with the bullet hole was the next project on his list. Taking two pieces of rawhide, he plugged the entry and exit holes, wadding the leather tightly into the spaces. It wasn't perfect, but it should hold most of the canteen's water. He filled both, then scattered the remains of his fire and headed twenty yards away. The plugged holes dripped a little, then stopped.

The location would give him a good view of the land from three directions. Tag curled up beside him and went to sleep. At Holt's side was his Winchester. Night sounds were gathering and comforting. Cicadas sang their lulling tune. A half dozen bats zoomed through the canyon, searching for insects for their dinner. Only half of an icy blue moon took position in the dark sky. Soon the Big Dipper appeared, supported by a hundred tiny stars.

Retrieving the medicine stone from his right vest pocket, he grasped it tightly. It was during a fierce battle against a Kiowa war party, his first Indian fight after the war, that he found it. Five Confederate guerrilla fighters had been surrounded by eighteen warriors. He saw the stone, laying at his feet, and decided to put it in his pocket. All of the Rebels survived and he had kept the stone close ever since. He knew the Indians believed in the strength of personal medicine, usually something of nature, something that gave them courage, strength, and protected them. Who was he to question the idea? Wasn't that really why he had carried that panther's claw for so long?

Their mother had loved the land and he supposed his feelings for it had come from her. He planned to ask his brother's wife about it when he next saw her. Bina was a Mescalero Apache, educated by missionaries, and a spiritual teacher in her own way. Her husband, Blue, said that being with her made him whole. He had used some of her views on life in sermons. Without the church members realizing it, of course.

Their father believed in the need for righteous behavior, but also in never backing down. Both parents had died when the boys were young. Deed, Holt, and Blue, with Silka's considerable help, had built up their family's ranch a few miles outside of Wilkon. Theirs was one of an original group of five ranches doing well in the region. Their mother and sister died of pneumonia when Blue was eighteen; Holt, sixteen; and Deed, ten. Their father died six months before their mother from a broken neck after a horse threw him.

Three years later, Blue and Holt had left to fight for the Confederacy while the much younger brother, Deed, stayed with Silka to keep the ranch afloat. While the older brothers were gone, Silka had honed Deed's fighting skills. Blue had returned after the war with his left arm missing; Holt hadn't returned and rode the outlaw trail for years, unable to accept the South's loss, before finally coming back.

He couldn't remember going to sleep, holding the stone. It was the middle of the night when he awoke and returned the stone to his right vest pocket, next to his watch. The night was cold and the shapes of everything appeared mysterious and strangely beautiful. He had slept longer than he wanted, but clearly he had needed the rest. From the roll of buckskin, Holt made four thick, crude socks and tied them over Tag's paws. The leather would help the dog's feet on the hot earth. It was the best he could do.

Gathering his things, he was on the march again in a few minutes, letting the pale moonlight guide his way. Tag was by his side, seemingly refreshed and enjoying his paw socks. Around the two of them, the land stretched forever. A curious nighthawk swooped low overhead and disappeared.

They walked on with Holt judging the direction from the fading North Star.

Red fingers of dawn crawled across the land and soon it was bright once more; heat taking control of the day. It was said an Apache warrior could make thirty-five to forty miles on foot. But not a white man.

His body soon ached from the heat and the walking, but it was either that or die. He didn't intend to die. Not here. Not now. He stopped at some thick cactus and cut off a chunk to suck on later. The cactus would be filled with water.

They crossed a dry lake bed. It was hard to tell how long ago water had occupied the bleak expanse. Scattered bones of animals looking for water that wasn't there were evident throughout the region. Foot tracks of the outlaws' horses were evident; they had made no attempt to hide where they were going.

"No need to," he grumbled. "If they want me, they'll find me."

At the northern end of the dry lake bed, a few scattered oaks stood forlorn and bent. Overhead a buzzard circled lazily.

"We'll rest there, Tag."

After giving the dog water, a piece of jerky, and a corn biscuit, he cut into the cactus's moist insides. He ate jerky and the remaining corn dodger, sucked on the cactus insides, and finally laid down to sleep. Tag would warn him of any danger.

Nighttime finally came and they were walking again, following the North Star. A stop beside a rancher's pond was brief; what water remained was brackish. Even Tag didn't want to drink it. Three cottonwoods stood over the sometime water, and Holt wondered how they survived.

To his left was a low set of rolling hills. In the dark they looked like a voluptuous woman lying on her side. He chuckled at the image as he kept moving. Would he ever see a woman again? He adjusted the saddlebags, canteens, shoulder holsters, and carbine sling on his shoulders. Yes, he would.

Tag brushed against him and he leaned over to pick up the weary dog. He trudged on into the night and his mind was numb.

CHAPTER SEVEN

When a new morning began to separate rock from cactus and shrubs, Holt Corrigan selected an old buffalo wallow to spend the daylight. It was a wide and shallow pit where the great beasts had once rolled. No trees were in sight, but the deepness of the wallow would provide whatever shade could be found.

"Tag, I'm ready to stop. How 'bout you?"

Sitting down with the dog in his lap, Holt poured water into the tin plate for his four-legged companion and drank from the canteen himself. After eating some jerky and giving Tag an equal amount, Holt stretched out with his hat over his face. His carbine rested on his stomach. The day's heat was already upon them.

It seemed like he had just shut his eyes when Tag began to growl, a teeth-tightened warning. Holt was awake in an instant and saw what was worrying his dog. In the distance were three riders, leading a fourth horse. Even without field glasses, he knew they were Indians by the way they sat their mounts. Field glasses yanked from his saddlebags told him precisely who was coming. Comanche. One was wearing Holt's left-behind long duster. Another wore the head of a wolf, and the lower half of his face was painted red. Even at this distance, the war chief's human tongue necklace was apparent. Most likely that was Achak himself. Holt recalled many outstanding warriors dressing distinctively so they wouldn't be missed. Part of their ego. Obviously, the Comanche had been following his trail since the ambush. He touched the stone within his pocket and grabbed his Winchester.

"I got 'em, Tag. Thanks, boy." Holt levered the carbine and squinted along its barrel, but a thought was pushing its way into his tired mind.

"Why are they leading a horse?" he asked himself. "Of course."

Laying down the rifle, he drew his revolver as Tag's growling resumed and the dog ran to the left side of the wallow. His white teeth became a snarl. The heavy cocking sound of the gun filled the quiet air and had barely disappeared when the fourth Comanche sprang at him from the left; the Indian's body was covered with dirt and sand. A knife flashed in his fist. The warrior had been crawling toward him a long way.

Holt's gun blasts tore at the man's face and chest; the Comanche was dead before his lifeless body hit the ground beside him. Tag snarled and grabbed the warrior's arm, shaking free the knife. Holt shoved the revolver into his waistband and grabbed his Winchester again. Two of the other three Comanche were galloping toward him, separating as they rode. The Comanche wearing the wolf's head waited and watched.

The coat-wearing warrior, to his left, had slipped to the side of his pony, making him a difficult target as he positioned to fire a rifle from under the horse's neck.

Holt had seen the maneuver many times before and had even used it himself. He stroked the cardinal feather in his hatband for luck and aimed. His first shot brought a scream from the Indian pony. It stumbled and fell, spilling the Comanche under him. The warrior's rifle danced in the air and thudded into the sand. Holt fired three more times, making sure the horse didn't suffer. The warrior under the horse was unmoving, dead.

Without waiting, Holt swung his attention to the remaining attacking warrior, now only fifty feet away and drawing an arrow back to shoot. The young lawman took careful aim and his shot took the Comanche from his horse. As soon as the Indian hit the ground, Holt fired two more times to make certain. Slamming new cartridges into the carbine, he returned his attention to the lone waiting Comanche, but he was already gone. So he turned his attention to the first warrior, the one wearing his coat, and fired into the lifeless body, then did the same to the second. There was no way he was going to worry about them trailing him again. Satisfied, he studied the dead Indian who had sneaked up on him; the warrior's face was gone, only a red mask remained.

It was over. If that was Achak, he had left for the time being. Maybe to get other warriors. Maybe to find an easier target, Holt hoped.

Across the hot land were two horses, looking for something to eat; the third was dying. Holt was more tense than during the fight. This was a very special opportunity to get a horse. Could he get close without frightening the animals and making them bolt?

The grain in his saddlebags!

Quickly, he took the small sack of grain kept for his horse, and poured some into his hat. The bay horse he had selected was the one led by the two Comanche. He hoped it hadn't been as agitated and would be easier to approach.

Holding his hat in one hand and his carbine in the other, the young lawman walked out of the wallow. The third horse was eating leaves from a scrawny bush. The mount was wearing a traditional Comanche saddle filled with buffalo hair and a bridle made of buffalo hair with a bone bit.

"Wait here, Tag. We need a new friend."

The process went easier than he could have hoped. The pony was interested in him as he spoke quietly to the animal, advancing slowly. His body smelled of sweat, smoke, and desert, and not that of a white man. After a few steps, he would stop until he was certain the animal was comfortable before moving again.

The bay horse whinnied softly as he came within four feet. Everything in him wanted to reach out and grab for the dangling reins. He resisted the impulse and, instead, stood without moving, except to hold out the hatful of grain. The warrior's horse shook its head and trotted toward the food. Holt gathered the reins as the horse ate.

A few minutes later, he led the horse toward the wallow. He stopped beside the dead Comanche wearing his long coat, then decided he didn't want it back. Three new bullet holes were evident. Holding the reins tightly, he smashed the warrior's rifle against close-by rocks and threw it as far as he could. Resuming his walk to the wallow, he called for Tag, who had gone to investigate the second dead Indian. The dog returned, limping slightly; one of the leather foot coverings was gone.

After laying his saddlebags across the horse, near its neck, Holt picked up his canteens and put them over his shoulder. He laid his Winchester on the edge of the wallow so it would be easier to reach from horseback. Then he turned to the tired dog lying near him. He knew his animal friend had taken great punishment in their trek.

"Stay real quiet, Tag. This may not go easy."

He patted the horse, talking quietly, and picked up Tag and placed him sideways on the bags. The dog sat quietly as if understanding the need to do so. Holt didn't know many Comanche words, but hoped the soft sound of his voice would be reassuring to the horse. It didn't react. Good. So far. The lawman led the horse close to the wallow's edge to make it easier for him to mount and swung onto its back. The horse grunted and Holt thought it was going to buck.

Instead, the pony whinnied softly and began to walk with the urging of his spurs. He leaned over and gathered his rifle as they passed. The other Comanche horse, a lighter bay, joined them twenty yards after they left the wallow, trotting beside Holt's new horse, as if it were planned. A strange sensation came over him and left almost as quickly. He had ridden an Indian pony like this in another life. More than that, he had been an Indian. Tag licked his hand. Having the dog with him didn't fit the fleeting image and he patted Tag to help him return to the moment.

That night they camped in a deserted ranch. Fire had long ago destroyed the buildings, leaving only a few crumbling stone walls. But there was a spring-fed well and it had water. Good water. He gave Tag a bath, sort of, using an old wooden bucket he found to pour water on the tired animal, then washed his own face and hands in the soothing wetness. The two horses were hobbled with leather strings from his saddlebags. Both were eager to be watered and to receive more of Holt's grain. Before he went to sleep, he thanked the spirits, tossed some tobacco as a tribute, and held the stone in his fist. Most would say it was a silly super-stition, he thought, but it seemed right. For him. His brother, Deed, would understand.

Two days later, Sheriff Holt Corrigan rode into Hammonds, a hardy settlement with a longer than usual main street. He had managed to alternate riding the two Comanche horses and that kept both healthy. He returned his badge to his vest. The business area featured three saloons, a sorry-looking bank, livery, a sorrier-looking hotel, a mining supply and assay office, barbershop and bathhouse, two churches, and an assortment of stores.

At the far end of the street was a marshal's office and jail that had once been something else, probably a warehouse. Behind both sides of the main street were scattered houses, mostly of adobe. A few tents were pitched on the north end of town. He headed for the livery, not wanting to make himself a target by riding down the main street.

A farmer in a buckboard rode past the tired lawman and gave a friendly wave. Holt returned the greeting and rode on. An empty freight wagon pulled out of the alley and onto the street, causing him to rein his horse hard to the right. Tag lost his balance, but Holt held him on the horse. The trailing paint horse jerked, but settled down quickly.

"Sorry 'bout that, Sheriff. Wasn't watchin'." The freighter yelled his apology.

"No problem," Holt said. He patted his dog and studied the street.

If he was lucky, the outlaw would still be in town, maybe waiting on the other two outlaws. Whiskey, women, and good food would be tempting for sure.

"Some good food sounds real fine to me, too." He chuckled and reined up at the livery.

A scrawny livery operator ambled out with a pitchfork in his hand. Taking off his ill-shaped, short-brimmed hat, he frowned and asked, "You musta had trouble, Sheriff. Or do ya jes' like ridin' Injun hosses?"

Holt explained the situation in a handful of sentences.

The liveryman's wiry eyebrows jumped. "Ya went across . . . without no hoss? Didn't ya know Achak's out thar, a'killin' ever'thang that's white? Raided two farms a day ago or so."

"Not my intention. Some Comanche were nice enough to loan me these fellas." Holt said as he swung down, then helped Tag from his perch.

"Really?" The liveryman took the reins of the two horses.

"Well, sort of." Holt didn't mention Achak himself was one of the Comanche, the one who got away.

The livery operator volunteered that two men had ridden into town from the same direction two days ago; another man came from there yesterday. His statement was a question as he led the horses inside to two empty stalls.

He rubbed his unshaven chin and looked away. "Thought you an' yur posse was a'lookin' fer four men."

"We were. I left one of them facedown about a week back. That's when they killed my horse. I might have wounded another." Holt followed him inside the sturdy livery, taking in the collected smells of horses, hay, manure, and leather. A loft was filled with fresh hay.

"Oh."

Reassured about the numbers, the livery operator continued as he unsaddled the first horse. "One were hurt. Said his hoss throwed 'im. They went to see our doc ri't away. Actually, Pete's also the town's dentist and barber."

He removed the simple bit and halter, laid them on the top board of the stall. "Sure ain't much fer a man to sit on, is thar?"

"Better than walking. Be sure to rub them down good and give them some extra oats. They earned it. I'll pay for it."

"Sure 'nuff." The livery operator picked up a brush and a bucket of water. "Ya think these Injun ponies are gonna be a problem?"

"No. Just talk nice and quiet to them," Holt replied as he untied his coat from his waist. "They'll be fine."

"Thar hosses is in hyar now. Real used up, they be. Fine animals though." He licked his cracked lips and poured some water on the horse's back. "They traded me for four o' mine. Paid an extry fifty on top o' that. Saddled 'em ri't then an' thar. Kept the bay fer their supplies, they said. Wanna see thar hosses? They're in the front stalls. Thar."

"No, that's fine. Know where they might be now?"

"Not for sur. They's in town. Prob'ly over to Aggie's." The liveryman pointed down the street. "She runs a cathouse. Three girls. Well, one's a Mex. Not bad lookin' though." His grin cut his long face in two. "Come to think on it, this time o' day, they's more likely in the Prairie Dog. That seems to be their drinkin' place o' choice, ya know.

"You gonna want another hoss? Got a

purty good bay I'd sell ya." The livery operator looked over at the dog's leather socks —
two were missing — and continued brushing the horse. "What about your dog?

Looking down at Tag, Holt grinned as he
shook out and put on his coat. His wolfish
smile returned. "Oh, I think he'll want to
go with me. Figures he might get a steak
outta the deal."

"Pepper Henry's, the best restaurant in
town. Fact is, it's the onliest. Henry's a good
cook, though. Bin up the cattle trails, ya
know."

"Sounds good." Holt walked over to the
stall and held out his hand. "Holt's my
name. Holt Corrigan."

"Heard o' you, Sheriff Corrigan. Not a
man to mess with, I hear tell. Folks say a
federal judge dun give ya amnesty if'n ya'd
be the county law. That's what I heard.
Folks jes' call me Pip." The livery operator
shook Holt's hand enthusiastically and
added almost sheepishly, "I dun fi't fer the
Union."

"You probably made the difference."

The liveryman smiled.

"How long you gonna be hyar, Sheriff?"

"Well, Pip, just long enough to arrest three
bank robbers, and get a bath and a good
meal." Holt draped his canteens over the

post of an empty stall. "I'll leave these here for later."

"Sur." The liveryman took the reins of the two horses. "Billy Ramschook's marshal hyar. He'll he'p ya. Lot older'n ya be. Bin steady, I reckon. Not much better with a gun than me, though." He smiled at the praise of himself.

Holt chuckled. "Heard of him. Billy's a good man. Even if he is . . . older. I'll let him know I'm in town. No need for him to get into this, though. It's Wilkon's problem. They shot Wilkon's marshal, so it's my problem." He rubbed his chin. "Might want to borrow Billy's jail while Tag and I get cleaned up and eat."

"Jail's only got three cells."

"Only need three. Hell, I only need one."

Holt added that he planned to head back to get his saddle and bury his friend and his dead horse's bones. He figured the outlaws could do the digging. The livery operator decided not to mention that the bones would likely be scattered all over by now. It was a strange priority, but the young lawman in front of him was a strange man. Maybe that's what it took to cross land like that on foot.

"Almost forgot. Did an Oriental fellow ride in a day or two ago? Scary-looking.

Carries a big sword," Holt asked. "Maybe another fellow with him, looks a little like me." He smiled. "Only not as handsome." He straightened his coat, making certain his revolvers were covered.

"No, sir, nobody like that. Leastwise, I didn't see them," Pip answered, rubbing his unshaved chin. "They some o' them outlaws, too?"

"No. The Oriental's my best friend. The other's my youngest brother. They'll be riding with another fellow. Nice-looking. Thin. Stern."

"Oh." Pip's eyebrows turned into a worry brow. "Ya ain't plannin' on takin' on three hombres by yur lonesome, are ya?"

"Don't have any choice, Pip. Unless the rest of the posse shows up real quick." Holt untied his saddlebags from the Comanche saddle. "Besides, Tag'll help me."

"Ya reckon they'll rob our bank, too?" Pip walked over to the water pump to refill his bucket.

"Yeah."

"Damn." Pip dropped the bucket.

"Yeah."

"How about I get my shotgun an' go wi' ya?" Pip picked up the bucket and began cranking the pump.

"That's a mighty nice offer, but I'll be

fine. You stay here."

The livery operator looked relieved.

"Let's get going, Tag. We've got work to do," Holt said, looking down at the dog. "Thanks, Pip."

Pip waved the brush.

CHAPTER EIGHT

Cradling his Winchester in his arms and throwing his saddlebags over his shoulder, Holt walked away. Tag trotted at his side, the two remaining leather socks flopping loosely.

As he stepped outside, a familiar voice teased him. "What's this about you being more handsome than me?"

Holt spun toward his youngest brother. Behind him stood Silka. "Deed . . . Silka! Man, I was getting worried."

After hugging each of them, Holt explained what had happened to him and his half of the posse.

"Real sorry about Ira. He was a good man. Had a bad feeling about Mason. Should've told you," Deed said, leaning against the livery wall. "Damn, you were lucky against Achak. I hear he's one bad hombre."

"Yeah, lucky."

"We just saw one of those boys come in from your direction. Only one. He was wounded," Deed said. "Figured you'd been in a scrape."

"Guess you could call it that."

Deed knelt to pet Tag and continued, "I see your buddy made it all right. We tracked the other two here. They just kept running. Didn't try to ambush us. We've been keeping out of sight. Hoping you'd show up." He took hold of one of the dog's leather socks. "What are these, Holt?"

Holt smiled. "Well, there used to be four. It was to help his feet when he walked with me."

"Should I take them off?"

"If you want."

Tag growled when Deed began to untie one of the leather pieces.

"Oops. Don't think he wants them off." Deed looked up, grinning.

"Yeah, Tag kinda likes them. Better leave them be."

Standing, Deed's eyes narrowed. "So you were going to face those bastards by yourself?"

"Aiie, that is not good," Silka added.

"Didn't see that I had any choice. Didn't know if you boys had run into trouble or what had happened. And I figured they

102

wouldn't stay in town long. Probably rob the bank and ride out."

"Malcom Rose is across the street right now, keeping an eye on them," Deed said, shaking his head. "We didn't think they'd recognize him. Right now they're in the saloon. Prairie Dog."

Heavy footsteps made them alert. A hard-breathing Malcolm Rose came around the corner.

"Two of them just went into the bank," the dry goods and clothing store owner reported. "The other one is on his horse waiting. Looks like their packhorse is carrying our bank money. Not sure though."

"Guess we'll find out," Holt said, levering his Winchester.

"Looks that way, big brother," Deed said and drew his Remington revolver.

"Nokorimono ni wa fuku ga aru," Silka said and touched the brass circle at his neck. Deed did the same.

Both brothers recognized the Japanese saying, that luck exists in the leftovers. Its meaning was clear, there is luck in the last helping.

"Let's hope there is a last helping," Deed said as they moved toward the street. "Malcom, you stay here."

"I didn't ride all this way to hide in a

livery. I'm coming with you."

"Got it. We're glad you're with us," Deed said and slapped the store owner on his back. He smelled whiskey on Rose's breath.

Quickly, they crossed the street, darting around, passing occasional buckboards, freighters, and riders. Lennie Kinney sat on his horse, facing the bank; his left arm was in a sling. The packhorse was on a lead rope tied to his saddle horn. The reins of the other two horses were looped around the hitch rack for quick release.

"Deed, take him out," Holt whispered. "Silka, move their horses. Malcom and I will go to the alley."

"Got it."

"I shall."

Like a wolf closing in on a wounded deer, Deed ran at Kinney and leaped onto the back of his horse. The outlaw was startled by Deed's arrival, but Deed grabbed his head with both hands around his neck before Kinney could move. A powerful snap and Kinney slid from his horse. Deed moved into the saddle, drawing his revolver to wait.

Silka grabbed the reins of the waiting horses, walked them away to the next hitch rack, and tied the leather lines tightly.

Holt and Rose slipped into the alley on

the south side of the unpainted bank building to wait. It wasn't long before Degory Black and Jethrum Pace slammed open the bank door, guns in hand. Black held a large sack. Both were laughing.

Holt stepped from the alley, raised his Winchester, and levered it. "Drop your guns. You're under arrest for murder and bank robbery."

Beside him, Tag growled, still wearing the two leather socks.

Black stopped and motioned for his outlaw friend to spread out. "Well, well, if it isn't Sheriff Corrigan. What rock did you crawl out from under? We didn't figure on seeing you again." Degory Black's words came out like they didn't taste good. "Lennie, you said he was a dead man. Lennie?"

Black looked at the rider in front of the bank. "Hey, where's Kinney?"

"Right over here. He wasn't good enough. Neither are you." Deed cocked his revolver and pointed it at the outlaw.

From the same alleyway, Malcom Rose appeared, brandishing his rifle. From the far hitch rack, Silka ran toward the bank robbers with his sword in both hands.

"Looks like you Corrigans got us outnumbered this time," Black snarled.

"Last chance. Drop your guns," Holt responded.

Behind Black, the bank door swung open and a squatty man with a centered part in his thick black hair jumped outside yelling that the bank was being robbed. The outlaw dropped the money sack, grabbed the bank president by the arm, and swung the surprised man in front of him. At the same moment, Silka bounded onto the boardwalk and drove his sword through Jethrum Pace. The outlaw grunted and fell against the building.

Without looking at his downed associate, Black yelled, "Back off or I'll shoot this little bastard. Do it now."

"Please . . . no!" The bank president pleaded.

Black shoved his gun barrel against the man's head.

Tag snarled and ran at Black before Holt could stop him. Surprised by the animal's sudden charge, Black swung his gun in Tag's direction. Deed, Holt, and Rose fired at once. Black's gun jumped in his hand. Tag whimpered and dropped as Black's bullet struck him.

Black lurched backward from the three shots and collapsed against the building. Holt fired twice more. Black's revolver popped from his hand and slid across the sidewalk. Silka pounced toward him, but there was no need. The outlaw was dead.

All over the main street, people began to look out of doorways and from behind wagons to determine what had just happened, unsure if the shooting was over or why it had begun.

Holt hurried to his wounded dog and knelt beside him.

Deed swung down from McKinney's horse. "How's Tag?"

"Looks like a nasty burn. Hurts, I'm sure." Holt patted the dog.

"We'll take him to the doc," Deed said and shoved a new cartridge into his handgun. "Where's the doc?" he asked the sweating president.

"Uh . . . uh, down the street. Where that barber sign is." The president straightened his coat and walked over to the money bag. "Uh, I'm going to take this back inside. All right?"

"Sure," Deed said. "Anybody else inside?"

"Uh, the Wilsons . . . and the Courtneys. My teller's in there, too."

"Tell them it's safe to come out."

"I will. I will," the short man swallowed. "Uh, thank you."

"You're welcome," Deed responded.

From his office, a bespectacled Marshal

Billy Ramschook came running with a double-barreled shotgun in his fists. When the gray-haired marshal saw it was Holt, he slowed down and adjusted his eyeglasses. Color began to return to his wrinkled face and the hint of a smile to his thin mouth.

"Sheriff Corrigan, what's going on?" Billy yelled as he advanced. "This is a quiet town, you know."

"Sorry, Billy," Holt replied, still beside the wounded dog. "That's Lennie Kinney . . . Jethrum Pace . . . and Degory Black. They robbed the bank in Wilkon. Killed the marshal there. We've been after them since. They didn't give us a chance to arrest them."

"Got papers on all of them. Bad ones. Looks like you saved us a bad time and a lot of money," Billy Ramschook said. "Got the wire from Wilkon a few days ago. Didn't figure they'd head this way though."

"Glad to oblige."

"That your dog?" Marshal Ramschook pointed at Tag, who was up and inspecting the dead outlaws, making certain they were dead by sniffing them, still growling.

"Yeah, that's Tag."

"He's bleeding. Hurt bad?"

"No, thank goodness. Just a bad burn," Holt said with reddened eyes. "I'll have the doc look at him."

Billy approached the bloody bodies of the outlaws, assured himself that they were dead, and looked again at the young sheriff. "The town thanks you, Sheriff. You and your friends." He turned to Holt. "Our town doctor is right down the street. He's also the barber . . . and the dentist. Tell him I said for you to come and the cost is on me."

"Thanks, Billy."

Holt introduced Deed, Malcolm Rose, and Silka, and the Hammonds lawman was appreciative of their help. Deed suggested they look in the outlaws' packhorse to see if the Wilkon bank money was there. Billy Ramschook waved at two men to come and drag away the outlaw bodies.

"It's here, Holt," Deed yelled and held up a large sack.

Even Silka smiled.

Two hours later, a bathed and shaved Holt Corrigan, wearing his one clean shirt with the pinned-on sheriff badge, walked into Pepper Henry's restaurant after telling Tag to wait. The dog was as clean as its master, enjoying the bath as much as Holt had. He was wearing a long bandage put there by the doctor. Holt had removed the remaining leather socks and put them in his saddlebags. This time Tag hadn't objected.

He paused inside the restaurant to study the situation. Deed, Malcolm Rose, and Silka were already seated. Only two other people were eating; a farmer and his wife, from the looks of their clothing. Holt was relieved to see that Silka had been allowed to come in. The group had had enough problems for one day.

A fat man with a greasy white apron around an ample waist greeted him as he entered. "Good day to you, Sheriff. Your friends are already here. You're a ways from home. How about a big steak — and some fried potatoes. Biscuits just came out of the oven."

"Sounds mighty good. Make it rare. Throw in some hot coffee."

"You got it."

Holt started for an open table, then stopped. "Say, would it be all right if I brought my dog in? He's been with me on a hard trip. Got wounded in the bank robbery today."

The fat man licked his lips. "Well, sure. Figure he deserves nice treatment, too. He'll be quiet, won't he?"

"If he isn't, we'll both leave."

Smiling, the restaurant owner declared, "Supper's on us, the town. I'm the mayor, so I've decided you men deserve more than just a few nice words."

From the doorway, Holt paused and said, "That's real neighborly of you."

He started again and the owner asked, "Pardon my asking, Sheriff, but aren't you the Confederate outlaw the army was chasing a while back?"

Touching the cardinal feather in his hatband, Holt nodded. "I am. Judge Pence decided I deserved amnesty." He cocked his head. "But he made me handle the county law duties as part of it."

"Sounds like the county got the best of that deal."

"Thanks."

CHAPTER NINE

A coyote jumped up as the four riders cleared a low hill and darted away from the tiny pool of rainwater. The Corrigan brothers, Silka, and Malcolm Rose were headed north, to Wilkon. They had wired Judge Pence and Blue that the bank's money had been recovered and they were returning. Nothing was said about Ira McDugal's death.

After buying supplies, grain for their horses, a shovel, and pickets, including a new long coat and replacement canteen for Holt, they had ridden out with two pack-horses and an extra horse for each man. Rose had managed to buy another bottle of whiskey as well.

As the days passed into October, a bright morning sun warmed the rough, broken land as they rode through. To their left was a cluster of arroyos, mixed with small canyons and a long finger of cliffs that barely cleared the horizon. They rode through two dry streambeds, bands of prickly pear, and huddled mesquite. No one was interested in talking, not even the store owner.

Holt rode and led the two Comanche horses. The others rode the outlaws' new horses and led their own tired mounts. The outlaws' packhorse had been turned into a packhorse for them. Tag was stretched out on top of the pack. The Wilkon bank's money was there, as well as food supplies, a large water bag, and two shovels. Holt had insisted on finding and burying Ira McDugal and his own horse, Buck. No one objected; Deed had quietly told him that the bodies would likely be torn apart by buzzards and coyotes. Holt didn't disagree, but felt it was important to give them as proper a burial as they could.

By midday, they were resting beside the only known water in this part of the region, a rock-rimmed pool that had once been the beginning of a stream. The water was low, but clear. Their meal was light, except for coffee. Their fire was a small one, made with dry wood that didn't smoke. This was Comanche country, especially so with Achak and his warriors ripping through it, and no one had to tell them of the need to be vigilant. They switched saddles to fresher horses before settling in to eat. It was safer that way, in case they had to run.

"How soon do you think we'll hit that abandoned ranch you went through?" Deed asked Holt as he sipped his coffee.

"It was two days out from Hammonds. We should reach it tomorrow at the pace we're going. It's a good place to camp." Holt lit a cigar he'd bought at the Hammonds general store and watched Tag dart after a panting lizard.

Malcom Rose stood and brushed dust from his pants with his hat, felt the flask against his chest, but decided not to get it out. "You think we'll have Indian problems?"

Deed shifted his feet and stood. "Never can tell about Indians. If we're lucky, no. If not, yes. Holt dropped three of 'em. They just might've set up business elsewhere."

Rose shivered, went to his horse, and yanked free his rifle. He looked down, leaned over, and held up a dust-covered horseshoe. "Look here. Somebody lost a shoe. Been a while ago, I suppose."

"Put it in your saddlebags," Holt responded. "That's good luck. You'll always have money as long as you have it. At least, that's what an old Gypsy told me."

"What about Comanche? Will it help keep us safe?" the thin-faced townsman asked.

"He didn't say anything about that."

Silka and Deed kicked out their fire and poured the remains of the coffeepot over the smoking embers. They were riding in minutes with Holt leading the way.

Deed's mind was wandering toward Atlee Forsyth, in spite of the need to stay alert. He missed her terribly, but this had been a necessary trip. As soon as they got back to Wilkon, he intended to head to the Forsyth stage station and see her. She ran the station after her husband had been killed by Comanche. He could see her children in his mind. He could feel her kiss and her hands touching his face.

"Over there." Silka's command broke Deed from his daydreaming.

A group of unshod horses had passed and the signs were fresh. The tracks were headed in the general direction of their own riding.

"Damn, they're headed the same way we're going," Deed said.

"I count twenty," Holt said. "Could be a few more."

"Maybe it's just a bunch of wild horses," Rose said and, this time, took a drink from his flask.

Deed cocked his head. "No. If it were just

horses, their dung would be together. It's not. It's scattered around. The Comanche were keeping them moving."

CHAPTER TEN

Holt reined up. "Not much we can do about it, except ride alert." He pulled his Winchester from its saddle boot, as did Deed and Silka.

Rose's face was tight. "Maybe we should turn back and wait."

"You're welcome to do that. We're going on," Holt said, then looked at Malcolm's horse with a pattern of large white and black spots. "But a piebald horse is supposed to be lucky." He grinned. "As long as you don't look at its tail."

"Where'd you hear such a stupid thing?" the store owner asked, more sternly than he should have.

Deed glanced at his oldest brother. Family could tease him about being superstitious. Not outsiders.

Holt's response was milder than Deed expected. "Every man picks his own way, Malcolm. I've picked mine." He kicked his horse into a lope.

Malcolm frowned, but didn't respond.

They rode on in silence with Holt in the lead. Each man watched the land in his own way. Deed's thoughts kept returning to Atlee, in spite of his knowing of the need to be alert. Silka rode up beside him and touched his shoulder.

"You think of her, the stagecoach lady."

Deed turned toward his mentor. "Yes, I think of her always, Silka. I want to be with her."

"So it will be." Silka smiled. "I see my wife and children each day. They smile at me. One day I will join them."

Deed looked over at his old friend. "Yes, my friend. Someday. But we need you here with us now."

Silka said something in Japanese that Deed didn't understand. Deed saw his friend's eyes fill and kicked his horse into a faster gait to leave Silka alone for the moment.

The four men cleared a slight rise that allowed them a view of miles of dry prairie. It was a risk because the Comanche could see them as well. They reined up to give their horses a rest. Nothing moved that they could distinguish. Fresh tracks of the war party continued to intrigue them, appearing to be riding ahead of them by no more than a day. But no signs of dust indicated riders were near. Holt took out his field glasses and studied the country more carefully.

Holt handed the field glasses to Deed. "Take a look. I don't see anything."

Deed's review of the land yielded nothing as well. "Let's spread out so we don't stir up as much dust."

Patting the rifle across his saddle, Malcolm said, "Let 'em come. We'll be ready."

"Ever been in an Indian fight?" Deed asked as he handed the field glasses back to Holt.

"Uh, no, but I was in the war. Took out a bunch of Rebels." Holt smiled, but it didn't reach his eyes. "I wouldn't wish a Comanche attack on my worst enemy. Or Apache, for that matter. And yes, I shot a lot of blue bellies, too."

Resting both hands on his saddle horn, Rose asked, "And they say you robbed a bunch of banks. Union banks. That true?" The whiskey was beginning to affect his judgment.

Smiling again, Holt said, "You sound like a man pushing for a fight. That true?"

"Damn it, that's enough," Deed snapped and eased his horse between them.

He glared at Rose. "You're a most fortunate man, Malcolm. If I were you, I'd just start riding again and keep my mouth shut."

The store owner glared at him, then spurred his horse into a trot. The others spread out behind him as Deed had suggested. A few minutes later, Holt and Rose were riding side by side talking. And smiling. The tension of the moment had passed.

Clearing a low hill, they startled three antelope and the lithe animals scampered away. Ahead was a long wash empty of anything growing except mesquite and brush. Holt swung his horse in that direction and the three men followed, strung out. The afternoon sun had found its strength and the day was hot. Signs of the Comanche appeared again in the soft sand: it looked like they were now riding west.

"Looks like that war party is headed west," Holt said and pointed.

"Good." Deed responded. "I like that. Think it's Achak?"

"Probably."

Malcolm Rose took a deep breath. "I like that thought, too."

"We'll stop by those rocks and give our horses some of our water." Holt pointed to a strange collection of large rocks at the end of the wash.

Reaching the stopping point, Holt asked

Silka to keep watch. They swung down and each man poured water into his hat for his horses. The animals licked up the moisture gratefully. After watering his horse and taking a swig himself, Deed replaced Silka while the former samurai watered his own horses. Holt lifted Tag from the packhorse, allowed him to drink, and returned the dog to its riding position.

The afternoon was long and fierce. By sundown, they were more than halfway to the abandoned ranch where Holt had camped coming into Hammonds. It was a dry camp and on an elevated plain. They could see in three directions with their camp settled against a low cliff of red clay. Anyone trying to advance from the cliff would not see them or be able to shoot down at them effectively. Just south of their camp was a cluster of buffalo grass that would provide grazing for the horses.

The animals were allowed to roll, rubbed down with saddle blankets, then picketed for the night. Water came again from their supply; their first canteens were empty and the second canteens were needed. Tag was moving stiffly, but his wound didn't seem to bother him otherwise. Deed built a small fire against the cliff and a coffeepot was quickly boiling. Dinner was bacon, cans of beans, and warmed-up biscuits from the general store.

"I'll take the first watch," Deed said. "Malcom, you can take over about eleven."

"Sure."

"I'll take the watch from two," Holt said, " 'til four, then it's yours, Silka."

Holt grinned and reached for the coffeepot. "Tomorrow night, we should be at that ranch . . . and some good water."

The camp settled into sleep quickly after a long, hard day in the saddle. Moonlight was dazzling and all of them slept with their hats over their eyes. Deed wandered away from the dying fire, taking his Spencer, and stood close to the horses. The Comanche horses were mustangs and should warn him if anyone tried to advance from outside the camp. Like his brother, he felt it was important to thank the spirits of the area and spread shredded tobacco around from the small pouch he carried. He thought his brother had done the same earlier.

Night sounds were comforting. Somewhere a coyote talked a lonely story. His thoughts danced away to the stagecoach station that Atlee ran. He could see the separate adobe home where her family lived and a small cooling house, a barn, corral, blacksmith shed, the relay station building itself, and its accompanying outhouses. He wondered if she was ready to leave that behind and help him operate the massive Bar 3. That was the plan; he and Silka would take over the management of this ranch. But none of it made sense to him if she didn't want to join him.

"Atlee, I love you." His whisper joined the other night sounds.

He took a deep breath and moved to a darker shadow not far from Holt's Comanche horses. "Going to count on you fellows to let us know if trouble is around."

The thought occurred to him that the horses might not react if it were Indians closing in. He grimaced and studied the surrounding land. At night, everything looked different, strange. Most Indians, Comanche and Apache, didn't like fighting at night. They believed a dead warrior's soul wouldn't be able to find the proper resting place in the darkness. He wondered if such bright moonlight changed that thinking.

He looked over at the sleeping men. He felt good that Malcolm Rose and Holt had gotten over their argument and was pleased to see the change in his brother. Holt was much more calm than he was as a younger man. Probably it was the amnesty, even with the burden of being a lawman. He smiled.

A lot had happened in a short time, thanks to the judge.

Deed hadn't told anyone, but he figured that some townspeople would challenge the amnesty and claim that Holt had robbed their bank and should pay for it. He didn't know if his brother had robbed any banks, or how many. The newspaper stories were, of course, all about Holt and his gang. Pence realized the stories had been generated by Agon Bordner and had not been crimes committed by Holt himself or any of his gang. Deed wondered if the judge had thought about the possibility. Legally, the amnesty cleared him of any such crime, but that didn't mean someone wouldn't try to change it. Maybe the army itself might challenge the judge. Deed shook his head to clear it.

He moved over to the Comanche horses and talked quietly to them. The animals were content and healthy. He figured they could run all day and all night if needed. Actually, he was more worried about Comanche finding them. There was no doubt of their fighting skill, their ferocity. There wouldn't be any safety until they reached Wilkon. Maybe they should consider traveling by night and avoid the obvious problems of day riding.

The taller Comanche horse's ears came up and it looked down at a fat mesquite brush twenty feet away. Something was definitely there. Deed cocked his Spencer and aimed it at the silent shape.

Nothing moved.

Deed stepped behind the horse to protect him from gunfire or an arrow. Yellow eyes appeared from the side of the mesquite and Deed breathed relief.

"My friend, go away from here. Staying around will only get you killed," Deed growled.

A moment later, the eyes disappeared.

"Thanks, boy," Deed patted the horse's neck. "Counting on you. Will you warn me if any Indians get close?"

Uncocking his Spencer, Deed moved again. He thought it was important to keep changing positions and trying his best to stay in the shadows. There was no indication of Indians close by, but he was worried. The moonlight had lessened somewhat with clouds cutting in front.

He looked up. "Wonder if we'll get rain tomorrow? That would help."

Of the three Corrigan brothers, he was the one most comfortable in the wilds and the one who seemed to connect with wildlife. Somewhere a nighthawk called out and he listened closely. Yes, it was real. No echo or anything human attached to the sound.

His mind slid from Atlee to the Comanche attacks. The war party would find them unless it was truly headed west. That seemed unlikely to him. Likely there was water in that direction known to only a few. It made more sense they would then turn back and head either south or east, where white settlements lay. Either way, the Indians would cut the posse's trail.

Most Comanche were in the reservation at Fort Cobb, but there were roaming bands causing problems at the edges of white civilization. Now Achak and his band of warriors had broken free. He didn't think they would have picked up their trail yet, or had they?

What could the four of them do if they did?

They could try to hide their tracks, but that would only slow them down. Any Comanche could see through the subterfuge. Deed touched the brass circle at his neck. Maybe they should travel at night. Tonight. They could make the ranch by midday according to Holt and, likely, get there before the war party did.

Yes.

He went to Holt. His brother was not

sleeping.

"Holt, I think we should ride for that ranch tonight," Deed said. "Got a feeling."

Without responding, Holt sat up and put on his shoulder holsters; his pants and boots were already on. "Had the same thought. Doesn't make sense for them to keep heading west. I'm pretty sure there's a small stream about a half day's ride from where we saw their tracks. They'll turn around after watering their horses."

"If they cut our trail, they'll know where we're headed."

"I'll wake the others. Water the horses good." Holt stood.

Walking over to Silka, Holt touched the former samurai on the shoulder and he was instantly awake, holding his sword with both hands.

"We're going to ride on now," Holt said. "Will you get the packhorse ready?"

"I do so." Silka was into the shadows in three bounds with no questions asked.

Malcolm Rose struggled to wake up. "W-what's the matter?"

"Nothing. But we're going to ride out. Now," Holt spoke almost gently. "Safer riding at night."

"Oh."

Rose grabbed his boots, shook them to

assure no small creatures had taken up residence, and stood, stomping them into place. Leaving the store owner to get himself ready, Holt went to Deed, now saddling their horses.

"Let's tie down anything that makes noise," the oldest Corrigan advised.

"Yeah. I've already shed my spurs."

Silka brought up the packhorse carrying their reloaded supplies and the bank's money. Tag was stretched out on top as usual. Holt noticed Silka wasn't wearing spurs, either.

Sitting on a rock, Holt removed his spurs and shoved them into his saddlebags, surrounded by an extra shirt. He avoided looking at Rose's piebald horse altogether, focusing on his own bay. Malcolm Rose came to the saddling area, dragging his blanket. He stumbled against a rock and almost fell. His rifle clattered against the rocky ground.

Deed looked at him and continued saddling.

"Damn, is this really necessary?" the thin townsman grumbled and leaned over to retrieve his gun.

"May not be, but better to be safe," Holt said in a low voice. "Take off your spurs."

CHAPTER ELEVEN

In minutes, they were riding again. Deed had added wood to the fire so it would burn well through the night. Sounds of their travel were muted. Only hoofbeats against soft sand and the occasional grunt of saddle leather. Each man had wrapped his bridle chains to keep them from making more than a whisper.

Holt led the way, heading straight for the abandoned ranch and good water. The night had darkened with clouds completely surrounding the once-dominant moon. They were thankful for the blackness. Soon the tensions of being awakened gave way to weariness. Several heads bobbed in rhythm to their walking horses.

False dawn was ushering in a new day when they pulled up among a gathering of scrub oaks. Four rabbits popped from cover as they rode into the area.

"We'll give the horses some water," Holt

announced, "and switch 'em. Should be at the old ranch in three hours."

Canteen water in their hats became welcome containers for the horses. Silka made certain the packhorses were particularly well watered. He helped Tag down and the dog began sniffing where the rabbits had been.

From his saddlebags, Rose produced a flask and took a long drink, then another. He offered the whiskey to Holt and Deed, who both declined. There was no attempt to ask Silka if he wanted any. The others began chewing on jerky and biscuits as they swung back into their saddles on fresh horses. Before mounting, Holt patted his hip for Tag and helped him onto the packhorse, then gave him a broken-up piece of jerky.

Holt studied their back trail but it was too dark to see beyond the outer trees. As he stepped into the saddle, a small toad hopped from a rock across his path and vanished into other rocks. He smiled. A sign of good luck. They would need it.

"When it gets lighter, I'll swing back and see if anything's coming," Deed said.

Holt nodded and saw Rose take another swig.

Dawn slipped into sight with rose and purple streaks announcing its advance. The men rode more alert than before, largely because of being able to see. Before them was an acrid land, laced with mesquite, cactus, and boulders. Before long, they took off their long coats and tied them behind their saddles with their blankets. Holt smoked a cigar and so did Rose, occasionally sipping on his flask.

"I'd go easy on that, Malcolm," Deed said. "We may be fighting Comanche before long."

"Oh, hell. You Corrigan boys see redskins behind every piece of mesquite," Rose blurted; the effects of his drinking once more beginning to show. "The only thing we have to worry about is water." He wiped his mouth and took another drink. "And coffee. Hot coffee would taste mighty good."

"Yeah, it would. We'll make some when we stop."

Deed loped up to Holt. "Take my backup pony, will you? I'll take a look-see at our back side."

"Sure." Holt held out his hand for the lead rope of Deed's second horse. His other hand held his own reins and his half-smoked cigar.

Swinging his horse around, Deed rode past Silka, smiled, and said, *"Hisashiburi."*

Basically, it meant, "long time no see."

Silka nodded and repeated the teasing greeting.

Deed kicked his horse into a hard lope and disappeared over the uneven ridge behind them. Minutes passed without any sign of him and even Holt was beginning to worry.

"If he isn't back soon, we'll head back and see if he's all right," Holt declared.

"He all right," Silka said. "He see something."

"Yeah, I was afraid of that."

Rose took another swig. "C-Comanche?"

"It ain't picnickers."

The words were barely out of Holt's mouth when the silhouette of a lone rider appeared behind them. Deed was riding hard. He reined up alongside the threesome.

"Dust behind us," he reported. "Has to be Achak and his bunch. They've picked up our trail."

"Can we make the ranch?" Holt asked.

"Yeah," Deed replied, "unless you're wrong about the distance."

"I'm not."

"Didn't figure you were," Deed responded. "They'll know where we're headed, but I don't see any shortcuts they could take."

Rose's face was stiff and his Adam's apple

132

bobbed rapidly. "H-how many, you think?"

"Unless they picked up some warriors at their watering hole, I'd say about twenty," Deed answered. "Enough."

"Yeah, enough for sure," Holt handed back the lead rope of Deed's second horse. "Let's ride, boys."

They rode hard to the burned-out ranch yard and decided to leave their mounts saddled in case they needed to make a run. Silka pointed at the tumbled walls of the adobe ranch house and declared they should make a stand there, bringing the horses with them. Silka and Holt began fortifying the broken walls with rock slabs while Deed and Rose watered the horses from the nearby well. Holt let the dog down and Tag ran around, happy to be moving again.

"Get all our canteens full. The water bag, too," Holt yelled. "I'll get the extra bullets from the pack."

After the horses were watered and grained, they were led into what once was a bedroom and tied to scraggly brush. A little grass had sprung up from the earthen floor, enough to keep the animals satisfied for a few hours. The abandoned ranch yard itself was nearly surrounded by tall buffalo grass and brush.

Rose was assigned to make a fire. He was uneasy in his walking, but determined to handle the task. He hurried around, grabbing what sticks he could find and a few larger branches. A small fire was going quickly and a coffeepot was soon boiling. The smell danced across the crumpled walls. At Holt's request, he went over to the supplies. Holt handed him a box of cartridges. Deed took a box of loading tubes for his Spencer from the pack.

"How soon will they come?" Rose asked, staring at the horizon, a little unsteady.

"Shouldn't be long now. Their dust is heavy."

"Silka, they know this place. Why don't you take a spot over there . . . in case they try to sneak behind us," Holt said, pointing to the far east side of the ranch yard.

"Aiie, that is good."

The youngest Corrigan was pleased to see that Rose was working his way through the impact of the whiskey. Malcolm Rose was a good man, Deed thought. This just wasn't anything the townsman was used to.

Rose shoved more sticks into the fire. "If I don't get back, I reckon the missus can run the store almost as good as we did together. She's a fine woman, you know."

"You'll be giving her a big kiss in a few days," Deed said.

"Thank you for that."

134

"Keep the fire going," Holt said, "and put a pot of water on. Might need it if anybody takes an arrow or a bullet."

"Sure. Sure. Hadn't thought of that," Rose muttered. He stood and retrieved a pot from their supplies and filled it from the well. After adding a few more sticks, and a fat branch, he placed the pot into the flames.

"Someone'll have to keep an eye on it or it'll boil away," he said.

No one answered.

"Coffee ready yet?" Holt asked, instead.

"Think so. I've got the cups from the pack."

"Good. I'll be over."

Holt walked over and poured coffee into a tin cup. The brew was scalding hot and strong.

"Why do you think it's Achak?" Rose asked, pouring a cup for himself.

"Hadn't thought about it. Probably. But it could be Kiowa. Or Apache. Hell, it might be Cherokee," Holt said. "Guess it's easier to say Achak 'til we know for sure."

"Guess it doesn't matter."

"Nope."

Holt walked back to his firing position, holding the cup and blowing on it. After he was in place, he yelled, "They're coming hard. Heavy dust."

135

In spite of the yell, Deed walked over and poured two cups of coffee and walked over to Silka. He leaned over and handed him a cup.

"It's mighty hot. Any thoughts, old man?" he asked between sips of the strong brew.

Silka took a drink and said one word. "Blankets."

"What do you mean blankets? You want one? I'll get it."

Silka took another sip and explained that he thought the Comanche would be split up, with the main group dragging blankets behind their ponies to create a bigger dust cloud. That way the defenders wouldn't notice several warriors had slipped away. He thought they might already be in the tall grass.

Deed patted Silka's shoulder. "I'll tell Holt."

"They will come at our edges."

"Got it."

As Deed turned to walk away, the former samurai motioned for him to touch the brass circle at his neck for luck. Deed nodded and did, walked past the fire, and paused, looking at Rose. "Don't drink any more 'til this is over. We need you sharp," he advised, holding his cup in one hand and his Spencer in the other. "Count on one or two of them crawling your way."

Malcolm patted the flask in his coat pocket. "I'll be all right."

Continuing over to Holt, Deed watched the war party advance and told him what Silka expected. They were still out of rifle range and knew it.

"Here, touch this," Holt said, holding out his hand. The small medicine rock lay in his opened palm. "Came from an Indian fight I was in. Five of us. We handled eighteen Kiowa. None of us were injured."

"Thanks." Deed touched the rock and patted his brother on the shoulder. "Silka had me touch the circle. Maybe you should, too."

Holt reached up and put his forefinger on the circle on Deed's neck. "Keep your head down."

"You, too."

The youngest Corrigan brother climbed through the crumbled walls to a place that was farthest south of the others. He settled down among the broken adobe; his reloading tubes were already there. He decided his coffee wasn't hot enough anymore and tossed the remains to the side.

Dust was high from the war party's charge. The Comanche were advancing confidently, their ponies strutting with feathers floating from their manes and tails. Strips of hair and flesh were tied to their horses' manes. New scalps. A fierce-looking band, most were painted for war. Achak was at the front with ribbons streaming down his bare back from his wolf's headdress. In his right hand was a Henry rifle, one of their few guns. Beside him rode a large warrior with vertical stripes of white down his face, wearing a military cavalry tunic with the sleeves removed. In his hand was an old Colt revolver. However, most were armed with lances, bows, and arrows.

Deed forced himself to watch the tall grass in front of him, instead of the Comanche riders, still a long way away. If Silka was right, warriors would be slipping through this cover to get close. His eyes caught movement. Nothing distinctive, more the sense of movement. He cocked the big gun, pointed it in that direction, and waited. And waited.

A brown body slithered through the tall grass. Slowly. Ever closer. It reminded Deed of a crouching panther stalking an antelope. The warrior was naked except for a breech-cloth, moccasins, and a scalping knife. An eagle feather fluttered in his long black hair, brushing against the grass.

Deed made a mental note of the warrior's

138

progress and moved his rifle to where he was likely to head. The young gunfighter began to tighten his finger against the trigger and sighted along the carbine barrel. He sensed the movement again before he actually saw it. The Spencer roared and the warrior actually stood, then collapsed with Deed's second shot.

Re-cocking the seven-shot Spencer, he studied the grass for other movement, glad there was no wind. Holt and Rose were firing their Winchesters at the band of Comanche dragging blankets behind their ponies to generate greater dust. Rose emptied his gun without hitting anything or anyone.

Achak raised his fist and yelled a command. Yelping, his men turned around and rode away. Two lay against their horses' necks.

At the far end of the camp, at almost the same moment, Silka greeted an advancing Comanche with the swing of his heavy sword and the warrior crumpled in the thick brush, spreading bright crimson streaks.

Tag sprang from Holt's side, growling and headed for the tall grass to Deed's right.

"Shhh, Tag. Stay here," Deed said.

A face-painted warrior lunged forward with a tomahawk in one hand and a knife in the other. Deed jumped sideways, cocked his right leg, and drove his boot into the warrior's face. A swift follow-through with his opened hand slammed into the Comanche's Adam's apple like an axe blade. Tag stepped from Deed's side to sniff the dead Indian. Satisfied, he trotted back to Holt.

As Rose turned to get additional bullets, a black-streaked warrior sprang from a shadow and drove his knife into the townsman's shoulder. He screamed. Deed and Holt turned toward his yell and both fired at the Comanche, driving him backward. Rose fell to his knees, holding his bleeding shoulder.

"T-they got me! T-they got me!" he choked as a crimson circle widened on his dirty shirt.

Holt told him to lie down so they could treat the wound.

"I'll get the hot water," Deed said and went to the fire.

As he hurried toward the hot water pot, Silka appeared from the far east side. A smear of blood decorated his right cheek.

"Malcolm's hurt. We're going to need your help."

Unspoken was the thought the Comanche had fled, not used to such high casualties.

"Yes, I do." The Oriental turned in mid-step to head for his horse and his saddle-bags.

An hour later, Rose was sleeping and Deed was preparing a meal for them. With his field glasses, Holt kept a steady lookout to make certain the Indians were not returning. Silka walked the rim of their camp, checking the downed Indians and making certain they were dead.

Smells of frying bacon and cut-up potatoes filled the temporary stockade. Deed had opened two cans of beans and they were cooking at the edge of the fire. A fresh pot of coffee was boiling. From their supplies, he had taken a loaf of bread and laid it open against a log near where he cooked.

"Might as well eat all that bread," he declared. "It's not going to keep. We're got powder for making biscuits in the pack. For later on."

"Sounds good to me," Holt said. "I'm hungry as a bear."

A mile away, in a narrow valley, the Comanche made a hasty camp. Achak was frustrated and worried. He had promised easy rewards to his band of mostly young warriors. Guns. Horses. White scalps. White women. War honors when they returned. The trills of impressed Comanche women. The appreciative stares of older men and younger boys. But so far, the three farms they had raided had produced only scalps and the women the men had enjoyed; one was still with them, little more than a whimper left in her body. But little else had been achieved. A gun they didn't know how to shoot, a shotgun without shells, and three old horses.

When he saw the tracks of the Corrigan party, he had been elated. Horses. Good horses. And, most likely, guns. He figured it was a white hunting party. But this small group had punished his men and had not been fooled by their blanket trick. He now figured that one of them had to be the white warrior who walked with a dog. Achak had been impressed with the way he fought.

Achak sat alone and smiled. His war medicine would be seen as invincible if he brought down these men. The white walker's tongue belonged on his necklace. His warriors had told him of a yellow man who killed with a long sword and another white man who fought with his feet. What kind of men were these? Their own war medicine was definitely strong. And different than any he had seen before.

Yet his men had counted nine good horses and more guns than his men had. They were excited about this challenge. Each man wanted the honor of killing the white walker or watching him die slowly from their torture.

This morning, before the battle, his brother, the wolf, had told him that his cunning was necessary to overcome this great enemy. To that end, he would send select warriors to steal the white men's horses and kill any of the white men they could. Even if they could only get the horses, the white men would be doomed. Even the white walker couldn't make it that far.

He chuckled and several of his men turned to see why their leader was pleased.

CHAPTER TWELVE

Late afternoon was closing in on the four men with no sign of the Comanche returning. They took turns sleeping while one stood guard.

Silka and Deed had dragged the Indian bodies away from their encampment, partly to remove the smell that would come soon enough and partly to let the warriors return for their dead as they usually did. Rose was sleeping, but it was a fitful rest with frantic words bursting from him occasionally.

Holt repacked the packhorse and refilled their canteens and the water bag. Nothing had been said, but he was planning on moving again when it was dark. They could make for the hills before daybreak. It wasn't as strong a position as where they were now, but it was closer to home. Of course, Achak would know where they were headed, but that couldn't be helped.

The immediate worry was Malcolm Rose.

Would he be able to ride? If not, they would have to rig some kind of travois and the pounding would be hard on him.

The oldest Corrigan brother walked over to the dying fire and lit a new cigar from one of its burning sticks. His leg wound had mostly healed, bothering only when he was very tired, as he was now. All of them were weary from the previous night's ride and the tension of the Indian fight.

But he didn't like staying in place where the war party knew where they were, and how many they were. They had been lucky. So far. Being tired was better than being dead.

Withdrawing his bag of tobacco, he spread a small handful of shreds in all directions and thanked the spirits for helping them. He looked around at the abandoned ranch and wondered what had happened to the people who built it, then wondered why they had done so there in the first place. The land was fit for coyotes, rattlesnakes, and Comanche, not cattle or crops. He was turning as Deed and Silka approached.

"Do you think Malcolm can ride?" Deed asked. The question held a built-in assumption that they would leave.

"Guess we'd better wake him up and see." Holt headed toward the sleeping man. Tag brushed against his leg for attention and got a quick pat on the head.

Leaning over Rose, Holt put his hand on the man's stomach. "Malcolm, we're going to have to leave here. Now. Can you ride? Or do you want us to rig up something you can lie on?"

Rose blinked his eyes and stared wide-eyed without moving. "I-I can ride." He started to get up and lost his balance.

"Easy now. Let me help you." Holt took hold of Rose under his shoulder and Deed came forward to take the other side, the wounded side.

Rose stood, shakily, with both Corrigans continuing to hold him in place. He took a step, tried to smile, but the pain was too intense. Holt held a canteen to Rose's mouth so that the wounded man could drink.

"You lost a lot of blood, man," Holt said. "Maybe we'd fix up something for you. Here, drink some more."

"N-no. Help me on my horse . . . I'll be all right." Rose pushed away the canteen.

Deed turned toward Silka and motioned for him to bring up Ross's piebald. Holt kept his gaze on the wounded man as they pushed him into the saddle. The first attempt ended in a groan from the wounded man. He was almost dead weight. He grunted and, finally, made it. He was pale and his shoulder was bleeding again.

"M-maybe you'd better tie me in place," Rose stammered. "I-I'm kinda dizzy."

"Makes good sense," Holt said and went for a rope.

They lashed his legs around the stirrup flaps and his wrists to the saddle horn.

"You look real hog-tied," Deed said, "but I'll keep you in the saddle. I'll take your reins so you don't have to worry."

"T-thanks, Deed. I'm sorry."

"We're the ones who are sorry," Deed responded, swinging onto his horse, "but we need to get out of here."

"I-I know. Y-you think they'll come back?"

"Hard to say." Holt mounted and took his rifle from its boot. "But we don't like the idea of them doing that. We'll be in the hills before dawn. Water's there. It's a safe place."

Gritting his teeth to hold back the pain, Rose looked at him. "What if my nose itches?" His smile was thin, but definite.

Holt chuckled. "Guess we'll have to take turns rubbing it."

At their fire, Silka placed the largest logs he could find to keep it burning all night. Satisfied, he took the lead ropes of his backup horse, Rose's backup horse, and the packhorse. He tied the ropes of the backup animals to that of the pack animal so he wouldn't have to handle three separate lines. The former samurai whistled for Tag. The dog came, knowing Deed and Silka were important to Holt, so he would respond to them as well. But Holt was still his first priority. Silka placed the dog on the top of the pack. Then, mounting himself, he declared he was ready.

They rode silently away with only the click of a hoof against rock to indicate their passing. The moon was barely a sliver of gold with a few aggressive stars rushing into the surrounding darkness. The trail was familiar to Holt, yet it wasn't. Going back never looked the same and he had been under severe stress, carrying Tag, his canteens, saddlebags, and rifle. But he kept focused on the North Star and slipped his hand into his pocket and felt the medicine stone there. It was oddly reassuring.

Deed rode beside Rose, holding both reins and making certain the townsman didn't start to slide off his mount. In spite of the situation, Deed's mind raced to find Atlee and kiss her. Did she miss him? Would she marry him? The Bar 3 ranch would take a lot of work and attention. But it would be oh so lonely if she weren't with him. He shook his head to clear away the images and glanced at Holt.

His brother was reading the area for landmarks. Deed was proud of him; Holt had stepped into the responsibility of being the county sheriff as if he were born to it. Deed couldn't think of anyone who could do the job better. When this mess was over, Holt planned to spend part of his time at their ranch, helping Blue. Being county sheriff wasn't a full-time job or expected to be.

Somewhere a coyote talked to a nonresponsive moon and the broken land took on a ghostly look in all directions. Bones of animals were radiant in the soft moonlight. Overhead an owl screeched and flew after a later supper. Holt avoided staring at the moon. That was bad luck. Besides, he needed to concentrate on where they were headed.

Rose's head bobbed and it looked like he had actually gone to sleep. Deed watched him slump forward in the saddle, then jerk awake. The process repeated itself several times as they rode.

They stopped to give the horses water from their canteens, and to sip some themselves. A cluster of wilted wildflowers provided something for the horses to eat.

Around them, the night had the usual night sounds, which were comforting. Silka helped Tag from the packhorse and the dog went to Holt. After giving his horses and Tag water from his hat, Holt loosened the rope around Rose's hands so he could exercise them and drink some offered water from his own canteen. He stayed in the saddle while the others dismounted. They decided not to switch horses; the trail had been relatively easy and level.

"How much farther?" Rose asked, after returning the canteen to his saddle horn.

"No more than three hours, I think," Holt said and rubbed his unshaved chin. "Only been this way once before . . . and that was walking. But I think we'll be there for breakfast."

Rose nodded and Silka retied his hands to the saddle horn.

"How are you doing?" Deed asked, shoving his hat back on his forehead.

"I'm all right. Just weak," Rose replied. "Guess I was lucky. That red bastard could've killed me."

"Yeah, they had that in mind for all of us," Deed said.

"W-will they follow us?"

"Hard to say. Hope not," Deed answered. "Of course, they aren't the only Indians in

150

this region."

Holt slapped his thigh for the dog and Tag reappeared with a dead field mouse in his mouth. Laughing, the oldest Corrigan put the dog back on the packhorse and let him enjoy his find.

Holt stepped into the saddle. "We stung them hard. They don't like that, especially a devil like Achak. He has to come after us, to prove his medicine is good."

"Where would they go if they didn't?" Rose asked, looking at his wrapped wrists.

"Oh, likely they would hit some ranch or farm at the edge of Hammonds. Someplace without a lot of firepower." Holt nudged his horse into a trot.

"Damn."

"The army is always going after the Indians to get them back on the reservation. Wouldn't those Indians worry about that?" Rose asked, worry in his voice.

Deed replied, "Yes, but they know the army is nowhere close now. So we'd be a nice prize with these horses . . . and guns." Deed looked around the quiet land.

"Wouldn't mind seeing some boys in blue right about now," Deed said.

"Actually, I wouldn't, either."

They rode on into the night. Morning light was teasing the hillside as they reined up among boulders and brush inside the narrow box canyon he had visited earlier. To his left was a low set of rolling hills. Holt remembered they had reminded him of a woman lying on her side. This time he didn't even smile.

"A spring's over there," Holt pointed. "It's fresh and cold."

"Sounds good." Deed eased from his saddle, feeling weary all over.

A field rat darted across the opening, followed by another. Holt helped Rose from the saddle after untying his restraints. The wounded townsman had difficulty standing. Holt held him in place until Rose insisted he could walk. The young sheriff guided him to a level place among the rocks where Deed had laid out a blanket for him. Rose was asleep in minutes.

Deed and Silka unsaddled the horses, including the packhorse. Tag went exploring. They watered the tired animals and rubbed them down with sacks empty from holding oats. After that effort, the horses were given nosebags of grain and picketed. Holt started a small fire, being careful to use wood that wouldn't smoke.

After the fire had steadied itself, he took the coffeepot from their supplies and filled it from the stream. The aroma of boiling coffee and sizzling bacon reminded all of them that they were hungry. Holt decided to make biscuits and soon his shirt was dotted with white flour.

"Going to have any flour left for more biscuits down the road?" Deed teased as he walked from the horses.

"If there isn't, you'll go without."

Breakfast was good, especially Holt's biscuits. Tag smelled the breakfast, too, and enjoyed his share. Silka took the first sentry while the Corrigan brothers slept. All of them were worn out. Carrying Holt's field glasses, Silka climbed up the rocky slope, blotched with patches of brush so he could get a view of what was happening, if anything, outside the small canyon.

It took time to get high enough, but his concern was on the prairie, not the canyon entrance. He was uneasy about them being in an enclosure with only one way out. Deed hadn't been concerned. Neither was Holt. His examination of the land was reassuring. No signs of dust in any direction. Yet he was strangely alert. Strangely worried. A sense of danger filled him and he didn't know why.

Behind him was movement. Slight but definite. Silka's fighting instincts saved his life. Without turning to see, he took a quick step to his left and then spun around. His movement was enough. A Comanche lunged at him, slashing his arm with his scalp knife, instead of catching Silka's throat as intended.

Silka slammed the butt of his Winchester against the warrior's head and looked up. Two more Comanche appeared like ghosts from thirty feet away. Both had drawn bows. An arrow hit Silka in the chest and a second drove into his right thigh. He fired his gun, levering it as fast as he could.

One Comanche was down and unmoving; the other was hit in the shoulder, but still shooting arrows. A third arrow struck Silka in his injured arm. Silka fired again and missed. A fourth arrow sang past his head.

From below came fierce yells. Deed bounded up the incline, appeared at the top of the hill, and fired his Spencer at the remaining warrior. His shot slammed into the Indian's stomach and drove him backward. A second shot from Deed toppled the warrior, headfirst.

"My God, Silka!"

Deed hurried to his friend and held him. Silka tried to smile.

"They surprise me. I am getting old."

"Lie down, my friend," Deed said and helped Silka to the ground. Half of the

Oriental's shirt was wet crimson. Deed knew the first thing he must do was stop the bleeding in Silka's arm. Using the throwing knife carried on a leather strand down his back, Deed tore away part of his own shirtsleeve and tied it tight around Silka's upper arm, releasing and tightening.

"Silka, I've got to stop this bleeding."

"I-I am in good hands. Yours . . . and God's."

After deciding the wound was coagulating, he took off the restraint.

"I'm going to make sure those bastards are dead, then we'll get those arrows out."

"I-I understand, son. Do not hurry." Silka mumbled something in Japanese that Deed didn't quite get, but thought it was that a warrior should die like this, fighting.

Holt appeared at the top of the hill with a revolver in both hands. Tag was at his side.

"There might be more of them," Deed declared. "Better go back to the horses. Uh, put a pot of water on the fire. I'm going to need something for bandages. Your medicine too."

"All right." Holt looked at Silka and grimaced. He wanted to ask his brother how bad the injuries were, but didn't dare, not in front of Silka. He returned his guns to his shoulder holsters and climbed down, talking to Tag.

Deed walked around the uneven hilltop, firing his Spencer into the heads of the downed Comanche. The anger in him was barely controlled. They had hurt, and hurt badly, his best friend, his mentor, his substitute father. After assuring himself there was no imminent danger, he returned to Silka, who was obviously suffering.

Deed removed Silka's sword from his back to make him more comfortable and ripped open Silka's shirt to examine the arrow in his chest. The arrow had entered his chest just under his shoulder blade. The wound was deep; the arrow had nearly gone all the way through his body. He felt along Silka's upper back and could feel the arrowhead just under the skin.

"I've got to push the arrow through," Deed said. "Then I can cut it off and pull out the shaft. It's going to hurt, Silka."

"I am ready."

"Wait, I'm going to get Rose's flask. Some whiskey will dull the pain," Deed said, putting his hand across Silka's forehead.

"Silka no need whiskey."

"Think of it as medicine, old friend," Deed said. "I'm going to need hot water and some of the salve you always carry."

"I see."

"I'll be right back."

Deed met Holt at the bottom of the hill, holding a jar of ointment and a shirt from Silka's saddlebags. At Holt's insistence, the dog stayed by the dying fire.

"I'll come up to help you make Silka comfortable and then head right back," Holt responded. "Like you said, they might not be alone."

They went back up to the top.

"Yeah, they were good enough, to get close to Silka without him knowing."

"I'll keep a sharp eye."

Propping up Silka's head, Deed offered him a drink from the flask. The Oriental grimaced at the taste.

"No like."

"Not giving it to you to like, you old dog," Deed said and held the flask to Silka's mouth. "Drink. It'll help."

Silka swallowed two more sips, then said he'd had enough. Deed made him drink one more; he knew what he had to do was going to hurt and hurt a lot. He picked up a thick stick and placed it in Silka's mouth.

"Bite down on this. I'm going to push this arrow through. It'll hurt."

"Aiie, a samurai is ready to die."

"You're not going to die. It's just going to hurt."

Deed took hold of the arrow shaft protruding from Silka's chest and pushed down with both hands. Silka's face broke out in sweat and his trembling hands became tightened into fists. Deed also shivered as he applied all his strength to forcing the point through the skin in Silka's back.

Finally, the arrowhead popped through. He drew the throwing knife hung behind his neck and made quick work of the arrowhead, severing it from the shaft. Deed took a deep breath.

"One more tough move," the young gunfighter said and grabbed the arrow protruding from Silka's chest and began to pull.

Silka passed out and the stick fell to the ground.

The shaft came free, bringing fresh blood and a little tissue. Deed cleaned the wound with whiskey and hot water. After applying some of Silka's salve to both wounds, he bandaged it with strips from the shirt, noting to himself that the shirt was Holt's. Deed moved his attention to the arrow in Silka's thigh. The arrow hadn't gone as deep as the chest wound, probably due to Silka's movement. Silka's pant leg cut open easily so Deed could get to the embedded shaft, then he made four cuts around the arrow to allow for easier withdrawal.

The arrowhead came free, bringing more fresh blood. He cleaned and bound the wound, then began removing the arrow in Silka's arm. The arrowhead had been driven through his arm. Deed cut off the point, removed the shaft, and cleaned and dressed the wound. He was glad Silka had passed out.

Finished, he laid exhausted beside Silka.

Below, Holt stared at the canyon's opening and the shadows beginning to sneak into the brush-laden corners. Anyone trying to enter the canyon would be subject to heavy rifle fire by him. From the tobacco pouch, he took a handful of shreds and tossed them in all directions, thanking the canyon's spirits for allowing them to stay and asking for their protection. Holt blamed himself for Silka's wounds; he had waited too long to give tribute to the spirits.

It was time to make supper and he welcomed the task. He went over to the stream with a pot from their supplies, his eyes alert for any movement. Their food was getting low, but should be enough if they could make it to Wilkon in a few days. Killing an antelope would be a nice addition to their menu.

Alongside the strips of jerky were the remains of a salted bacon slab, cans of beans

159

and peaches, a handful of carrots and six potatoes, dried fruit and apples, a small sack of salt, a half sack of flour and another of sugar. There was a sack of coffee and a sack of crackers. Two large sacks of oats remained for the horses. The large sacks carrying the Wilkon bank's money were set off to the side, along with a shovel, a hand axe, extra picket pins, and hobbles. Three "good 'nuffs," slip-on substitutes for horseshoes if any were lost. Three boxes of cartridges, a waterproof container of matches, and a small bird's nest of tinder and sticks were also part of their supplies. Personal items were carried by each man in his own saddlebags.

He would make a broth for Rose and Silka, and later, a heavier stew for Deed and himself. Some small sticks made the fire stronger. After the water was boiling, he shaved jerky into the pot, offering an occasional morsel to Tag, and stirred the broth with his knife. Later, he would add bigger chunks of jerky, a cut-up potato and three carrots, and a few wild onions he had found to make a hearty meal.

Checking the broth, he decided it was as good as he could make it. He tasted the hot liquid and decided the broth was definitely worth eating. Putting on his gloves, he poured some into a tin cup and took it to Rose. Tag trotted along as if on a wonderful adventure.

CHAPTER THIRTEEN

"Malcom, can you eat something?" Holt said, leaning over the sleeping townsman. "I made some broth. Be good for you."

Malcolm Rose pushed himself up from his blanket and looked around. "How long have we been here?"

"Since morning. Six hours or so," Holt answered. "How are you feeling? Better blow on it. She's hot."

"Sure. Sure. Thanks." Rose blew on the brew and tasted it. "Say, that's right good."

"There's more."

"Was I dreaming . . . or did I hear gunshots a while ago?"

Holt glanced up the hill. "Deed and Silka shot some Comanche trying to sneak up on us."

"C-Comanche? Oh, Lord, how many?" Rose almost dropped the cup, spilling some of the broth on his blanket.

"Three. They're dead." Holt wasn't sure if

he should tell Rose that Silka was badly wounded.

Rose wiped his hand across the blanket where he had spilled. Tag inspected the spill and licked it. The townsman watched the dog, then looked up at Holt. "I'm going to be all right. Just a little weak, that's all. Should be just fine in a few days." He took a sip of the broth. "How long are we staying here? Are we in danger of being attacked?"

"Tomorrow, we'll ride to Turkey Wing," Holt said. "I hope we don't run into any more Indians, but nobody can say for sure, you know that."

Rose nodded and drank more, then patted his coat pocket. "Wonder where I put my flask? A little sip would taste good."

Holt licked his mouth. "It's up with Silka and Deed. I took it when you were sleeping."

"What?"

"Silka's been hurt. Bad. The Comanche ambushed him when he was standing guard," Holt said. "The rest of us were sleeping. We used some of your whiskey to clean his wounds."

"I thought you said the Comanche were dead."

"They are. Silka killed them, even as they were shooting him."

"Oh." Rose put his hand against his injured shoulder. "Was he hurt worse than me?"

"Yes. A lot worse." Holt was sorry to have stated Silka's situation that way, but it was true.

"I see. So my wound isn't bad."

"I didn't say that, Malcolm," Holt said, getting irritated. "But Silka had an arrow in his chest, another in his arm and a third in his thigh. As well as a deep knife gash in his arm."

Rose stared at Holt without speaking.

Holt folded his arms. "Deed's going to stay up there tonight. We can't move him. I'm going to take Deed's horses up there. They'll warn Deed if anybody tries to sneak up. I'll stay down here and guard the rest of our horses."

"My Lord! We're all going to be killed!"

"That's not our plan."

Rose began babbling and waving the cup in his hand.

"Careful there. You'll spill your broth." Holt was trying hard not to be disgusted. "Tag'll be happy if you do, come to think of it."

Rose stared at him. "What difference does it make! We're all going to be dead by morning."

"Stop being a stupid little kid," Holt blurted. "I've got to take some broth up to Deed, so he can give it to Silka." He turned toward the fire.

"B-but what about me?"

"I'll bring back your whiskey if there's any left."

"There better be."

Holt spun around. "Drink your broth and shut up. I've got to help a *brave* man." He walked over to the fire, put a spoon in his pocket, and filled another cup of broth.

Picking up a canteen with his other hand, he headed up the hill, then stopped. Tag was surprised, but came to a stop a few steps behind. Holt yelled, "There's more broth if you want it . . . and you're not afraid to get it."

Holt fought to regain his temper as he continued walking up the slope. Deed was sleeping next to Silka. Tag's lick on his face brought Deed awake with a start, fumbling for his holstered revolver.

"Easy, little brother. Looks like you did well. Silka's sleeping good," Holt said and handed him the flask. "Here, there's some left. Take a drink of Rose's whiskey. You could use it."

Deed sipped the offered flask and handed it back. Without drinking himself, Holt pushed the stopper in place and shook it to see how much remained. Very little. Rose would have to do without. He hoped the townsman would complain.

"Here's some broth and some water for Silka. You'll have to give it to him with this spoon."

"Thanks. I'll wait for him to wake up." Deed shook his head to clear it. "How far to Turkey Wing?"

"Not far. Half a day, maybe."

"You wanted to bury McDugal and Buck."

"Yeah, but that was before this," Holt said, motioning toward Silka. "Might not be the smart thing to do now."

Deed was silent, staring at the unconscious Silka. "He's hurt bad, Holt."

"I know. But he's a tough man."

"We can't move our camp," the youngest Corrigan said, putting his hands together as if to pray. "We can't move him. Not yet."

"I agree, but the horses will be out of grass soon. We'll leave tomorrow. We have to." Holt walked across the rocky hilltop, examining the dead Comanche, and returned.

"Here's what we'll do. You rest and I'll bring two horses up here. They'll make good alarms. One of us will stay up here tonight. The other, below. Tag'll help, too."

Holt and Deed talked a few minutes

longer. Moving the entire camp to the hilltop wasn't practical. Any fire this high would be seen for miles. Silka needed rest, maybe for days, but they would have to move before he could ride. There was no doubt they would have to build a travois and should start looking for any poles that would suffice. Holt said he would fix them some stew and bring it up when ready.

Deed mumbled something about the stew sounding good, then said, "He can't die. He can't."

"Silka's going to be fine, Deed. You did well treating him. No doctor could've done better."

"I'll stay here with him," Deed said, looking at Silka.

"Sure. I'll bring up your ponies," Holt responded, "and some blankets for both of you. It'll be cold tonight, especially up here. Hard to believe, but it will."

"Let me know when it's ready and I'll come down. I can bring up the ponies then." Deed bit his lip. "How's Malcolm doing?"

"Good enough to know his flask is missing," Holt said, shaking his head. "If he's not careful, he's really going to have something to whine about."

"He's a good man, Holt."

"Maybe." Holt put his hand in his pocket and withdrew the small red medicine stone. "Got something I want to leave with Silka. It'll help bring him back. It's done that for me, you know."

"He'll appreciate that, Holt."

Stepping over to the prone Silka, Holt laid the stone on his bloody shirt. As he turned away, Silka's eyes fluttered open. He took the stone with his left hand, squeezed it, and said, *"Arigato."*

"You're welcome, my friend," Holt said softly. He patted his brother on the shoulder and retreated down the hill with Tag bouncing behind him.

After a few minutes, Deed focused on the wounded samurai. "Silka, you need to drink some water. Have some of this broth Holt made for you."

He put his hand on Silka's forehead. It was hot. Very hot.

"I not thirsty."

"Please, for me. Take a swallow or two. You've lost a lot of blood. Your body needs this."

The severely wounded Oriental swallowed six spoonsful of water and broth, then shook his head. "Where is my gun?" His hand patted the ground.

"It's right here," Deed said and moved

the Winchester beside Silka.

"Is reloaded?"

"Uh, no."

"What have I told you?" Silka's breathing was labored.

"Sure." Deed shoved new cartridges into the gun.

"Is cocked? We may have more fight tonight. Must be ready."

"It is now," Deed said. "How about some more broth?"

"Where is my sword?"

"It's right beside you. Now, how about some more broth?"

"No. I sleep now."

"All right. Sleep, my good friend," Deed said and stood, checking the load in his carbine.

The heat of the day was leaving when Holt called to Deed that the stew was ready. The meal was good, and so was the hot coffee. Rose was asleep again or pretending to be. Earlier, Holt had laid the nearly empty flask next to him.

The brothers talked quietly, looking forward to the coming dusk. Much of their talk was about their ranch and taking over the Bar 3 as well. There was no mention of their dangerous situation. Both had been in similar situations. Both had survived. Neither looked into the fire. To do so would blind a man for an instant that could mean the difference between life and death if he had turn around quickly and shoot.

A quail called out for company, but none answered. Holt and Deed listened carefully and decided it was, indeed, a real quail. No echo that would have come from an Indian. Tag seemed to listen for a moment, then stretched out beside Holt. Holt thought they should secure the horses more than usual and Deed agreed.

Silka needed sleep, but they wouldn't be able to give him much.

"I looked at those scrawny cottonwoods by the spring," Holt said. "A couple should work."

"Good. Thanks for the stew," Deed replied and laid back on his elbows. "You'll make somebody a good wife one of these days."

They both chuckled.

"When we get back, I think you'd better get yourself hitched up to that fine stage-coach lady," Holt said and poured more coffee for both of them.

"Guess that'll be up to her."

"Well, don't make her guess."

Deed smiled. "Since when have you become the expert on marriage?"

"Since I didn't . . . and didn't ask." He

scratched Tag's back with his fingers.

Deed studied his brother's face, painted by the low orange of their fire, and changed the subject. "I'll take my horses back with me. That'll stretch our grass a little."

"Some, but we'll be gone by noon. I was going to suggest taking my ponies, but they wouldn't be worried by Comanche." Holt motioned toward the horses. "Rather not use our grain if we don't have to."

"How much is left?"

"Two sacks."

The brass circle at Deed's neck glinted in the glow of the fire. As if on signal, the two gunfighters moved away from the fire.

"Reckon I'd better get back," Deed said. "See you in the morning. You're in charge of breakfast." He chuckled.

"If that quail's still around, we might have him."

Both men headed for the picketed horses and hobbled them as double protection. Deed took his two horses with him up the slope. They made the climb easily and immediately took to the clumps of grass. After settling the horses, Deed covered Silka with a blanket and managed to put another under him.

Silka looked past him, holding the medicine stone in his right fist. "Horses?"

Deed told him what they had done, and why. Feverish, Silka insisted that the animals be tied and hobbled both. He reminded Deed that Comanche were magicians when it came to stealing horses. The youngest Corrigan promised to do so, deciding not to tell him that they had already done the extra step.

He soaked the folded shirtsleeve with a canteen and placed it on Silka's feverish forehead. Deed tried to get the Oriental to drink some water and the now-cooled broth with a spoon. Silka accepted three swallows, two of water. He muttered a woman's name and fell into a troubled sleep. Deed recognized Toshie as the name of his late wife.

Waiting beside Silka for a few minutes, he decided the Oriental was going to stay asleep. Taking his Spencer, he sat with his back against an upright boulder. After an hour, he got up and inspected the two horses. Late afternoon was bringing a cooler temperature and a frisky wind. He wrapped his own blanket around his shoulders and considered building a small fire. If he put it against the boulder, a hatful of flame, it wouldn't be seen far, or would it? He recalled seeing a campfire ten or fifteen miles away on a still night. No, it wasn't worth the risk.

His thoughts moved to the dead Indians. Were there more around? Likely. Achak would be a shrewd enemy.

What if they moved in below, trying for their horses? Would Holt stay awake all night? He was as weary as Deed was. Maybe they should have tried to bring Silka below. Would they have been able to do so without hurting him more? Not likely.

To his right, a quail called out.

He was immediately alert. It wasn't a quail.

A second quail answered from somewhere on the other side of the boulder. The horses' ears were up.

Two Comanche!

CHAPTER FOURTEEN

Two Comanche crawled toward Deed, one on each side of the large boulder. The warrior to his right was headed for the two horses and they were agitated. More might be closing in below.

Deed stood, pulling the blanket from him and holding a corner with his left fist. His Spencer was in his right. He spun to his right, around the boulder, and threw the blanket in the direction of the darker shadow where the horses were tied. The blanket surprised the Indian as it settled around him. Deed's Spencer roared in the night, fired like a pistol with his right hand and the butt braced against his thigh. Pushing wildly at the blanket to get it away from him, the Comanche stiffened. His knife clattered on the rocks. Deed levered the big gun and fired again.

Turning back to his left, the second warrior ran at him, knocking Deed's carbine from his hands. He fell backward, kicking up as he fell, catching the warrior full in the groin and slamming his hand against the man's wrist, driving the knife from the Comanche's hand. The warrior groaned and staggered away. Deed drew his revolver and fired. The Comanche's eyes were wide and fierce as Deed's shots rammed into the warrior's stomach. He folded to the ground.

Standing with his revolver at his side, Deed jumped as a shot rang out and the first Comanche, wounded but not killed, took a step and fell forward. The shot had come from Silka's rifle.

Deed shook his head. His mentor had actually come to his rescue in spite of his serious condition.

From below, Holt yelled out, "Deed, are you all right?"

"Yeah. Watch yourself," came his brother's echoing reply.

After assuring himself that both Comanche were dead, Deed walked over to Silka lying on his back as before. Only now he held a smoking rifle in his hands.

"You saved my life, my friend," Deed said.

"Aiie, just as you saved mine."

Holt Corrigan sat below, away from their small fire, and deep in a long dark finger of a shadow finding its way in the dusk. Every handful of minutes, he had been getting up and checking on the horses, then on to Rose. The activity kept him awake, along with cups of strong coffee. Comanche would attack until dark, he was certain. He had thought about having Tag stand guard among the horses, but that would only sacrifice the dog. The gunshots from above brought Holt to his feet, cocking the hammer of his already levered Winchester.

Tag growled and attacked the shadows behind them. It was enough.

Holt spun and saw a Comanche trying to push Tag off his forearm holding a tomahawk. The dog's jaws were clamped tight; the rest of Tag's body dangled in the air. The young sheriff was amazed at how close the Indian had come without him hearing his advance. He fired, holding the gun against his hip. Five quick became one long explosion and the bullets became a square in the warrior's heart. The Comanche stiffened and fell face-first into the dirt.

"You made the difference, boy. Thanks, Tag." He moved beside the dead body and coaxed the dog into releasing his grip.

Turning his attention to the horses, Holt told Tag to stay by the fire and hurried past the slowly arousing Malcolm Rose and toward the picketed animals. Three Comanche were moving among them. Three mounts stomped their hooves, whistled, and snorted.

"Deed, I need help! At the horses."

To his right, he saw Deed coming down the hillside. Holt glanced toward him and held up three fingers. Deed took two more steps, knelt, aimed, and fired at the closest shadow who hopped onto one of Holt's Comanche horses. Deed's bullet drove into the small of his back and the warrior slumped against the horse's neck. As the Corrigan brothers had guessed earlier, the two mounts were not disturbed by the appearance of the Indians.

Holt fired an instant behind his brother and fired five more times as fast as he could lever the gun. All three Comanche were hit, but not downed. The other horses reared wildly, pulling on their restraints. Only the hobbles had been cut but the pickets were holding.

Running closer, Deed stopped and fired, ripping lead again into the mounted Comanche and at the fleeing warriors. Holt ran beside the horses and levered shots at the two escaping warriors. His first shot caught the farthest Indian in the hip and spun him sideways, but he continued running. His second shot missed the remaining

Comanche limping into the night. From the opposite side, Deed levered his big Spencer and fired. If he hit the Comanche, he couldn't tell.

Frustrated, he yelled a fierce samurai challenge.

"What the hell was that?" Holt asked, firing once more at nothing.

"Oh, that's something Silka used to say. It was a toast. 'Long live death, long live war, long live the cursed mercenary.' I was mad and it just came out," Deed explained.

"Well, they got away," Deed said, "but we stung 'em some."

"Yeah, don't think it's smart to trail them," Holt declared.

"Good way to run into an ambush."

Behind them, Malcolm Rose staggered to his feet, grasping his rifle. "W-where they are?"

"It's all right, Malcolm. Go back to sleep," Holt yelled and began reloading his rifle.

Tag barked and came running to Holt's side.

"They're gone, Malcolm," Deed said, shoving a new loading tube into his carbine.

The two brothers dragged the dead Comanche from Holt's horse and into a ravine and began retying hobbles.

"We're going to need some new hobbles.

No way we're going to save these." Deed held up a cut hobble and headed for their supplies.

"Damn, those devils came out of the earth," Holt said and checked on the pack-horse, who seemed especially agitated. "Tag saved my life back yonder. The bastard was close enough to shake hands. He had other ideas."

"Good for Tag," Deed said and slapped the back of a long-legged bay.

Deed returned with three sets of new hobbles and they reworked the animals where necessary. The horses seemed to like the attention and soon settled down. The Comanche horses were never bothered.

"How far away do you think they left their horses?" Deed asked and replaced a hobble on a gray.

"Farther than a white man, that's for sure." Holt stood, then rechecked a bay's picket. "How many?"

"I think that was it. Wouldn't be traveling with a larger group," Deed said. "I could be wrong. Wouldn't be the first time."

"Are we making a mistake splitting up?" Holt pulled on his hat brim and picked up his Winchester.

Deed rubbed his nose. "No, it gives us a little advantage. Besides, I don't want to move Silka until we have to."

"Agree."

As they walked back to the fire, Holt noticed it had a dark hole in its middle, a sure sign of death. He nodded to himself and dragged a branch over the coals. The deaths were Comanche deaths, he assured himself. Looking down at Tag, he brushed the dog's head with his fingers and the animal responded with a wag of his tail.

Rose stood, watching them. "Did you get them all?"

"No. Two got away," Deed said without glancing up. "We put some lead in them though."

"W-will they come back?"

"They might, Malcolm, but we'll keep watch," Holt growled, "and ride out come morning."

"Is there any coffee?" Rose asked, swallowing his fear.

"Just put a new pot on, before all the noise. Bring your cup." Holt motioned for him to advance.

Holt poured coffee for the three of them.

With a cup in his hand and rifle in other, Rose said, "I can stand guard for a while . . . if you trust me."

Holt sipped the hot coffee and grinned. "That would be great, Malcolm. We could use some sleep."

"Thanks, Malcolm. That would help a lot," Deed added.

After drinking a little from his cup, he asked Rose if there was any whiskey left. Surprised, the townsman told him that he didn't know, that he hadn't touched the flask since Holt brought it back.

"I want to add a little in this coffee for Silka," Deed explained. "And some sugar. He loves sugar." He grinned.

Rose went over to his blankets, retrieved the flask, shaking it as he returned.

"Here, Deed. There's some in there. Please take it. I've got a full bottle in my gear."

"Thanks.'

Deed poured a little whiskey into the coffee and resealed the flask.

"There's sugar with the supplies." Holt motioned with his rifle.

"Good. I'll see you boys in the morning."

Above, Deed went over to Silka and checked his forehead. The former samurai stirred and gazed at him.

"There were more." Silka said. It wasn't a question.

"Yes. Four."

"You and your brother got them."

"No, just two," Deed said.

"Have you reloaded your gun?"

"I have."

"Have you reloaded mine?"

"I did earlier. How about drinking some of this coffee? Holt just made it. Got lots of sugar in it."

"I will do so. It sounds good." Silka accepted the cup with his left hand.

Back at the Comanche camp, the two warriors reported their failure to Achak. His eyes flashed a hatred that went beyond sanity. Five of their fellow tribesmen had been killed by these white devils. And now these two came back wounded. The two warriors weren't sure what Achak would do next. More words might bring death from their leader. One held his wounded arm and shivered. The taller warrior, next to him, shook his head for silence.

From their tied ponies came the large-shouldered warrior wearing the sleeveless army jacket. Hakan's face was streaked with vertical lines of war paint. In his belt was a big Colt.

"Achak, is your medicine broken?" Hakan declared. "Many warriors have died under your leadership. Warriors whose names will no longer be spoken. Before long, the blue-eyes will find us and then we will all die.

Without glory. Without honor. What are we going to do?"

He took two more steps toward Achak. "It is time for the old Achak to return to us. It is time for you to lead . . . and win." He placed his hand on the handle of his revolver for emphasis.

Slowly, Achak got to his feet. He looked at each warrior watching him from around the fire, then he smiled. It was an ugly, vicious smile.

"Your words ring with truth, Hakan. You are truly my blood brother," the Comanche war chief snarled. "I, for one, realize the white devils we are fighting are too important to let live. I, for one, want to see the white walker beg for mercy in front of us, *The People.* If you will ride with me, this will happen." He crossed his arms and walked away.

Hakan studied him for a moment, then came to him and embraced him in a warrior's salute.

Achak returned to the fire. "Now, my brothers, let me share with you what the spirits have told me and how we will achieve the honor of all honors. How we will destroy the white walker and his followers. It will be grand." He made a special motion toward the white woman. "Go now and have your

183

way with the white woman, then kill her."

Night passed slowly and dawn finally came with both Corrigans tired, but pleased to see the welcoming sun. The sky was yellow and streaked with gray. Deed checked on Silka, getting him to drink some water, and told him they planned to move. Silka understood and asked for some coffee. With sugar. The samurai was pale, but trying to appear in better shape than he was.

Deed brought him the coffee, laced with whiskey and sugar, and a plate of cooked food. The wounded samurai picked at it, but managed to eat some. The coffee was savored. As he ate, Deed returned with a pot of hot water and new bandages, strips from a towel, to clean and change Silka's bandages. The wounds were red and angry, but, so far, not infected.

"Thank you, my son." Silka handed back the emptied cup.

"You rest," Deed said, completing his task. "I'm going to grab some breakfast at the fire. I'll be back."

"Do not hurry. I have your brother's medicine stone." He held up the small stone in his left hand.

Deed led his two horses downhill and saddled the gray. After a breakfast, they started work cutting poles for the travois. The poles were placed through the stirrups on the saddled dun. They decided it was the sturdiest horse for carrying the travois. Two blankets were tied to the poles. While they worked, Rose packed their supplies.

The wounded townsman brought the readied packhorse and asked if there was anything else he could do. Both Corrigans were surprised and pleased at his help.

"Tell you what," Holt said. "I'd appreciate it if you made sure our fire was out and all of our canteens are full. Water bag, too. All right?"

"Sure."

"Great. Deed and I will be bringing Silka down and putting him on the rig." Holt pointed toward the quiet horse with the prepared travois.

Deed walked over to Rose, who was pouring handfuls of dirt on their small fire. "Malcolm, do you want us to tie you on your saddle, like before?"

"No. Thank you. I can ride." Rose looked up. "I'm sorry to have such a drag. I had no idea what this would be." His manner had turned timid again as if the whiskey had worked its way through him.

"Don't apologize, Malcolm," Deed said. "You've been an important part of this posse. We're proud to have you riding with us."

"I appreciate that, Deed. A lot." Rose picked up a canteen and sprinkled water on the dead fire. "How soon before we get home?" He tried not to show his weariness or react to the pain in his shoulder.

"Well, we'll hole up at Turkey Wing for the rest of the day," Deed explained, adjusting his gun belt. "Then, if Silka's doing all right, we'll head out from there. Probably at night again." He rubbed his unshaved chin. "If everything goes right, we should be home in two days." He smiled. "You'll be in your missus' arms in no time."

"Reckon the town'll be glad to get the money back."

"You bet. You'll be a hero."

Rose grinned and headed toward the spring to refill the canteens.

With a pat on the back as he walked past, Deed rejoined Holt and they headed uphill with Tag jumping around them as they walked. Silka was sleeping. The coffee cup was empty, but only a few bites of the breakfast were gone.

"He didn't eat much," Deed said, lifting the rag on Silka's forehead. "His fever's down. A little."

"He's a tough man," Holt replied. "Why

don't you eat that, we'll just have to throw it out."

Picking up the plate, Deed tossed the food in several directions. "I'll leave it as a thank-you. To the canyon spirits."

Holt chuckled. "That's what I would've done, little brother."

"Think we can carry him down?"

"Sure. Put that plate and cup on the blanket, along with his sword and rifle," Holt said. "We'll put them in the pack after we get him settled."

Deed put Silka's sheathed sword on his shoulder and laid the rifle beside the sleeping man. The two men lifted Silka by the shoulders and upper legs, and started down the slope. The plate started to slide. They stopped.

"Can you reach it?" Holt asked.

"Yeah, I think so. Let me cradle him on my knee."

Silka stirred and muttered something in Japanese that neither understood.

"What was that? Some kind of secret samurai code?" Holt asked.

"Wasn't that. I know all of those." Deed stretched out his hand, resettled the plate, then retook Silka's shoulders. "Ready."

"Easy does it. He's one heavy boy."

Deed grunted agreement.

Minutes later, Silka was resting on the travois, still muttering. Tag checked him and Holt picked up the dog and placed him on top of the packhorse for traveling.

"Holt, we're going to leave a trail that a child could follow." Deed pointed at the travois.

"You're right, but I don't know what to do about it."

Cocking his head, Deed suggested they should put the two Apache horses in their rear. Any Indians seeing the tracks of unshod horses would assume it was Indians.

"Interesting idea," Holt said. "Can't hurt. If they don't get rid of all the travois marks, maybe they'll think it's Indians with their families." He patted his horse's neck. "I'll ride Silka's other horse."

CHAPTER FIFTEEN

Back in town, Wilkon was trying to return to normal, but it was difficult. Men and women were doing the things of everyday life, getting horses shod, buying what they needed in the town's stores, having saddles and harness repaired. Men were spending time in the saloons talking crops, cattle, weather, horses, Comanche, and Agon Bordner's men and the bank being robbed, and whether or not the posse would get the money back.

That was the most important topic, although it wasn't the one most frequently discussed. The facts were obvious: the posse hadn't come back yet.

As soon as the posse rode out, Judge Pence conducted a brief hearing that became a full trial of the just-arrested Bordner outlaws. They were convicted of murder of a peace officer, attempted murder of a county sheriff, and assault against a citizen.

The sentence for each was life in prison. Pence wired the authorities immediately and made arrangements for these outlaws to be taken with the others when the Rangers came.

Underneath the normal activity was tension. Would the Rangers arrive soon enough to take away the arrested Bordner men, or would there be more violence in the street from other members of the old gang? Would the posse be successful? Would Blue Corrigan and his friend, James Hannah, be able to stop any attempts to hurt the town? There was also worry about Comanche and where they might be. Few wanted to express the possibility that the posse might be in danger.

At least there was no problem with the bank itself, for now. Before his brothers rode out, they had agreed to reopen the bank with whatever money they could put in from the ranch. The Sanchez family had since agreed to do the same and the bank was operating as if nothing had happened.

Blue Corrigan sipped coffee and read the newspaper as he sat behind the marshal's desk. He had already made his rounds of the town; only two drunks had spoiled his walk and he decided to tell them to go home, instead of jailing them. James Hannah hadn't yet appeared at the marshal's office, but he would soon. Hannah wasn't an early riser even when he was healthy. Blue shifted the heavy Walch Navy 12-shot revolver at his hip to make him more comfortable. He would much rather have been at his ranch than here, but it was his duty.

Blue's mind wandered easily to his wife. Bina was a remarkable woman, he thought. As a full-blooded Mescalero Apache, educated by a Jesuit priest, she was at home in both the white man's and red man's worlds. Her insights had showed up in many of his sermons as the town's part-time minister. The fact their two children were half-breeds didn't bother Bina or him.

"Hey, Corrigan, you know there's more of us coming. Save your life and let us go," Rhey Selmon yelled from the cell. He had been loyal to one man, Agon Bordner, and one cause, helping Bordner become a cattle baron, and that was over. Only a long prison term waited.

Blue didn't respond.

Ice-cold eyes, slightly crossed, stared at him beneath a narrow-brimmed hat and stringy black hair. Rhey still wore his bear-skin coat. But he looked naked without his double-crossed gun belts and their silver-plated revolvers with pearl handles.

"I said let us go and save your life. You ain't got much time. Nobody's going to help you . . . and your brothers are gone," Rhey repeated, yelling louder. Macy Shields and Sear Georgian joined in.

Blue looked up as if he were observing a horse acting up, then went back to reading the newspaper. Holt's telegram lay on the desk. Blue was worried, but didn't act like it. His brothers, Silka, and the two townsmen were crossing bad country, made worse by the news of Achak and his warriors raiding in the region. He had heard something about Mason Mereford that he didn't like. A local rancher had told him that he didn't think Alexander Mereford had a brother.

It was like him to worry. He couldn't get the thought out of his mind. What if this Mason was a plant to set up the posse? Why hadn't he paid more attention? No one seemed to know where Mason had come from. There was no question Blue was the most stable of the three brothers and the least violent. Even so, he couldn't get Mason out of his mind, and the thought of them being ambushed somewhere out on prairie. He would talk to Judge Pence about it, but had already decided to take a posse out tomorrow. Pence had stayed in town to help quell any sense of instability and, without saying so, felt guilty about making Blue take charge of the town's law, but he knew the town would be in good hands.

Bina had been in town for a few days and that had made his heart jump with happiness. She and their children went back to the ranch yesterday. It was quiet on their ranch at this time of the year. Nothing had been done with the Bar 3 yet, but that would wait until Deed and Holt returned. He laid down his coffee cup and patted his coat pocket where the small edition of the Bible was usually carried. He enjoyed serving as a part-time minister along with another local man. But now he was uneasy and wanted comfort.

Taking the Scriptures from his pocket, he flipped it open and saw a familiar verse: "If God be for us, who can be against us?" (Romans VIII, verse 31) It gave him a comfort he couldn't explain.

From the cells, Rhey yelled again, "Hey, Bible thumper! You'd better let us out before our friends hit town. They'll tear off your other arm and shove it down your throat." The rest yelled similar threats.

Blue stood and looked at Rhey, then the others. "You boys are through, you know. Your time of evil is over. No one is coming to help you. No one even cares about you."

He adjusted his heavy gun belt. "You'd be much better off praying for forgiveness."

Rhey was silent for a moment, then cursed and declared, "Bullshit! You'd better let us go, Corrigan. I mean it. There are twenty riders just outside of town. They're going to burn down everything."

Blue laughed and walked over to the small stove, which was belching nearly as much smoke as heat. He picked an ironware cup from the shelf above it and poured fresh coffee.

Rhey and the other continued their verbal barrage, but Blue ignored them as he walked back to the desk and resumed reading his Bible.

After a quick knock on the door, James Hannah strolled into the marshal's office. His Victorian black suit coat was draped over his bandaged shoulder. His bowler hat was cocked forward and he pushed his glasses in place as he entered. An ivory-handled revolver was evident in his waistband. A shiny deputy badge was displayed on his vest. His smile was confident and warm.

"Morning, brother. I see Rangers coming down the street with a prison wagon," Hannah said. "So we'll be able to clean out this jail soon."

Blue looked up and smiled. "Good. I've been getting a lot of threats from the bear boy back there."

"Rhey Selmon, eh?" Hannah chuckled. "Rhey, if you were half as good as you think you are, you wouldn't be behind bars."

"Shut up, Hannah!" Rhey pounded his fist against the cell bars.

"Sure. Sure. Look me up in twenty years . . . when they let you and your buddies out of prison." Hannah walked over to the small stove and poured himself a cup of coffee. "Or, if Marshal Corrigan would oblige, he can hand you a gun right now and we'll see if you're as good as you think."

Before Rhey could respond, there were heavy footsteps on the boardwalk outside, followed by a pounding on the door.

"Texas Rangers. We're here to escort prisoners to the prison," came the hard call.

"Come in."

Blue recognized Rangers Williams and Rice from earlier. He didn't know the square-shouldered man with thick eyebrows, a matching mustache, and a slight limp. The man stepped toward the desk and held out his hand.

"I'm Captain Palerns. This is Ranger Williams and Ranger Rice."

"Glad to meet you, Captain," Blue said,

extending his lone right hand. "I've already had the pleasure of meeting your two associates." He turned toward Hannah. "This is my deputy, James Hannah. We're sitting in for the real sheriff while he's running down some bank robbers." His presentation was more confident than he felt.

Palerns, Williams, and Rice took turns shaking hands with Blue and Hannah.

"Heard about your brother," Captain Palerns said, stepping back toward Blue. "Holt Corrigan was given a pardon, I understand."

"Yes, by *federal* judge Oscar Pence." Blue emphasized the word "federal" to make it clear the pardon was valid. His manner was casual, but he was primed for the lawman to disapprove of the pardon.

"I know Judge Pence. Good man."

"I agree. He's around town somewhere. It's been a rough time."

"Heard that, too," Palerns said. "When you expect your posse to return?"

"Be a handful of days, I suppose. Got a telegram they had retrieved the bank's money . . . and the robbers had resisted." The pinned sleeve of his left arm fluttered as he motioned toward the telegram on the desk.

"And?"

"And they weren't good enough."

Captain Palerns looked over at his fellow Rangers and back to Blue. "You know Comanche are raiding down through there. Achak and a bunch of heathens."

"Had heard, but it didn't make any difference to Holt and Deed . . . or our friend Silka."

"Heard that about them, too," Palerns said. "We may want to recruit those boys one of these days." He cocked his head. "You, too."

"Not me. I'm a rancher."

Palerns smiled awkwardly and presented papers for Rhey Selmon, Sear Georgian, Willard Hixon, and Macy Shields. "I'll take these fellas off your hands." He stared at the cells. "We don't have papers for the other three, but our orders are to take them, too."

"Yeah, they were just tried and convicted. Killed our town's lawman. Wounded another. They wanted to bust out these other boys." Blue smiled. "They weren't good enough, either."

"Well, Judge Pence swings a lot of weight, otherwise we wouldn't be taking them now," Palerns snorted.

Blue accepted the papers and got the cell keys from his desk, then looked up. "Say, Captain, could I talk you into staying in town for a couple of days? I'd like to take a posse out to meet my brothers. As you said, that's nasty country they're coming through."

"Marshal, I wish we could," Palerns replied, rubbing his hands on his shirt. "But we're expected at the prison in three days. That doesn't give us much time."

Both Williams and Rice expressed their disappointment at not being about to stay. Blue thanked them and told them he understood. From the wall next to the door, Hannah watched quietly. The prisoners were released from their cells; all were wearing handcuffs and leg irons.

As they were marched out of the jail, Rhey turned toward Blue. "You know your brothers are dead, don't you, Blue? Who the hell do you think Mason is?" His laugh bounced around the small room. "Mason is Agon's brother."

Hannah came off the wall, pulling his gun from his waistband. The Rangers warned him not to act.

"Don't, James. He isn't worth it," Blue said. "Besides, Deed knew who Mason was before they left."

Rhey's face was a mixture of surprise and hatred. "We'll be back, Corrigan. Count on it."

Hannah laughed and Blue ignored the taunt. As the Rangers led the prisoners into the prison wagon, people began to gather and watch. No one noticed a short man in a black tailored broadcloth suit and black hat standing among the townspeople. His right hand rested on the butt of one of his two pearl-handled pistols carried in a green brocade sash. Light green eyes studied the exiting prisoners.

Rhey Selmon saw him and held up his right fist with two extended fingers for a brief moment before stepping into the wagon. His reaction wasn't missed by Hannah, who looked into the gathered crowd to see whom Rhey spotted. He glimpsed the black-attired man with the blond hair and green eyes and knew he'd seen him before. But where?

They watched the Rangers move the prisoners into the prison wagon, lock them in place, and remount.

Captain Palerns gave a command to the driver and the wagon rumbled into the street. Williams and Rice turned to wave as they rode out. Hannah eased into the crowd, hoping to get a better look at the stranger. But he was gone, moving with the crowd as it returned to normalcy. Hannah stood, studying the street and boardwalks in both directions. Who was that stranger? Where did he know her from?

Returning to the marshal's office, he told Blue about the stranger and the likelihood that Rhey Selmon knew him. Blue poured a cup of coffee and handed it to him, then poured another for himself.

"Saw him." Holt responded. "I'm guessing he's a gunfighter. Maybe a friend of Selmon's." He swallowed a mouthful of the hot brew. "Doesn't matter now. The Rangers are taking that bunch to a hard place for a long time."

"Do I need to find him?"

"Sure. Take a shotgun with you."

Hannah frowned at him. "You think I'm not good enough with a handgun?"

"You know better than that, James," Holt said, pushing his hat back on his head. "But a Greener will stop a lot of trouble before it starts."

Without answering, Hannah went to the gun rack, lifted free a double-barreled shotgun, cracked it open to check the loads, and clicked it shut again. He pulled open the top drawer of the cabinet below the rack, grabbed a handful of shotgun shells, and shoved them into his coat pocket.

"See you later," he said, walking toward the door.

"Sure."

At the doorway, Hannah stopped and looked back. "Deed didn't know who Mason was, did he?"

"No."

"Look, Blue. I can hold down the town for a few days," Hannah said. "Some of the Sanchez boys are in town for supplies. Saw them earlier. They'd be happy to ride out to meet your brothers. It'll be all right, I promise."

Chapter Sixteen

The trail left by Holt, Deed, Silka, and Malcolm Rose was an obvious one to follow with the double lines of the travois, somewhat blurred by the unshod hooves of the two Comanche horses led by Deed. It was the best they could do. The land was yellow and brown with outcroppings of sandstone and battalions of sand. It was hard to believe great cattle country was a few days' ride to the north. In the distance, rain was turning the horizon into a sheet of darkness.

At mid-morning, they stopped to give the horses a breather and canteen water from their hats. Tag was happy to get down and trotted around the area. Rose was weak and had to be helped from his horse and gladly accepted Holt's canteen. Afterward, Holt rode back to check their back trail while Deed tended to Silka, who had gained consciousness. Each man chewed on a piece of jerky and Holt fed half of his to Tag.

"We're about two hours from Turkey Wing," Holt said.

"Oh, that's good to hear." Rose took another swig and handed back the canteen.

His flask was in his pocket, refilled from his remaining bottle, and he was tempted to have a drink, but forced himself to think of something else.

Holt continued, "Up ahead is a cluster of rocks. That's where they ambushed us and killed Ira . . . and Buck. I'm going over there. Maybe I can bury them."

"We're all going," Deed said and looked at Rose.

"Yes. We should all go," Rose added.

Holt bit his lower lip and swung into his saddle. It wasn't long before they saw the remains of the ambush. The bones of those involved were spread about the area. Coyotes and buzzards had long ago cleaned the bodies of flesh.

Jumping off his horse, Holt took Tag from the top of the packhorse and led his own mount toward the skeleton of his dead buckskin. His saddle was weirdly wrapped around the white rib cage. He took off his hat and muttered to himself. Tag began sniffing at the bones and Holt called him back. The dog dropped his tail and returned to the young sheriff's side. Meanwhile,

Deed found the torn head of Ira McDugal; the rest of his bones were scattered. The bones of the dead outlaw and Mason were spread across the area.

"Let's dig a hole and put Ira's bones in it, the best we can," Deed said, moving toward the packhorse. "We can do the same with Buck's remains. All right?"

Holt nodded and returned his hat to his head.

Pulling the shovels from their pack, Deed told Rose to stand guard and began shoveling. After ten shovelfuls, Holt took the second shovel and continued.

"Any signs of dust?" Deed asked Rose.

"No. Nothing out there that I can see."

"Good."

The holes they dug weren't deep, but the sun dictated they should quit. With care, Deed picked up the bones of what he thought belonged to the dead townsman while Holt unstrapped his saddle and carried the bones of his horse to the intended hole. They placed the remains in their respective graves and covered them.

"See anything for a headstone?" Holt asked. "I should've brought something from town."

"It won't last but a few days," Deed said.

"I know, but it'll make me feel better."

"Sure," Deed said and motioned toward the pack. "Look in our supplies. We might have some large sticks that will work."

Holt took a deep breath, went to their packhorse, and withdrew two larger sticks and found two more near the rocks. After tying the sticks into a crude cross, they placed them at the foot of the graves. Holt took off his hat, so did Deed. Rose realized what was happening and did the same.

From the travois, a weak Silka offered the same toast that Deed had yelled as a challenge to the fleeing Comanche, only his weak presentation had the air of a prayer. Both Corrigans looked at each other and nodded. They returned their hats to their heads, thanked Silka, and mounted their horses.

Silka waved weakly for their attention and held out Holt's medicine stone. "C-come, Holt. Y-you must carry this."

"No, you keep it for a while," Holt said.

"Its power needs to be in your hands now," Silka said weakly. "It is best there."

"All right." Holt took the stone, held it a second. and returned it to his coat pocket.

"Are we going to leave the bones of those other two?" Rose asked.

"Yeah," Deed said. "They tried to kill Holt. Let them rot."

It was late afternoon when they approached the rocky area known as Turkey Wing. Holt recommended they spread out in case the Comanche were waiting. As they cleared the last shallow ridge, they saw an antelope drinking. Deed swung his readied Spencer to his shoulder and fired in one motion. The animal lifted its head, took a step, staggered, and fell.

"There's dinner, boys," Deed said.

"Wait," Holt commanded. "What if that antelope was tied there to fool us?"

Deed shrugged his shoulders. "I didn't see any rope."

Without saying more, Holt lifted his Winchester and began spreading lead across and into the rocky formation. Bullets ricocheted off the rocks and whined away. He lowered his rifle and smiled. "All right, let's go in."

A cooking fire was quickly built and cuts of antelope meat were soon broiling on spits above the flames. Holt and Deed rubbed down the horses, let them roll, and picketed them among what little grass existed. The shirt Silka had shoved into the crease to silence its moaning was still there. Tag enjoyed exploring the pockets of water in the rocks around the main basin. They were well visited by animals in the region. The painted buffalo skull with its tied eagle feather reminded them that Indians considered the area haunted and usually stayed away. It was as comforting a thought as they were going to get.

A magpie jabbered its day song and strutted across the rocks in front of Holt, as if daring him to shoot again. He grimaced. A magpie crossing in front of someone meant bad luck. Unless that person made a quick cross from two sticks or bowed three times, repeating "Good day, your Lordship."

He tugged on his hat and bowed. "Good day, your Lordship," then repeated the action and greeting two more times. From the skull, Tag bounded toward the bird. Squawking loudly, the magpie flapped its wings and flew away.

Deed looked over and laughed. "What the hell was that all about?"

Sheepishly, Holt explained that a Gypsy had told him about the superstition. Deed shrugged his shoulders and motioned toward the fire.

"We got anything to eat with this meat?" he asked.

"Not sure. Maybe some beans," Holt replied. "Hey, Malcolm, see if there is a can of peaches in our stuff, will you? I'll look around for some squaw cabbage."

"Sure thing."

"Should've shot that damn bird," Deed teased.

Holt froze and Deed laughed.

Off to the west, thunderheads were meeting and gathering strength. Their growl was menacing and rain was headed their way as dusk hovered over the land.

Holt looked up, glad to be on a different subject. "Looks like we're going to get real wet."

"Yeah. There's nowhere to go. What say we do something with our tarp? Might keep us a little dry. Maybe." Deed headed for their unpacked supplies.

"Good idea. You check on Silka. Malcolm and I will get something rigged up."

"Better get our slickers, too."

While Deed tended to Silka, Rose and Holt took the tarp that had covered their supplies and put up a temporary shelter for the coming rain. It covered their small fire and offered a dry space for them, but not their horses. Their meager supplies were moved under the tarp as well, then Silka himself. Deed was happy to see that none of the samurai's wounds were infected. A testament to Silka's own ointment.

Holt handed Deed a slicker and glanced over at their picketed mounts. "It's going to be a gully washer, Deed. Any thoughts about the horses?"

"The best we can do is to move them under those cottonwoods," Deed responded, slipping into the long coat. "That'll keep the worst of it off them."

"Let's go," Holt said. "Hey, Malcolm, give us a hand with the horses. We're going to move them under those trees."

Soon the horses were picketed under the windbeaten cottonwoods. Some grass was waving from a narrow hollow, along with willows, catclaw, Spanish dagger, and Apache plume. To be on the safe side, they decided to hobble them again as well. Large raindrops pelted their hats and shoulders as they made their way back to the tarp and the welcoming fire.

Holt clapped for Tag and the dog appeared with a prairie dog in his mouth as he dashed across the wetted rocks.

"Good boy. You got your own dinner for a change."

They laughed and it felt good. The antelope meat and coffee smelled delicious. Even the pot of beans looked inviting. The opened can of peaches made the moment even better. Beyond the tarp, the rain seemed to separate them from the rest of the world.

Rose stared at the pouring rain. "This'll wipe out our tracks, right?"

"You're right," Deed responded. There was no reason to tell him that any Indian around knew they would be at Turkey Wing.

CHAPTER SEVENTEEN

The cooked meat, beans, peaches, and a few stalks of squaw cabbage and coffee were savored by the three men, eating silently and staring into the hard rain. It was the last of their food. Deed made a meaty broth and served it to a reluctant Silka a spoonful at a time.

After taking care of his mentor, Deed returned to the fire.

"Were you surprised Achak wasn't waiting for us here?" he asked.

"A little," Holt answered. "It's scary."

"You don't think they went away."

"Do you?"

Deed shook his head. "No."

"You don't think we've lost them?" Rose handed him a cup of coffee.

"Thanks. Got to figure we haven't," Deed said and pushed a stick toward the middle of the fire. "We killed a bunch and that makes it a badge of honor to kill us. Achak has to kill us or be seen as a failure by his people." He sipped the coffee.

No one spoke.

"They know where we are and where we're headed . . . and what our strength is," he concluded.

"A-are we . . ." Rose stammered.

Deed interrupted him. "Not hardly."

Holt stirred his coffee with his finger. "Thinking of pulling out tonight?"

"Yeah. Like we did before. No use staying here."

Holt patted Tag on the head. "We can't reach Wilkon by dawn. Not with the travois. Not close."

"I know, but we'll be a helluva lot closer," Deed said. "I expect Achak will be waiting for us somewhere up ahead. He's got to kill us or lose all respect from the tribe."

"That's a nice thought."

"Yeah, isn't it."

Malcolm Rose stared at them, unsure of what to say or do. What had seemed like a fairly simple civic duty had turned into a nightmare. He touched the healing knife wound on his shoulder, then considered taking a little drink from his flask.

Holt broke into the townsman's thoughts. "What do you think, Malcolm?"

"I . . . uh, I don't know. I just want to get home."

"That's the idea, Malcolm. That's the idea."

They talked about how much water they could carry and in what containers. A coffeepot and three cooking pots would hold water, in addition to their canteens and the water bag. The pots could be pushed down into empty saddlebags. That way most of the water would remain, if they didn't have to run. The coffeepot would be all right if it didn't tip over. Besides that, the heavy rain would likely leave runoff water in places as well. They should have plenty of water to get to Wilkon.

Holt stared at the fire, but saw nothing to guide his thoughts, or warn him of danger. It did remind him to leave a tribute to the spirits.

He shook his head. "Deed, they'll catch us out in the open . . . and tear us apart. We can't move that fast." He glanced at the sleeping Silka. His leg ached from the damp weather, but he ignored the pain.

"Got a better idea? We've got to assume they'll swarm this place at dawn."

"No, not really. I guess it's a risk we'll have to take," Holt said and studied the heavy rain. "Achak isn't going away."

Rose was suddenly alert. "Something's out there!"

Holt and Deed grabbed their rifles and spun away from the fire. They squinted into the downpour, but saw nothing.

"I-I saw something moving. I'm sure of it," Rose said and cocked his Winchester.

"Wait. I see it." Deed said. "It's a toad."

"A toad?"

"Yeah, a toad. Had one come our way yesterday," Deed chuckled. "Probably loving this weather."

Holt sat up and grinned as the toad ambled across their camp, headed for somewhere else. A sign of good luck, for a change, Holt thought. He looked over at his brother.

"I suppose that's some kind of symbol." Deed smiled.

"Yeah, a good luck sign."

"Well, there you go." Deed grinned. "Let's get ready to ride. It'll be totally dark in an hour."

Holt stood. "What do you say we put the travois on my paint? He seems real steady. Give the dun a break."

"Sure."

After a brief exchange, they decided to create the impression that they remained in camp. They would leave the tarp where it was and leave their cooking gear behind. The food was gone anyway. Three blankets were rolled and tied into long, tight appearances, as if they were bodies. The fake bodies were rolled to look like sleeping men. It wouldn't fool the Comanche for long, but for a while. They saddled their horses, prepared the travois for traveling, and placed Silka into it. His mumbling was incoherent.

Deed walked over to Holt. "Got a thought, big brother."

"I'm listening."

Shifting his feet, Deed said, "I figure they'll try to fool us. We'll see a bunch of them ride at us . . . from behind." He motioned toward the dark. "Try to get us distracted. But the main bunch will hit us from the front, probably hiding on the ground."

"Makes good sense," Holt said. "We can't charge them, Deed. Not with Silka." He lowered his voice. "And we can't leave him with Malcolm while we charge, either. So, nothing's changed from what I said before."

"Maybe. Remember when we walked right through that bunch of warriors?" Deed asked. "With me yelling all kinds of stuff? Like I was some kind of mystic."

"Of course I do. It was my idea."

"It might work again."

Deed explained his idea. They would ride into the night as planned. When they stopped several hours from town, they would build as big a fire as they could with flames jumping high. Holt would stand near it, yelling strange things, like he was calling forth great powers. Deed thought they should make their stand in one of the old buffalo wallows along the edge of the dry lake. The deep indentation would give Rose and him a good place to shoot, as good as there was in that area.

Holt took a deep breath. "What if that doesn't work? I'm standing out there in the open, waving my arms."

"I'll do the mystic if you want. Just thought you would have a reputation with them from earlier. Thought they'd remember you walking with a dog. That by itself would make them wonder." Deed rubbed his boot along the wet ground.

"I don't have a problem doing that," Holt said. "I was asking what happens if it doesn't work."

"You jump into the buffalo hole with us and we keep shooting." Deed tried to grin.

Rose waved his arms. "Why don't we stay here?"

"That's what they expect us to do," Deed

replied. "And our old friend Silka likes to say, never do what your enemy expects. Find a way to attack."

"But that's absurd!" Rose's face reddened. "There's only three of us . . . and there's a whole lot of them."

"Right."

"What do you mean 'right'?"

Deed's eyes narrowed. "Malcolm, we're in a fix. My brothers and I have been in them before. We'd like you to help, but you're welcome to stay here."

Rose stared at him and, finally, gulped, "Of course."

"What about taking along that skull?" Holt pointed at the tribute from another time, breaking up the conversation.

"Yes. Good thought. You can hold it up like you're praying," Deed responded.

"Better take along as much firewood as we can," Holt added. "We can't assume there's going to be any . . . or that it's going to be dry."

"Get that axe and we'll cut up some of that downed tree, too."

Quickly, the three men shoved chunks of wood, a few pine knots, and fat branches onto the otherwise empty pack of their packhorse, along with a small nest of starter twigs. Both Corrigan brothers left tributes of tobacco to the spirits of Turkey Wing. Rose watched, but said nothing. He was scared, totally scared. Holt put Tag in his usual position on top of the packhorse. They banked their fire so it would burn for a while, although they had stripped it of most of the wood, and slipped into the darkness.

Night was long, wet and tiring, but the rain had turned into only a nuisance of fat drops. The ground was soggy and silent. The North Star seemed like the only visible light and it was wobbly, but it gave the direction needed.

In the middle of the night, they crossed the dry lake and stopped beside the bigger of the two old buffalo wallows. A yellow moon was sheepishly trying to get around a dark cloud. Night sounds were nonexistent, reinforcing their sense the Comanche were just ahead, waiting.

"Well, little brother, what do you think?" Holt asked as he gave his horse canteen water from his hat and gazed out at the ominous land.

"I think we should build a fire. A big one." Deed patted his horse.

"Let's do it."

Assignments were quickly given and undertaken. Deed and Rose moved all the horses away from where the fire would be built, and watered and picketed them. Holt started constructing the fire with Tag darting around him as if it were a wonderful game.

Deed decided to use their saddles as extra protection against the Comanche bullets and arrows, and began unsaddling the mounts. Rose argued that it would leave them unable to run if necessary. The young gunfighter made it clear they wouldn't be running. Rose bit his lip and nodded.

Two saddles were propped on the south edge of the wallow; the other two, on the north side. Rose gathered a box of cartridges and his rifle and knelt behind the saddles. His job was to watch their back side, where the Corrigans expected to see Comanche on horseback, creating a diversion from the main attack from the other direction.

Deed held a similar position, studying the gray, empty land. Beside him, Tag had been encouraged to sit. And next to them was a prone Silka.

The old samurai raised a trembling hand. "M-my son, w-where is my sword? My rifle? I must help." He tried to raise, but couldn't.

The youngest Corrigan walked over and handed Silka the great sword lying beside him. "Here. Your gun is beside you. Loaded. But you must rest now. You have taught us well. It will be all right." He sounded more confident than he felt.

"No, I must do this. Help me stand beside you where I can shoot." A tear straggled down the side of Silka's face as he took the weapon with both hands.

Deed patted him on the shoulder and assisted Silka to his feet. There was no use in arguing about it. The former samurai was nearly dead weight, but Deed managed to move him a few feet and prop him against the side of the wallow.

"You can see from here . . . and shoot," Deed said, whispering a Japanese saying, and added, "I'll be right over here."

He moved closer to Rose and asked, "Do you have plenty of cartridges?"

"Uh . . . yes. I do," Rose said. "D-do you think I'll need more?"

"I'll bring you some. I've got to get more for me."

He slid out of the wallow and went to the picketed horses. At their packhorse, he filled his pockets with bullets for Rose and shoved four reloading tubes for his Spencer into his belt. He started to leave, then looked in the pack further and withdrew a large piece of linen they'd cut up to hold coffee grounds. He looked over at his brother adding wood to the yet-to-be burning fire.

"Hey, Holt, got an idea. Make you look scary," Deed said is he pulled his throwing knife from behind his collar.

"What?"

Deed cut two squares from the linen and shoved the balance back into the pack. Taking a handful of cartridges, he began separating the shell from the bullet with his knife and pouring the gunpowder into one of the squares. Holt came over, nodded, and began to help. They created two small sacks of gunpowder and tied them tightly with rawhide string.

"Not a bad thought, little brother."

"Anything to help." Deed smiled and patted Holt on the shoulder.

"See you in a little while."

"You bet." Deed returned to the wallow, handed Rose two handfuls of cartridges, and went to his original site, where he took up his Spencer. Glancing sideways, he saw Silka slowly cock his rifle.

The horizon was about to belch its first streaks of gold and rose when their fire roared into existence.

"Well, get it done, big brother," Deed said. "Make 'em scared."

"Just keep a place for me."

"You got it. Right beside me."

Holt lifted the buffalo skull into the air

with both outstretched arms and began chanting as loud as he could.

"*Nakuhitu,*" he yelled. The Comanche word for "listen" was one of the few he knew, including "food" and "friend." Licking his lips, he began, "Eye for an eye, tooth for a tooth, bacon and beans, beans and bacon, eating goober peas, eating goober peas, all that glitters is not gold . . . oh, Lord, makes this work, long live the Confederacy, yea, though I walk through the valley of the shadow of death, I will fear no evil." He swallowed and glanced at the darkness ahead. "To be or not to be, that is the question. Song of the South, awake to glory, a thousand voices bid you rise . . . now I lay me down to sleep, I pray the Lord my soul to keep . . . The way to dusty death. Out, out, brief candle." He swung the skull in a circle and, dramatically, pushed it high in the air again and started his chant again. Holt was no longer a county sheriff, he was a shaman. A shaman to be feared.

As if from the earth itself, brown bodies began to appear from their positions fifty yards away. One warrior was only twenty yards from their campfire. They seemed mesmerized, stunned by Holt's unexpected performance. His drone was constant, dramatic, and having the hoped-for effect. Holding the skull with one hand, Holt swung his free hand across the flames as if caressing them to do his bidding. He dropped one of the gunpowder pouches into the fire as he moved.

A roar followed with a billow of smoke rising above the fire. Deed kept his attention on the warriors. All but one jumped when the powder went off. Achak stood alone and screamed at his men. None responded. Achak's leadership was fragile; his seeming invincibility had been tarnished by "the walking white man." Now his warriors were puzzled by this unexpected display.

Of courage, yes, but more than that. Of the spirit. This white walker was calling forth powers they did not understand.

None of the Comanche on the north side made any attempt to attack. But, from behind the buffalo wallow, six Comanche warriors rode into view as if on cue, whooping and waving their weapons. All were painted with their war medicine.

"Open up on them," Deed yelled.

Gunfire from the wallow surprised the Comanche. Deed's .52 caliber Spencer was accurate and deadly. Arrows and bullets flew from the back side, slamming into the saddles and landing in the wallow itself. Deed moved quickly from one side of the wallow to the other, shooting and returning. The Comanche in front remained confused. Three went down as the others sought hiding places. Deed pushed a new reload tube into place with practiced ease. He wondered what had happened to Achak. Where was the Comanche madman? He had disappeared.

As he stepped around the far edge of the flame, Holt jerked and began walking in a strange, halting manner. His chanting changed and became clusters of unusual sounds, none familiar to Deed. It was as if he were another person. He pointed at the pale moon and tossed the second pouch into the fire. Moments later a second burst of smoke and flame exploded. Across the way, the terrified Indians retreated. All but one. Achak was now clearly visible in the pale moonlight. He was shaking, not in terror, but in absolute anger.

"I-I don't see any of them!" Rose stammered and fired into the morning.

"Just keep at it, Malcolm," Deed assured. "Keep putting in new loads when you can." He saw what looked like a leg exposed near some mesquite and fired. The resulting scream was testimony to the accuracy of his hunch. Levering his big gun, Deed studied the prairie for more opportunities. So far, the warriors hadn't run; they just hadn't dared. He fired again, but missed a darting figure. He heard Silka fire and curse.

"H-help! They're coming in!" Rose yelled.

From behind him, Tag snarled and charged in Rose's direction. The youngest Corrigan brother spun to see two Comanche diving between the saddles and attacking Rose. The dog grabbed the closest Comanche's arm, keeping it from slamming a tomahawk against Rose. But the second Comanche hit the townsman along his right ear with his war club, then again. Rose whimpered and dropped his gun.

Deed fired, shooting his Spencer from his hip, missed, and fired again. The first Comanche's face became crimson, just in time to keep the warrior from drawing his knife to gut Tag.

"Get back, Tag!" Deed yelled, firing at the second Comanche. The shot thudded against a saddle.

The second Comanche dove for Deed, swinging his war club. Deed's rifle clicked on empty as the Indian slammed into him. Stumbling backward, Deed's left hand stopped the downward swing of the warrior's weapon. His open right hand slammed against the warrior's neck like an axe. Deed's left fist followed with a drive into the man's nose. The Comanche's eyes met Deed's as he collapsed.

Shaking his head, Deed stood, reloaded his carbine, and fired into the bodies of the two downed warriors as Tag came to his side. The dog was bleeding along his back. The wound was slight, Deed hoped.

"Good job, Tag." He patted the dog's head and confirmed the wound was a long scratch.

Deed started toward the unconscious townsman, but was stopped by a rush of movement behind him. Expecting to face another Comanche, he turned and saw a warrior on top of the prone Silka. The samurai's bloody sword protruded from the Comanche's back. The Indian was dead, but Silka was too weak to push the body away. Deed stepped over, grabbed a fistful of the warrior's hair, and yanked him from the old samurai. The dead warrior wore a sleeveless army jacket. His face was streaked with vertical lines of war paint. In his dead grip was a big Colt.

"I could not remove him," Silka muttered weakly. "Help me, please. He smells."

"Well, you did the important job," Deed replied. "Are you all right?"

226

"I am samurai. I fear nothing."

Deed laid his carbine against the wallow's wall and helped Silka to his feet. "I know you don't." He noticed fresh blood on Silka's shirt; it was coming from his reopened shoulder wound. He would treat it later.

He encouraged Tag to come to Silka's side and started again to look at Rose, when he heard his brother yell, "Come on, you bastards!" and then a phrase Deed didn't know. It sounded like something in Comanche, but he wasn't sure.

Looking up, Deed saw Holt firing with a revolver in both hands; the skull lay at his feet. His target was Achak himself, charging on a black horse, screaming and firing his rifle. Beside him rode a menacing-looking warrior in black-and-white face paint, wearing a white woman's dress. The rest of the Comanche hid in a shallow ravine forty yards north of the buffalo wallow, refusing to ride with him because his war medicine was broken.

"Stay, Tag." Deed grabbed his Spencer and jumped out of the wallow. Quick strides put him alongside his brother.

"Leave Achak for me," Holt yelled.

Calmly, Deed knelt on one knee, aimed, and fired at the dress-wearing Comanche. Almost at the same moment, both Comanche were jolted from their horses by Corrigan bullets.

Acting as wild as the Comanche war leader, Holt charged toward the downed Achak as his black horse thundered past. A few strides behind was the other warrior's paint horse. Leaning over, Holt shoved a revolver into his waistband and yanked hard on the dead Comanche's tongue necklace. It popped free. He held it high and screamed into the morning.

"Holt. They've gone," Deed said. "But I think Malcolm's dead."

Holt stood as if not hearing. Deed repeated what had happened. Tag bolted from the wallow and went to Holt. Deed surveyed the area to make certain the Comanche had fled. None remained.

"Hey, little buddy, you're bleeding," Holt said as he knelt beside the happy dog. Deed studied his brother.

"I've looked at the scratch, Holt. It's not deep," Deed said. "Wait! Holt, you're bleeding. You've been shot."

"Damn. That crazy Indian was a better shot than I thought."

"Lie down and let me take a look." Deed put his hand on Holt's shoulder.

"All right. All right. It's just blood, you know."

"I know. We need to know where."

Pulling up Holt's bloody shirt, Deed found the wound. A long, ugly crease along his side, above his hip. He was pleased to see it wasn't serious, but it was bleeding hard. Tag stuck his nose close to the wound and seemed to be concerned. Holt patted the dog and held him away as Deed cut off a portion of the shirt to help stop the bleeding.

Taking out his throwing knife from down his back, Deed cut a large piece of Holt's shirt and held it against the wound.

"Hey, that was a good shirt!" Holt growled.

"Yeah, and right now, it is good for stopping the blood. You've already lost a lot."

Holt was quiet a moment. "I do feel a little dizzy."

"Well, you'd be feeling a lot worse," Deed said, pressing the folded shirt fragment against the bleeding, "if that bullet hole in your hat had been an inch or two lower."

Holt reached for his hat and examined it. "What? Again? That's my second hole. Now that damn good hat is totally ruined."

"You've got another hole in your coat." Deed motioned with his free hand toward a hole in the lower flap of Holt's coat.

"*Good* thing I got him when I did," Holt

mumbled and grinned at his reuse of "good."

"Agreed. Hold this while I go get some bandages and some of Silka's medicine."

"Sure."

Deed grabbed a clean shirt from his saddlebags, then the jar of Silka's salve and a long bandage roll from their nearly empty pack. Spotting a cluster of long-leafed plants near the horses, he tore off six leaves and continued back to Holt. His brother lay with his eyes closed; Tag was curled up next to him.

Deed said, "Brought you a new shirt. It's mine. Was, now it's yours. Might not fit real well, but it's in better shape than yours."

"Hey, good enough. It's stopped bleeding." Tearing the bloody shirt away, Deed said, "I'm going to put some of Silka's magic stuff on it, along with these leaves."

"What's with the leaves?" Holt asked.

"I've seen Apaches use it that way."

"Probably will turn me into a vegetable." Holt watched his brother apply the salve and the leaves and began wrapping the wound.

"More likely a weed." Deed finished wrapping his brother's stomach. "When you're ready, I'll help you put on that shirt."

Holt put his hand on his brother's arm.

"Thanks, little brother."

"You bet," Deed said. "You know, there was a time there when you went into some sort of trance and began yelling out some real strange stuff. Words I'd never heard before. You even moved different."

Holt looked at his brother without speaking, as if trying to bring back the situation. He felt for the medicine stone in his pocket. It was there and felt warm.

"I'm not sure I really remember that," he finally said, "but I sort of recall doing something . . . like it was a different lifetime. Don't laugh."

"I'm not," Deed said. "The last time you said something like that . . . and I laughed . . . you broke my nose."

"Sorry."

"No, you're not."

Holt chuckled.

After helping Holt change shirts, Deed said, "I'm going to check on the horses and Silka. If you're up to it, we'll start for town after that."

"Got anything to eat?"

"Don't think so. An old biscuit or two, maybe. We can have some coffee though. How's that?" Deed smiled.

"Better than nothing."

Deed added the last of their dry wood to

the fire and put the coffeepot at the edge of the reborn flames.

"Holt, look!" Deed pointed toward the horizon where six riders were advancing.

"More Comanche?" Holt asked. He picked up one of his revolvers and tried to thumb cartridges into the empty gun.

"No. It's . . . it's Blue! And Taol Sanchez with some of his men."

In the morning light, the Lazy S riders were distinctive with sombreros, bandoliers, and leather hoods over their stirrups.

"Well, I'll be damned." Holt knelt beside the dog. He looked over at his brother. "Better get some coffee on."

"Already done."

CHAPTER EIGHTEEN

Blue Corrigan slid from his horse and hurried toward his brothers. His smile took over his face and he hugged Deed with great enthusiasm and went to the prone Holt to determine how badly he'd been wounded. Behind him, the Lazy S vaqueros were combing the brush for any remaining hostiles.

"You missed all the fun," Deed said, stepping back from Blue. "You would've loved seeing Holt perform." He told Blue what had happened, then about the deaths of Ira McDugal and Malcolm Rose, and that "Mason Mereford" was actually one of Bordner's gunmen.

After Blue was satisfied that Holt's wound was not serious, he helped Holt stand up, at Holt's insistence. The second Corrigan was wobbly from the loss of blood, but was determined to stay on his feet. He insisted that Deed treat Tag's wound and the youngest Corrigan did so with care. With the dog beside them, the three brothers walked together to examine the dead Achak; his necklace of human tongues lay next to his bloody chest where Holt had dropped it. He shot it full of holes.

"Do we need to take that damn thing along to prove he's dead?" Dead asked, pointing at the necklace. His gaze took in the empty prairie and the vaqueros riding through it, like some river taking over the parched land.

It was Holt who answered, "I don't need to prove anything. Leave it . . . and him . . . for the vultures and coyotes. Any Indians that might come along will see that his medicine was not strong."

Deed did most of the talking about their difficult ride as they walked back to the wallow. Holt thought he would sit down at the edge of the deep incline and did so with Tag next to him. Deed jumped into the wallow and Blue followed. They went first to Silka. The proud Japanese warrior was leaning against the side of the wallow, his head resting against the bare earth.

In a handful of sentences, Deed told his brothers how Silka had insisted on helping and had killed a brave who managed to get into their defense. The dead Indian lay a few feet away with Silka's bloody sword extending from both sides of the warrior's stomach. Deed put his hand on the older man's shoulder and Silka looked up, his eyes glazed.

"Are they stopped?" Silka asked.

"Yes. We did it," Deed replied and motioned toward Blue. "Blue and Taol Sanchez and some of his men are here, too."

Silka smiled. "I smell coffee. I would have some. With much sugar."

That brought laughter from all three brothers and a happy bark from Tag.

"And so it will be," Holt volunteered, feeling light-headed, but trying not to show it. "Maybe you should rest until it's ready."

With a twinkle in his eyes, Silka responded, "Is this the command of the great white medicine man?"

They laughed again, Holt the loudest, holding his hand against his side.

"Well, sure. I'll bring down the powers of Shakespeare, if you don't."

That brought more laughter. The discovery that Malcolm Rose was indeed dead returned their solemnity.

Deed and Blue helped Silka back to his travois bed. Before he lay down, Silka turned toward them and said, "I will ride my horse to town. You can place Malcolm's body there." He punctuated the statement with a Japanese oath.

"We'll need to tend to your wounds again," Deed said and described how the old samurai had been wounded.

"There is no need. I am healing."

Deciding not to argue with the great warrior, they moved to Malcolm Rose's body. Blue suggested covering him with a saddle blanket and Deed got one from what remained of their gear. They would take the body to town for a proper burial. Blue said Malcolm's wife had been very worried about her husband. They would report that he died a hero, fighting well.

As they cleared the wallow, Taol Sanchez and his riders rode up, rifles in their hands.

"They is gone," Taol said and warmly greeted Holt and Deed. "It is good you are well, *amigo,*" he said, his white teeth setting off his hard brown face. "*Mis* sisters were worried about Señor Holt."

Everyone laughed. Gathering around the fire, they enjoyed the hot brew. Taol produced a bottle of tequila and passed it around. None of the Corrigan brothers drank much, but it seemed appropriate to celebrate their survival with a hearty toast.

They were surprised as Silka, bloody shirt and all, walked toward them. He raised his right hand in a salute and shuffled toward the fire. Deed and Taol were the first to him.

"You shouldn't be up, Silka," Deed said sternly.

"I am samurai. I want to join victory celebration."

"Sure. Let me put my coat around you. You need to stay warm."

"Get sugar first."

They helped him to the gathering and eased him into a sitting position between Blue and Holt.

From the new posse's packhorse, food was pulled and soon the good smells of frying bacon joined that of the boiling coffee. The men ate heartily of fried bacon, beans, and biscuits from town, washed down by the hot coffee. They ate in silence as was the custom of western men. After finishing their meal, two of the vaqueros talked of taking scalps from the dead Comanche; another mentioned taking Achak's tongue necklace.

None of the Corrigan brothers responded. But Holt decided to take along the buffalo skull and placed it in their pack. Getting ready to leave took longer than usual, as they lifted Malcolm Rose's body onto the travois and attached the frame to the packhorse. Deed helped Silka mount his horse, trying to do so casually so the older man wouldn't object to the assistance. Light-headed, Holt managed to get on his horse without help. Deed brought Tag over to him so the dog could ride home with his master. Both were pleased.

Holt reached into his coat pocket and withdrew a few tobacco shreds from its pouch. He tossed them into the air and said his thanks to the spirits. Before mounting, Deed did the same. Blue saw the tributes and offered a silent prayer. Only Holt noticed a chickadee calling out a sweet morning song as they rode out. Definitely a sign of good luck.

The solemn group rode past the bodies of several Comanche, including Achak's and the warrior in the dress. Both had been scalped and the tongue necklace had disappeared. From among the riders came a triumphant yell that was embraced by the others. Deed and Holt joined in. Silka blurted a samurai victory cry. Only Blue was quiet.

They rode with their rifles across their saddles, wary of some last-ditch attack by the Comanche. As they approached a thicket of juniper bordering a long wash, Taol ordered two of his younger men to ride into the thicket in case Indians were waiting. It was an honor to be chosen. Each had a bloody scalp tied to their saddles.

Spurring their horses, the two vaqueros raced for the junipers, carrying their rifles in one hand like pistols. Bandoleers of bullets bounced off their backs. Their yells snapped through the air as they disappeared into the thicket. The others reined up and waited with rifles ready.

Assured of safety, the group rode on. Gradually, the conversation turned to ranching. Deed was eager to see Atlee and could barely keep his mind on anything else.

"Harmon Payne is at the Bar 3," Blue advised. "He'll stay there until you're ready to take over."

Harmon Payne was a longtime hand, a well-built cowboy who liked to spout phrases from Sir Walter Scott and Tennyson.

The comment drew Deed back from his daydream. "You think any of the Bar 3 hands are around, the honest-to-goodness cowhands?"

Riding next to him, Silka smiled as if he knew what Deed was thinking about.

"Quite a few," Blue answered. "You might want to hire some of them. Remember Luke Pennegrit? He's around. Saw him in town yesterday. So's Pete Williamson."

"Good. Maybe he can help us round up some more. They were good men."

Blue studied the land as they rode. The day was solemn and overcast. Rain was coming again.

"Harmon said the Bar 3 herds are in good shape. Plenty of calves. Branded. Going to need to take the older stuff to market." Blue pursed his lips.

"That sounds better than I'd hoped. At least Dixie was a cowman," Deed responded.

"The only problem he's found so far is no preparation for winter," Blue continued. "No hay cut and put up."

"Damn. What was Dixie thinking?"

"My guess is he couldn't get any of Bordner's gunmen to do that kind of work." Blue glanced at his younger brother and smiled.

"Yeah. I'm sure you're right," Deed said. "We'll have to get on that fast."

Blue nodded agreement. "Harmon's already working on it. That far section is fat with hay-making grass."

Deed looked over at Blue, rolling the reins in his fingers. "You think Harmon would make a good foreman? We're definitely going to need one."

"I was hoping you'd come to that idea."

Silka added a Japanese affirmation.

Riding next to Taol, Holt called out, "Hold up a minute."

All of the riders raised their rifles and reined their horses.

"What's the matter?" Deed asked, turning in the saddle.

Pale but grinning, Holt waved his hand. "No problem, boys. I just spotted a button. In the dirt."

"A what?" Deed frowned.

"A button."

"A button?" Deed shook his head. "Is it one of ours?"

Holt swung stiffly from his horse. "Don't think so. But picking up a button is good luck. We can always use that."

Deed looked at Blue and bit his lower lip. How like their oldest brother. "Sounds good to me." He patted Silka on the shoulder and the samurai tried to smile. Deed looked back again as Holt held his side as he retrieved the button. The wound was bleeding again, a little. Other wise, the Apache leaves were doing their job. He wiped the pearl button on his shirt. He thought it might have come from a woman's dress. Could the warrior in the dress have come this far before turning around? He shook his head. It didn't matter. He shoved the button into his pocket, next to the medicine stone.

Remounting wasn't easy. The strain on his

wound triggered intense pain. He winced as he pulled himself into the saddle. Glancing up, he saw Deed watching him. Holt smiled, trying to mask the pain.

"You all right, big brother?" Deed asked.

"Good as gold."

"Fool's gold, maybe."

Holt nodded. "Maybe so, but let's ride. Luck is with us."

"Sure enough. Maybe you should put your badge on, Holt," Deed suggested. "A nice way to hit town.'

"Hadn't thought about it," Holt said, remounting. "But I like it."

Hours later, the two posses rode into Wilkon and the celebration of their return was instantaneous. People lined the street, applauding and yelling their gratitude. Tag got excited and barked, but Holt told him to be quiet.

James Hannah met them in the center of the street, along with Judge Pence. Both were carrying shotguns. Silka was feeble and in considerable pain, but remained upright as they walked their horses down the main street.

Mayor Patterson Cooke hurried to Holt's side and asked, "Do you still haff de bank's money?" Cooke was the German owner of the lumber mill at the edge of town, a man with a constant forced smile and ever-sweaty hands, but a man who loved Wilkon. Currently, he was trying to raise funds to paint all of the town's commercial buildings and had started the drive with five hundred dollars of his own money.

"Every damn cent of it, mayor."

"Danke, Herr Corrigan. *Ja*, 'tis *sehr gut*," Patterson said. "Now we can plan our town celebration . . . for *der gut.*"

"We lost two good men, Patterson," Holt said, studying the busy street. "Malcolm Rose and Ira McDugal."

"Ja, das ist schlecht . . . uh, bad. Too bad. Such things do happen. *Ja.*" Cooke patted Holt's leg and turned away.

"Thanks for asking," Holt snarled. "And Mason Mereford turned out to be one of Bordner's men. He killed Ira McDugal."

Cooke smiled and waved.

Holt looked over at Deed and Blue and shook his head.

Their arrival was halted when Flavian Rose screamed in horror. She ran toward the travois where Malcolm's covered body lay and threw herself on it. The frame cracked under the added weight and both the grieving widow and her late husband's body thudded to the ground.

Blue swung from his horse and went to

the distressed woman. "Mrs. Rose, we're so sorry. Malcolm was a brave man. He died fighting for Wilkon. For all of us."

She looked up, through tear-glazed eyes, said something unintelligible, and returned her head to the covered body.

"Men . . . I'm going to need help. We need to take Malcolm to Claude's."

Three men came from the crowd; a fourth hesitated and then hurried to catch up. A fifth joined them as they carried the body to Claude Gausage's store. Flavian walked beside them with her hand on the body as Blue and Judge Pence held her up. Deed and Holt stayed with Silka, who was lying against his horse's neck.

James Hannah strolled over to the Corrigans. "What do you say we get the money back into the bank?"

Deed shook his hand, then Holt greeted the gunman.

"You two do it," Deed said. "I'll stay with Silka. We need to get him to the doctor."

Holt tugged on his hat brim, dismounted, and walked with Hannah to their packhorse. They carried the saddlebags filled with gold and certificates into the bank and the waiting hands of the tellers and the new bank president, Simpson Wade.

Ira McDugal was a bachelor, so no one

waited for him except three quiet friends. They asked Holt about him and he explained his death. The friends left for the saloon.

After leaving the body at the undertaker's, Blue and Judge Pence walked back with Blue filling the magistrate in on what had happened on the trail, based on Deed's report.

Taol told his men to take the old posse's horses to the livery and see that they were cared for. While that was being done, Deed and Taol helped Silka limp toward the doctor's office. A townsman with a thick mustache, big belly, and derby hat walked past the threesome. Behind him walked a prune-faced woman wearing a big brown hat with a fake yellow bird perched on its front. Her manner was that of someone who felt few were her equal, socially or financially.

The townsman stopped, yanked the cigar from his mouth. "You're not taking that yellow-eyed heathen to our doctor, I presume. Or that filthy Mex, either."

Deed's face tightened. "Excuse me a minute, Taol. You go on ahead."

Without waiting for his reply, he spun and walked after the now strolling man. Deed grabbed the well-dressed townsman's shoulder and he stopped, turning toward the pressure. His eyes widened as he realized who was behind him.

"W-what's the matter?" he asked, shoving the cigar into the corner of his mouth.

"You're the matter," Deed growled. "Silka risked his life for you, your town, and your money, you fat sonuvabitch. And Taol is one of my best friends, a far better man than you'll ever be. Get away from me. I'm too tired to mess with something like you."

"Unhand me, sir, or I've have you arrested for assault," the townsman blurted.

"Assault?" Deed snarled. "You mean like this?" He backhanded the man savagely across his face, smashing the cigar against his teeth.

"Or this?" His follow-up backhand against the man's face covered his teeth with blood and the man yelped.

"Or how about this?" Deed's right fist slammed into the man's belly. He bent over, retching onto the boardwalk.

Deed stepped back and growled loudly, "Don't ever call that fine woman a name like that again." He motioned toward the prune-faced woman who had stopped behind the fat man.

Her face reddening, she demanded, "What did he say? I wasn't listening. I-I thought it was a fight."

"Oh, I couldn't repeat it, ma'am," Deed bowed. "Wouldn't be proper, you know. It was my pleasure to defend your honor."

"Oh, thank you, sir. You are indeed a gentleman."

She walked over to the retching businessman and clobbered him with her heavy purse. "You should be arrested for doing that in public." She looked up at Deed, straightened her hat, and smiled.

Repressing a chuckle, Deed Corrigan touched the brim of his hat, returned the smile, and went to catch up with Taol and Silka. His made-up story would keep the businessman from making an official complaint, he thought.

Smiling, the bronzed rancher thanked him for his reaction to the townsman's words.

"You are the true *amigo*. It is my honor to know you," Taol said as Deed rejoined them.

"No problem, Taol. I don't have a long fuse when I hear fools talk."

"So I saw." The Mexican rancher laughed.

Silka glanced at both. "He is samurai."

At the judge's insistence, Holt had joined them to be seen by the doctor. Deed told him what had happened with the fat businessman. Holt's eyes flashed hot.

"When we get through here, I'll go arrest

247

the bastard."

"For what?" Deed asked.

"Being fat . . . and foul language."

Deed grinned. "Let's go see the doc."

Dr. Wright was impressed to see Silka's wounds healing so well. He was equally surprised to see Holt's wound laced with leaves.

"Well, gentlemen, whoever treated you did well," Dr. Wright concluded after cleaning and re-bandaging the wounds. "There are no signs of infection. The wounds are healing well. You both just need rest. Lots of rest."

CHAPTER NINETEEN

After leaving the doctor's office, Holt and Deed bought new clothes at the general store, while Silka stayed at the doctor's and napped. They bought new clothes for him as well. Tag trotted between them, proud of his association and the opportunity to show it off in town.

"Guess there's nothing I can do about my hat," Holt said, wiggling his finger through the hole in the crown. "Don't think a sheriff should go around wearing a hat with a hole in it. Might invite other folks to try."

Deed agreed and waited for his brother to select a new one. The selected bowler was almost identical to his other hat, especially after Holt moved his lucky cardinal feather from the old to the new. Then they dropped off Holt's suit coat at the tailor's to mend the bullet hole. At the doctor's office, Silka was awake and showing the doctor his samurai sword. Deed and Holt thought he was trying hard to show he wasn't seriously hurt when he was.

The trio — Deed, Holt, and Silka — left for the barbershop to get shaves and baths. Holt took Tag with him and washed the dog down. A young Chinese woman assisted Silka with his bath. If he was aware of her attention, it didn't show.

Dressed in new clothes and feeling clean again, Holt and Deed helped Silka to the hotel. Tag spotted a dog and ran ahead to greet the black-and-white animal. In the lobby, a salesman sat reading a newspaper. He didn't look up. Sitting next to him was the thin-faced reporter from the *Wilkon Epitaph.* He jumped up from a sofa as the threesome entered.

"Holt Corrigan! Deed Corrigan! How great to see you made it back," the reporter gurgled, reaching for paper in his pocket.

"Sit down, sir. We're on official business," Holt barked.

The salesman continued to read.

"Oh, I just wanted to ask you a couple of questions. Everybody wants to know if you killed Achak."

"Did you see him riding with us?" Holt turned to the hotel clerk, looking stunned behind the check-in desk. "We need rooms for tonight. Two for sure, maybe more." He turned to Deed. "I'll sleep in the sheriff's quarters. You think Blue will want a room? Or Taol?"

"I'm guessing they'll ride out after eating."

"Uh . . . uh, we don't allow . . . foreigners to stay in our place," the clerk blurted.

Silka frowned at him. "I not foreigner. I samurai."

Deed stepped next to the desk. "There you go, pardner. Two keys. Now."

"B-but . . ."

Deed took a deep breath. "Look. We've been fighting Comanche for a week to get Wilkon's money back. Our friend was hurt bad in that. So we're in no mood to be messed with." His eyes narrowed. "If we have to go to the owner of this place, you're going to be fired. Your choice. Make it now."

"Uh, would you like the two rooms in a row, sir?"

"Sure."

Grabbing the offered keys for 215 and 216, Deed started upstairs with his right arm around Silka. Holt was on the other side.

The reporter hurried beside them. "So you're saying you killed Achak, right?"

Holt glanced at Deed. "He's dead. Now leave us alone."

"Sure. Sure. Uh, which one of you did it?"

Deed stepped in front of the man. "It's been a long day, mister. You're pushing when you should be backing up. Go away."

"Sure. Sure. What a story! What a story!"

At the first room, 215, they unlocked the door and went in. The room was simple, with two chairs, one straight-backed and the other upholstered, a lone French-styled dresser with its bottom drawer nailed shut, a narrow bed, and a pitcher and basin for washing. The window, overlooking the street, was flanked by yellowed curtains rippling with a late afternoon breeze. They helped Silka to the bed and left him stretched out on it. He was asleep before they left.

"Buy you a steak," Holt said.

"All right. Let's get the others." Deed paused at the check-in desk and told the nervous clerk that Silka was expecting a visit from a relative and to give her his room number. He winked at Holt.

It didn't take long to gather at the Silver Spur restaurant. The Corrigans liked the place because the owner had no problem serving Mexicans. The group sat around a long table in the restaurant, laughing and talking. In addition to the Corrigan brothers, Judge Pence, James Hannah, Taol

Sanchez, and his vaqueros enjoyed their meals. The three Corrigans sipped hot coffee while Hannah, Taol, Judge Pence, and the Lazy S riders savored tequila. Taol and his men planned to ride for their ranch at dusk. Blue was eager to return to the Rafter C and had decided to ride out after eating. Deed said he would bring Silka to the ranch in the morning. Holt planned to sleep in the sheriff's quarters as he had been.

Three men, supported by earlier whiskey, sauntered into the restaurant and headed toward their table. The tallest of the three, a dog-faced man with ears like opened doors, spoke for them.

"We'd like to know why yah all made it back . . . an' our friend Malcolm didn't. How come?" He looked at the other two for support.

Glancing at Deed, Holt stood and proceeded to tell the three what had happened in great detail, making it clear that Rose had not been able to do his share of the fighting, put the others at risk, and finally failed to keep watch as he was expected to do. Only quick action by Deed and Silka kept them from also being killed.

The man with the ears winced as Holt outlined the running fight across the open prairie. The shortest man looked like he was

253

going to vomit. The third, with a heavy dark beard, looked at his dirty boots, unable to meet Holt's eyes.

Finishing his recital, Holt folded his arms. "Any questions?"

"Uh, no . . . no, sir," the eared man said. "We thank yah fer yur time. Yas, suh, we do."

"Good. You're dismissed," Holt growled.

The three men walked away in silence. A few minutes later, two older couples entered the restaurant. With a nudge from his gray-haired wife, the stocky man took a step toward the table, removed his misshapen hat, and proclaimed, "We are sorry to bother your supper, but we wanted to thank you for what you did for Wilkon." He motioned toward his wife and the couple with them.

"We're the Graveses . . . an' this is the Seldons. We, uh, just wanted to thank you. That's all." He glanced at his wife to see if he had forgotten anything. She smiled.

Standing, Deed held out his hand. "That's mighty kind of you folks. Wilkon means a lot to us, too. Would you care to join us?"

Without looking at his wife, Huston Graves declined, as did Jake Seldon. Holt rose and joined Deed in shaking hands. As the two couples nervously started to leave,

Mrs. Grave smiled and said, "And we're very happy to have Holt Corrigan as our county sheriff. He did the Confederacy proud."

Holt bowed. "Those are the nicest words I've heard in a long time, ma'am. I thank you kindly."

The couples added further exclamation of gratitude as they left, almost shouting through the doorway.

Judge Pence beamed and spat into his ever-ready cup. "Thar ya go, boys. Yah are 'preciated. Yas, suh."

Settling back to the table, Holt noticed Hannah was unusually quiet, drinking tequila and talking only when he was asked a question. The oldest Corrigan said, "James, this town is going to need a marshal. A good one. How about you staying on? I'll put in a word to the mayor. So will Deed and Blue."

Spitting into his cup, Judge Pence almost hollered, "Well, dammit, boys, I'm ahead o' ya fer onces't. Dun already talked to Patterson about it. He likes the idea, too."

Holt looked at Hannah. "Well, my friend, what do you say?"

Smiling widely, Hannah pushed his glasses back on his nose. "Yeah, I like the idea, but I'll have to talk it over with Rebecca. It'll be her decision, too, you know."

"Of course," Holt said. "Will you know tomorrow?"

"Sure. I think she's grown quite fond of Wilkon."

"Great."

Outside was the clatter of a fast-driven buckboard. It rattled to a stop in front of the restaurant. Into the gray room came Atlee Forsyth. Her face was taut with worry. Holt saw her first.

"He's right over here, ma'am. Ornery as ever," Holt greeted her and stood.

Deed met her a step later.

"Oh, Deed, I was so scared," Atlee said, looking into his eyes. "I hadn't heard from you. For years, it seemed." She brushed away a tear escaping down her right cheek. "I-I left the Beinrigts in charge of the station and rode to your ranch. Bina told me what was going on. I saw Rebecca in the general store and she said you were here."

"Shhh. It's all right now," Deed whispered. "All I could think about was getting back to you."

"R-really?"

"Ask Holt. He teased me about it," Deed said and brushed back a curl from her hair. "I love you."

Her eyes locked onto his face. "Oh, and I

256

love you, Deed Corrigan."

Holt, Taol, Blue, and the judge winked and chuckled. The vaqueros joined in as Deed and Atlee hugged.

Taol and his men excused themselves and headed out after exchanging warm good-byes with the Corrigan brothers. Atlee joined them at the table, but said she wasn't hungry and only wanted coffee. At Deed's insistence, she ordered a piece of fresh apple pie.

A few minutes later, Blue, Holt, Hannah, and Judge Pence excused themselves. Blue wanted to head for home now that he wasn't needed as the town's interim lawman. Holt said he wanted to check on their horses and then go to bed. Judge Pence said he wanted to discuss some official business with Holt and Hannah.

Deed watched them leave, grinned, and said, "Got a feeling they thought we wanted to be alone."

"I had the same thought," Atlee beamed. "And I do."

Deed reached across the table to take her hand. "You are the most beautiful sight I've ever seen."

"Oh, Deed . . . I missed you so much."

They held hands and lost themselves in each other's eyes. The waiter came and went, delivering her coffee and pie, and taking away the emptied dishes of the others. Atlee tasted the pie, said it was good, and drank some coffee. He asked about her children and the stage station, and she told him that Benjamin and Elizabeth missed him greatly. Benjamin was twelve and Elizabeth, six. The boy had initially resented Deed helping at the stage station after their father was killed by Comanche.

Deed smiled again. "Now, I can believe Elizabeth might miss me a little, maybe . . . but Benjamin? I doubt it."

"Oh, not so, Deed. He talks about you every day . . . and cares for that horse you gave him like it was a gold statue. Every night, he includes you in his prayers. It was his idea."

"Don't think I've ever had anybody do that before, unless it was Blue."

She smiled. "Well, I do it, too. Every night."

Their conversation became easy, like that between husband and wife. They talked about the Corrigan ranch and the Bar 3 that had also become theirs, at least partially so. He told her about the court's rulings on Agon Bordner's ill-gotten holdings.

The only thing they didn't discuss was the awful trip Deed and Holt had just completed. It wasn't necessary and wasn't anything he wanted to relive.

"I hope someday you'll join me at the Bar 3," Deed said. "You, and Elizabeth, and Benjamin . . . and Cooper, too. He's a great dog."

"We would love that," Atlee said. "Anywhere you are is where I want to be."

They talked on and on. Finally, Deed looked around and realized they were the only people in the restaurant. The waiter returned to tell him that the meal was on the house, a thank-you for getting the bank's money back. He said people were talking about it all over town and calling it "the great prairie fight."

Deed smiled, handed the waiter several coins for a tip, and said they would be leaving.

"Atlee, we need to go. They want to close up," Deed said. "I'm staying the night at the hotel. Silka's already there." He stood, walked around the table, and pulled back her chair. "How about we get you a room as well?" He examined her face. "Tomorrow I'm planning on taking Silka home. He was badly hurt during our return." He bit his lower lip. "We can ride there together and I'll go with you to the station, if you want."

A tear escaped from her eye and hurried

down her cheek. "You are so brave."

"Shall we head for the hotel?"

"Yes."

At the hotel, the clerk was eager to provide Atlee a room and avoid another confrontation. She and Deed walked up the stairs without talking, and went directly to her room, 235. His lodging was down the hall, 216, next to Silka's room. He told her to come and get him if she needed anything. They kissed and kissed. Neither wanted to end the evening, but they finally did, with Atlee going into her room.

His walk down the hall was a daze. He was weary, but excited from being with Atlee. Her appearance washed away the awfulness of the Comanche fighting. It was hard to believe how their day had begun, with his oldest brother playing medicine man and killing the wicked Achak. He stepped into the darkened room, not bothering to light the lamp on the table. He unbuckled his gun belt and took the heavy Remington revolver and laid it on the bed. The gun belt and empty holster were tossed on a chair. His hat followed.

One boot came off easily and he dropped it on the floor. A small chunk of dried mud popped from the heel and dribbled away with the jingle of his spur. Then came the second. After taking off his shirt, he laid back on the bed and closed his eyes without taking off his pants. Just for a moment, he told himself. Just for a moment.

An hour later, he heard a soft knocking on his door. He sat up, shook his head, and grabbed his gun. Opening the door slowly, he saw Atlee.

"I didn't want to be alone tonight," she said. "I want to be with you." Her hands went to his bare chest.

CHAPTER TWENTY

Early the next morning, Deed and Atlee were eating breakfast in the hotel's restaurant. They had already taken food to Silka. He ate some oatmeal and drank coffee with lots of sugar. His eyes stayed focused on them, and he whispered a sweet Japanese blessing on their relationship.

Outside, a bugle cut through the quiet town. The waiter went to the window and exclaimed, "There's a bunch of soldiers coming in!"

Deed sipped his coffee and smiled at Atlee. "Looks like those boys are trying to catch up with Achak. A little late, I'd say."

Silka put two more spoonfuls of sugar into his coffee. "Soldiers may want to talk with Holt. Not so good, maybe."

"Hadn't thought of that," Deed said. "I'd better go and check." He reached across the table and touched Atlee's hand. "Will you excuse me for a minute?"

"Of course, my dearest, if Silka promises to tell more about you. I love it." Her eyes caressed his face.

Deed shook his head and glanced at Silka, who appeared busy stirring his coffee. "Don't believe everything that old samurai tells you."

Outside, a column of uniformed cavalry pulled up in front of the jail in a tight file. A heavy wagon carrying a mounted Gatling gun pulled up next to the troopers. Dismounting, a young lieutenant with a razor-thin mustache stepped onto the boardwalk and stomped his boots. His uniform looked like he had never left the post. He slapped his glove against his thigh to pop away what dust dared to rest there.

Scrambling to catch up, a skinny man appeared with a lopsided face tanned by long days in the saddle and grizzled with graying beard. He was the opposite in appearance to the young officer. Smoking an old corn-cob pipe, the sloppy-looking man wore a wide-brimmed hat with an eagle feather fluttering from a beaded hatband. At his waist was a bullet belt holding a large knife in a beaded sheath. He wore a sweat- and dirt-stained buckskin shirt and striped pants stuck into knee-high boots. Deed guessed he was a scout for the patrol. His smile showed many yellowed or missing teeth.

Behind them, horses snorted and stomped, spurs and bits jingled, saddles creaked. One man coughed and another spat. A second wagon pulled up alongside the first, packed with supplies, ammunition, tents, and bedrolls.

Holt met the officer and scout on the boardwalk. "Morning, gentlemen. I'm the sheriff of Cassidy County. How can we help you?"

"My men and I have been trailing a renegade Comanche named Achak and his men since they left the reservation," the lieutenant said stiffly. "From the looks of it, there was a fight a few hours south of Wilkon. Another fight back at" — he looked at the scout, who told him — "Turkey Wing. Riders headed this way after that last fight. Know anything about it?"

"Yeah. My brother and I were in all of them." Holt touched the feather in his hat-band.

Holt told them what had happened in a few sentences. The scout was impressed; the lieutenant tried not to act so.

"Do you know if the Comanche leader known as Achak was with them?" the young officer asked, taking off his hat and wiping his brow with his sleeve and attempting to act nonchalant.

"Yeah. I killed him and we killed a bunch more."

"How do you know it was him?"

Holt cocked his head. "Ever see another Indian . . . hell, another anything, wearing a necklace of human tongues?"

The scout turned to the side, took out his pipe, and spat toward the ground. "That's the he-devil all right. You was lucky."

"Never hurts."

Returning the pipe to his mouth, the scout said, "Didn't find no Injun bodies, 'ceptin' one. Couldn't tell much 'bout it. Buzzards were workin' it over, ya know."

Holt folded his arms and saw Deed coming from the hotel. "Yeah, they usually drag off their dead. Bet they left Achak because his medicine had gone bad. He couldn't take us, even though they had us outnumbered."

The scout nodded agreement and relit his pipe. Behind him a trooper mumbled, "Damn." The scout turned toward him and said something Holt didn't hear.

The lieutenant held out his hand to Holt. "I'm Lieutenant St. John of the Tenth Cavalry. This is my chief scout, Eagle Jones."

Holt shook both men's hands, but didn't give his name. "Glad to know you." He

265

glanced down the street and saw Judge Pence headed their way from the other part of town. Occasionally, he spent evenings with a widow who lived in a small cottage there. Holt glanced in the other direction and saw Silka exit the hotel, carrying his Winchester. He was twenty feet behind Deed.

From inside the jail, a crisp voice yelled, "What do these boys in blue want?"

Holt grinned. How like James Hannah. Holt turned toward the unseen voice and reported, "Lieutenant St. John and his men are after Achak and his Comanche."

"Typical army. You've already taken care of the problem," Hannah yelled again. "Did he think they're going to sit and wait while he got that Gatling gun in place?"

The scout chuckled, removed his pipe again, and wiped his mouth with the back of his hand. A trooper in the third row laughed out loud. A cavalry horse whinnied and its rider cursed. The man beside him yawned. It had been a long, hard ride for nothing so far.

Lieutenant St. John stiffened; the heels of his boots clicked together. "We have our orders and we will carry them out."

"I'm sure you will, St. John," Holt said, "but my friend is right. Those wagons only slow you down. Comanche can live off the land. What's left of them will be split up now, looking for easy targets . . . or sneaking back to the reservation."

The scout stepped forward, partly to change the subject and partly to keep his young officer from saying something foolish.

"Came across two graves. Outside o' Turkey Wing. Looked new." The question was implied.

Holt leaned over to pat Tag, who had just burst out from the marshal's office. Looking up, Holt said, "We did that, too. One was a friend who was riding with us." He licked his lower lip. "The other was my horse, Buck." He straightened his back. "Comanche didn't do it. They were killed by bank robbers we were trailing."

"They get away?"

"No."

"Good for you."

"Guess you'd say we were lucky." Holt tugged on his suit coat, covering his twin shoulder-holstered guns.

Eagle Jones grinned like a jack-o'-lantern.

Folding his arms, the scout said, "Had me a hoss like that once. Used to eat carrots ri't out of my mouth."

Holt nodded and looked away.

A few feet away, the trooper holding the lieutenant's horse, his own mount, and the scout's shifted his feet, put all of the reins in his left hand, and reached for a wad of tobacco from his shirt pocket. As he pulled it free, the lieutenant's horse stomped its feet and shook its head, causing the trooper to drop the chaw. Looking around to see if anyone was watching, he picked up the tobacco, wiped it off against his pants, and bit off a piece, returning the rest of his pocket. He savored the taste and went back to daydreaming.

Several stores away, Judge Pence went into Howard's Real Estate, Insurance, and Telegraph office.

Recovering his poise, Lieutenant St. John slowly put on his gauntlets, tugging them into suitable position. "Are you saying that you and your brother . . . and two other men . . . fought off twenty Comanche?" he asked, his thin eyebrows jumping. "That doesn't seem likely, sir. Are you sure? I must know for certain."

"Didn't have much choice," Holt said and shifted his feet. "We lost a good man and our best friend got shot up."

"Amazing."

"That's one word for it."

St. John wiped at some dust on his tunic.

"There was another really bad heathen . . . named Hakan . . . riding with Achak. Did you see him?"

Holt glanced at the scout who was relighting his pipe. "The only Comanche that stood out was wearing a woman's dress. He was riding beside Achak when I killed him. My brother shot up the one in the dress. Was that Hakan?"

"Probably not, Sheriff. The last time he was seen, Hakan was wearing a cavalry officer's coat with the sleeves cut out," St. John replied. "He favors war paint in long stripes on his face." He looked at the scout for verification.

"Kinda hopin' you boys got him, too," Eagle Jones said, reinforcing the separation with his hands.

Deed strolled up to his brother. The handle of his revolver was apparent above his belt.

"Well, Lieutenant, here's my little brother, Deed. You might learn more from him." Holt reached out and put his arm around Deed's back.

"Deed, this is Lieutenant St. John and his scout, Eagle Jones. They're wondering if we saw another killer Comanche with Achak . . . uh, his name was . . ."

The lieutenant finished the statement.

"Hakan. Wearing an officer's coat with the sleeves cut off. We think he serves as Achak's right-hand man."

"Yeah, saw him twice. Big fella. His face was painted in black-and-white stripes. He was leading a bunch dragging blankets to make us think there were more with them than there actually was. That him?"

"Sounds like it. When was that?" the lieutenant asked, aware that his scout was staring at Deed.

"Early on. We were holed up in a deserted ranch."

"You said you saw him twice."

"Second time he was laying on top of our friend at our last stand. This Hakan was dead. Silka killed him with his sword."

Taking his pipe from his mouth, Eagle Jones said, "Well, good. Makes our job a helluva lot easier. Say, ain't you the one who took down two bank robbers, one holding a gun in your belly? Austin, I think it was."

"Something like that."

Holt laughed. "My brother's modest. That story's been up and down all of Texas."

"That makes you Deed Corrigan, right? And you're Holt Corrigan," the lieutenant said, his eyes widening.

"It does. Thought I said that earlier."

The lieutenant turned toward his men,

then spun around. "You are under arrest, Holt Corrigan, for the robbery of a United States payroll wagon and the murder of two soldiers and an officer." His eyes were bright with anger.

A slight twitch caught the corner of Holt's mouth. "When did this supposedly happen, lieutenant?"

"Three years ago. Near Fort Worth," St. John blurted, his face beet red. "You and your Reb cowards murdered my brother."

"Sorry about your brother, but I wasn't there."

Without responding, the young officer turned again toward his men. "Sergeant, take three men and place this man under military arrest. We'll take them to the fort for processing."

"Sergeant, you move from that saddle and it's the last thing you're going to do." In Deed's hand was his Remington. Cocked.

The sergeant froze and the lieutenant was surprised. "Sir, if I give the command, you and your brother will be shot down."

From the barely opened door of the marshal's office came a curt response from Hannah. "Blue boy, if you do, you'll never know what happened. This double-barreled shotgun'll blow you to hell. And I'll get the next five or six."

Kneeling with his Winchester propped against a horse rack ten feet away, Silka yelled, "I have the second three. Say the word."

Holt remained calm. "Lieutenant, I didn't rob that pay wagon. Even if I did, that was considered an act of war. I was given a full amnesty a month ago."

"An act of war? The war's been over for years. What amnesty?"

Leaving the store, Judge Pence walked down the sidewalk, holding a piece of paper in one hand and his spit can in the other. He stopped a few feet away and declared, "Officer, I am Oscar Pence, judge of the federal circuit court." He spat into the can. The handle of a shoulder-holstered gun was evident under his coat. "I gave Holt Corrigan full amnesty as is my authority to do so."

"I-I don't believe it." The officer shouted back, barely able to contain himself. His body shook with rage.

Eagle Jones told the lieutenant to settle down and St. John glared at him.

Deed growled, "Sergeant, tell that fool next to you that if he moves any closer to his rifle, you both will die."

The sergeant turned to the man beside him and snarled, "Don't you move a muscle,

272

you stupid sonuvabitch. Don't you know who that is? That's Deed Corrigan, for God's sake."

The soldier swallowed and put his hands against his chest.

Walking toward the lieutenant, Pence held out the paper. "Had me a feelin' ya weren't up to knowin' . . . so I stopped in the telegraph office. This here's from yur commandin' officer, Major Foutant, a good friend o' mine."

The lieutenant grabbed the paper and read it.

TO JUDGE PENCE STOP LT ST JOHN KNOWS OF AMNESTY STOP HIS ORDERS ARE TO CAPTURE ACHAK AND HAKAN STOP NOTHING ELSE STOP

MAJOR FOUTANT

He crushed the paper into his fist and ordered, "Sergeant, prepare the men to ride out."

"Hold on, lieutenant," Holt said. "Your boys have left quite a mess in our fine street. Better leave a patrol behind to clean it up." He cocked his head and glanced at Deed, who turned away to hide his chuckling.

Lieutenant St. John stared at Holt as if he

273

hadn't heard correctly.

"There's a city ordnance against leaving excessive horse manure in the street," Holt said. "Keeps cowboys from driving cattle through town. Your boys are going to need shovels and a tarp." He pointed at the supply wagon. "You can drop it outside of town."

Judge Pence held his hand over his mouth to cover his own tickled response. Eagle Jones smiled as he took the reins of his horse from the trooper with a huge chaw pushing out his cheek. Inside the marshal's office, Hannah hooted and stomped his feet.

Mumbling orders to his sergeant, St. John took the reins of his horse and climbed into the saddle. The trooper followed, mounting his horse and leaning over to spit.

The young officer nudged his horse into a trot and yelled out, "Forward . . . at a trot." He never looked back.

Four troopers pulled aside from the leaving column and went to the supply wagon. Each man grabbed a shovel, carried there for burial detail. A large tent was dragged out of the wagon to serve as the receptacle for the horse manure.

From down the street, a lone rider loped toward the marshal's office. It was the mayor, Patterson Cooke. He was clearly excited and spitting German phrases as he approached. Holt told him what had happened and that the army had volunteered to clean the street of horse manure. Cooke stared at the men working in the street, then back to Holt, and smiled.

"Dos ist gut."

"Yeah."

Looking around, Cooke asked where Hannah was, and Holt told him that he was inside the marshal's office working on some papers. The mayor seemed quite pleased. He excused himself and went into the office.

Deed slapped his brother on the back. "I'm going back to finish breakfast with a pretty lady. Then we'll take Silka and head for our ranch. After he's settled, I'll probably ride with Atlee back to the station."

"Of course you will," Holt said. "I'll be along in a day or two, need to let the rest of the county see their law in action."

"Good idea."

CHAPTER TWENTY-ONE

The brisk ride to the Rafter C ranch went happily as Deed and Atlee spent the time talking about her children, the stage line, ranching, and, coyly, about a life together. Deed insisted that Silka stretch out in the back of Atlee's buckboard. The former samurai was asleep before they left town.

As he drifted off, Silka mumbled, "Raise legs. Curl them. Strike. Again. Be quicker. Always attack . . ."

Deed smiled. "I've heard that a few times. He was quite the teacher. After I drop him off at the ranch, I'd like to go by the Bar 3," Deed said. "Check in and see how things are going. One of our men is running things there, Harmon Payne. Going to make him foreman there."

"Oh, I'd like that very much."

He explained that Harmon Payne was an interesting man who liked to spout phrases from Sir Walter Scott and Tennyson. The

Corrigans knew he had been a teacher in Ohio before coming to Texas. Something had happened there, but no one asked. He was loyal to a fault and tougher than his polite manner would indicate.

The land was showing signs of a coming winter. Several meadows were flushed with a light frost that disappeared as the morning sun took control of the day. Overhead, vees of geese flew toward warmth. A fat stream ran along the trail. Cattle moved contentedly about open meadows, enjoying the fine grass, although most of it was now brown. The herd was the Rafter C's and mostly Durham and Shorthorn with a few longhorn scattered around.

A hundred yards from the road was a large boulder, bigger than three men, that didn't seem to belong there. The closest rocks were in the blue hills, shadowy in the distance. It made a man wonder and feel small and Deed said so.

As they rounded a slow curve, two calves bounced for joy in front of them. Deed reined to a stop and they watched the young animals cavorting across the land. After enjoying a laugh together at their playfulness, Deed explained where they had stored hay for the winter months. Hopefully, there wouldn't be a blizzard this year like there was four years ago. That extreme cold had hit all of the area ranchers hard.

The Corrigans had been fortunate. Three protected valleys were rich in grass and water. A healthy stream cut across two of their main grazing areas and the rest of the land was dotted with springs. Five thousand head of cattle and a string of mustangs, were spread throughout their acres. Acres that were owned by them, truly owned with all of the necessary ownership files. Their third valley had been bought from another ranch just after the war and it, along with the other two valleys, gave them a fine operation. The herds were shifted from one valley to another as needed. Blunt hills and long benches offered natural fencing to keep the animals from drifting.

The ranch itself lay in one of the valleys with a well-built two-story ranch house featuring a porch and a second-story balcony. Silka had directed the construction of this larger house after the war; most of it was built by Blue and Deed. The one-armed rancher surveyed the ranch and took satisfaction in its appearance; they had painted all the buildings a year ago.

Atlee looked over at him, studying his tanned face. "Deed, will there always be trouble with Comanche? With Indians?"

"Most likely. We grew up believing everyone thought like we did, but they don't," Deed said, snapping the reins to keep the horses at an easy trot. "Human nature isn't what everyone believes. Just us. Indians grew up with different beliefs, different ways. Unfortunately, for them, their ways won't last." He shook his head. "Too many of us. They're nomads and need a lot of land to survive. Land that'll hold thousands of white folks."

"But can't we talk to them? Find ways to get along?"

"If you only had to talk to the old men of the tribe, I'd say yes," Deed continued, "but the young men won't listen. They live for war, only for war. Their whole society is built around it. The young men want their turn, like their fathers and grandfathers had."

"What a shame."

"Yeah."

They rode on, passing a tree that had been ripped apart by lightning years before. Four antelope darted away. In this stretch of the road, many dead trees lay about the land, as if God had decided he needed their energy elsewhere. A few minutes later, Deed Corrigan cleared the half-moon hill rimming the southern lip of the Rafter C ranch yard. He reined up the team to enjoy the scene below and explain the ranch layout to Atlee. The sight never grew tiring to him and he said so. Nearby cottonwoods whispered their welcome. Overhead, an October sun was easing toward noon.

Behind the main house they could see the bare limbs of the old oak tree that overlooked the graves of their father, mother, and sister. How long ago that seemed, almost like it was part of another life. None of their faces came distinctly to his mind anymore. Only blurred images. Silka had become a father — guiding, teaching, caring. He touched the brass circle at his neck. Atlee noticed and took his hand.

The ranch itself was quiet; the corrals, empty. Their horses had been unshod and allowed to roam, except for the handful kept for daily use. Next to the closest corral, two dogs rested from their labors. One looked up, then went back to sleep. Not far from the southern corral was the chuck wagon now closed up for the winter. Their few full-time cowhands were distributed about in line cabins or were over helping Harmon get things in order at the Bar 3. Deed felt guilty about not being at the Bar 3 before, but it couldn't be helped. He, Silka, and Holt had saved the town's money.

The only things moving around the ranch yard were some chickens pecking the ground on the south side of the main house. Atlee and Deed didn't see Blue or Bina, but saw the children playing on the east side. It looked like a game of cowboys with imaginary cattle being rounded up.

He clucked the wagon horses forward and hailed the ranch. The buckboard creaked and groaned as it eased down the hill. Aroused from their naps, the dogs barked and headed toward Deed. The three children stopped playing, recognized their uncle, squealed, and came running and laughing toward the buckboard.

Behind them, Silka was muttering again. "Sun, moon, mountains, river. All divine. Skills and inspiration to develop self also divine. Remember this, Deed . . ."

As they neared the ranch, Blue and Bina came from the main house, waving cheerily. The children were soon beside the wagon, all talking at once — Matthew, Mary Jo, and the now-adopted Jeremy.

"Uncle Deed! Uncle Deed! What's the matter with Uncle Silka?" Ten-year-old Matthew asked.

The Corrigans didn't believe in keeping the harshness of life away from children, so Deed told him what had happened. The children's eyes widened as the story was simply told.

"Pa told us you, Uncle Holt, and Uncle Silka are heroes. You caught bank robbers . . . an', an' fought off some bad Indians," the boy blurted.

It always amused Deed that none of Blue's children seemed to connect their mother to Indians. She didn't hide her Apache heritage; it just didn't connect. Of course, that meant they were half-breeds, but that didn't register, either. Deed figured at some point Matthew would be teased about it and forced to fight. He reminded himself to teach Matthew good self-defense skills, as Silka had taught him.

"How many Injuns did you kill?" Matthew asked.

Blue stepped beside the boy and put his arm around his oldest son. "That's enough, Matt. Indians have their ways and we have ours. Both are good under God's eyes." He also didn't mention their mother was an Apache. Probably because it didn't occur to him.

Satisfied, the children ran away to resume their game. Deed pulled the buckboard to the reining post at the main house and helped Atlee down. She and Bina began chatting and went inside, returning with a bowl of dried herbs to treat Silka's wounds.

Blue and Deed helped Silka from the wagon and walked with him to the small house where the samurai and Deed lived. Along the way, Silka mushmouthed, "Now, fall back. Hit the ground with your palms first. Keep chin tucked so you don't hit your head. No raise legs. Curl them. Be quick. Quicker. Attack. As hard as you can. Drive through enemy . . ."

"I'm worried about him, Blue," Deed said. "I think he's hurt worse than he lets on."

"Well, he's home now and there's nobody better than Bina to care for him."

"I know."

After getting the wounded Japanese warrior into bed, Bina and Atlee began cleaning his wounds. So far, none were infected, but the old man had lost much blood and was quite weak. As they tended to him, Silka alternately mumbled and chanted. None of it was in English.

Later, Deed and Atlee joined Blue's family for a noon meal. Blue asked them to stay for dinner and the evening. Atlee could sleep in the spare bedroom in the main house. After all these years, Blue still couldn't bring himself to call it their parents' old room.

"No thanks, Blue," Deed said. "We need

to get back to the station. Maybe next time."

"Sure."

"I'll take Warrior with us," Deed continued. "Then I'll ride on to the Bar 3. Lots to do, I'm sure." He had told Atlee about the special Comanche warhorse that had shown up at the ranch along with a bunch of mustangs. With help from Bina, the animal had become an exceptional mount, but was ridden only by Deed.

Blue told him of Harmon's progress at the big ranch, including cutting hay and checking on the line cabins. Taol Sanchez had sent over three hands to assist. The herd was in good shape and all the calves were branded. There was plenty of food in the ranch house kitchen, a tribute to Agon Bordner's appetite.

Soon, Deed and Atlee were on their way again, with his saddled paint horse trotting behind the wagon.

"I thought you said we were going to the Bar 3," Atlee asked when they were out of earshot.

"We were, but your eyes told me we needed to get you back," Deed answered.

"Was it that obvious?"

"Only to me. I miss your kids, too."

He kept the wagon on a main road, rather than cutting through wilder country. The buckboard would have had a difficult time going through places where a horseman could easily pass. It was longer this way, but it made sense.

He found himself telling her about Silka and how the former samurai had taught him to defend himself with any weapon, including his hands and feet. How the older man had instilled a spiritual sense within him.

"He's been a father to me," Deed said, "to my brothers, too."

She asked about Holt, saying all she had ever heard about him was that he was an outlaw. Bristling at first, Deed settled into an explanation of how his older brother couldn't deal with the South losing, and that he and other former Confederates tried to fight on, long after the war was over. Judge Pence had saved Holt from himself, and the Corrigans would always be grateful.

Atlee was silent, looking down at her hands. Finally, she said, "Deed, I love you. I think I have since I first saw you." She paused and tears formed in the corners of her eyes. "I-I loved Caleb, too. I shouldn't feel this way . . . about you. My husband has been dead only . . . a short while." She wiped her eyes. "What kind of person am I?"

"You are the most wonderful woman I've

ever known, that's what," Deed said in a soft, even voice. "I didn't know Caleb, but he was obviously a fine man . . . or you wouldn't have loved him." He tugged on his hat brim. "And I think you should go on loving him. Who says we can only love one person? You love two children."

"B-but that's different."

"Not, it's not. Love is love." He smiled. "And if you ask my brother Blue, he'll deliver a mighty fine sermon on the matter. As in God is love."

Atlee looked up at him, tears sliding down her cheeks.

He smiled. "And I love you."

They rode on again without talking. The land was changing, easing from meadows of grass into broken spaces of rock, stunted cedar, chickweed, and prickly pear cactus. Two unmarked graves beside the road were indications of much earlier pioneers whose names were now lost. At the farthest point of Rafter C grazing land, a lone longhorn steer stood as a sentinel, watching them pass. A jackrabbit bounced in front of the buckboard and scurried out of sight.

To their left, a winding trail appeared from among a cluster of trees. Blue and Deed had used this trail when coming and going from the station. It kept a rider out of sight most of the way. Ahead of them, tracks of a recent stagecoach swerved from the south, cutting over earlier marks along the established path. Familiar cottonwoods signaled the advent of the stage station yard.

"Pull up here, please, Deed," Atlee said and moved close to him. "I may not have a chance to do this for a while."

As he halted the horses, she put her hands to his face and her mouth sought his.

CHAPTER TWENTY-TWO

Deed and Atlee finally pulled into the station yard, both red-faced and warm. A dust devil danced across the open ground as the station door swung open and Atlee's two children came running toward them. From the barn came the eye-patched Mexican horse wrangler Billy Lee Montez, and the German farmer Hermann Beinrigt.

Billy reached the buckboard first. "*Es bueno* to see you, Señor Deed." He waved his hands. "One of the passengers say you and your brother are *los* heroes *muy grandes*. Catch bank robbers. Kill Achak and his Comanche. *Bueno!*"

"We didn't have much choice, Billy. They came at us. We were lucky."

Behind him came Hermann. The wrinkle-faced German hurried to the back of the buckboard and examined the supplies. "*Ist gut du bringst* supplies. Ve vere getting low. *Ach, ja,* ve need . . . everyting."

Deed smiled. How like the German to focus on what was needed, never mind greetings or conversation.

Benjamin, looking older than his twelve years, came from the barn and walked to the buckboard. "Well, howdy, Deed. We heard you were in another fight with Injuns. Wow! That must've been something."

"How are you, Benjamin? You look like you've grown a foot," Deed exclaimed as he set the brake and wrapped the reins around the brake handle.

The boy smiled. His dog, Cooper, bounded from the barn and skidded to a stop beside his master.

"Hey, you should see Chester. Him an' me get along just great."

Atlee frowned and corrected her son, "He and I."

"Yeah, that's what I said."

"Glad to hear it," Deed said, climbing down and then helping Atlee.

Without hesitating, Benjamin held out his hand and Deed took it vigorously. The boy told him what he had been doing with the horse Deed had given him. Atlee walked over to greet her son, who stepped back, embarrassed by her show of affection. He glanced at Deed, who nodded, and the boy returned his mother's hug.

"Mommy!"

Watching from a few feet away, Elizabeth held a doll against her chest.

Eagerly, she waddled toward the buckboard with her arms now outstretched. In one hand, the six-year-old held the doll Deed had brought her. Atlee turned to Elizabeth and took her in her arms, hugged her, and let the excited girl down.

"Good afternoon, Miss Forsyth," Deed said politely. "How have you been?"

"I'll bet you don't remember the name of my doll," Elizabeth pouted.

"Hmmm, let's see. It isn't Mary Louise." Deed knelt and the little girl wandered closer. "And it isn't Rebecca." He rubbed his chin. "And I know it isn't Olivia."

She frowned.

"But it is Jessica. Jessica Forsyth."

She ran to him and he took her into his arms and stood. Without his asking, she told him in exhaustive detail what she had been doing and how her doll had been.

"That's enough, Elizabeth," Atlee said. "Mr. Corrigan's head will be buzzing for hours."

Deed laughed and kissed Elizabeth's cheek. "Not at all. I enjoyed it. Every word. Seems like I haven't seen you or your brother forever."

"It has been a long time," Elizabeth declared. "You shouldn't stay away so long." She wiggled to be let down.

Deed released her and asked the two men how the operation was going. Atlee came and stood beside him. Since Deed left, they had replaced one team of horses with a new set, purchased from August Magnuson in El Paso. Hermann emphasized they had gotten a good deal.

"*Es bueno* hosses," Billy added proudly. "Strong. Steady. Nuthin' scares them. Nuthin'. You should see them."

"I'd like that. We bought a stallion from that man. Excellent animal."

Beinrigt agreed with Billy's assessment; his response laced with German phrases.

Benjamin leaned over to pat Cooper and they wandered back to the barn. Elizabeth meandered away, singing a song about Jessica and Deed. Atlee asked if there had been any signs of Indians while she was gone. Both men assured her that there hadn't been. Billy added that he kept a shotgun handy.

Turning to Deed, Hermann said, "Ve just heard of *du* and *dur* bruthur fighting redmen. *Du* are *sehr* brave, Herr Corrigan."

"Well, thank you," Deed said, glancing at the smiling Atlee. "Just lucky."

"Is they be gone now?"

Deed told them what the lieutenant had said about trying to round up the few remaining renegades from Achak's band.

"So, da heathens still be about?"

"Only a few as far as we know," Deed responded and adjusted his heavy gun belt out of habit. He stomped his boots to clear them of dust. His spurs sang. "But I'd stay alert. They'd love your horses."

Billy shook his head and declared they intended to keep the animals in the barn most of the time, until needed.

"That's smart, Billy."

The Mexican grinned.

The station doorway swung open and Olivia Beinrigt appeared, wearing a fresh apron over her gray dress. The green scarf Deed had given her was around her neck. Her hair was pulled back in a bun and a smudge of flour adorned one cheek.

"It *ist du*, Herr Deed! *Guten tag!*" she said. "*Valkommen!* Coffee *ist* on and a fine stew *ist* ready. We need to hear how *du* are." She looked at Atlee and smiled.

"It's good to see you, too, Mrs. Beinrigt."

CHAPTER TWENTY-THREE

Back in Wilkon, Holt Corrigan was regaining his strength and catching up on the area news from James Hannah, now the permanent town marshal. Judge Pence had resumed his circuit responsibilities and was out of town. The *Wilkon Epitaph* was doing well and had taken on some regular advertisers. A new couple in town from San Antonio had opened a small drugstore. The funeral service for Malcolm Rose had been well attended, and it sounded like Mrs. Rose was leaning toward staying and running their store. A series of lyceums, with their regular rounds of debates, lectures, and songfests, was being planned for the winter.

Miss Temple had resigned as the schoolteacher and was leaving town. It was thought she was getting married to an Ohio businessman. Hannah's wife had agreed to fill in until a permanent teacher was secured.

To celebrate the mostly successful return of the posses, the special day of fun that was canceled earlier was now reorganized for the Saturday after next, still having all the events planned before.

Drinking coffee, Holt noticed a Bible laying on top of the cabinet under the gun rack. He wandered over, knowing it had to be Blue's.

"Looks like my brother forgot his Bible," Holt said, picking up the scripture. "Not like him to forget the good book."

"Well, he was mighty worried about you boys," Hannah said without moving. "Might've forgotten it then. Sure isn't mine."

Patting the Bible, Holt said he thought it was a good time to take a tour of the county so folks would know there was law in place. Hannah agreed.

The door slammed opened and both young lawmen drew and swung their revolvers toward the entrance. An arrogant and bullish Scotsman stomped into the office. Sleeping in the corner, Tag growled as he stormed inside.

"Be quiet, Tag," Holt commanded, and the dog was silent.

Kornican Tiorgs, a local horse rancher, was mad as hell and certain that Henry Welton, a clerk in the general store, had stolen his horse. The powerfully built Scotsman had nearly killed another horse riding into town to find the county sheriff and demand an arrest. The madder he got, the thicker his brogue became. There was no doubt the store clerk had a new horse in the town livery. Both Holt and Hannah had seen it. The animal was carrying the accusing rancher's brand. Welton said he had a bill of sale.

"There's got to be a mistake, Tiorgs," Holt said, returning his gun to its shoulder holster. "Welton is a good man."

"Nae, that tae be bullshit. He is thae hoss thief. He is tae be hanged. I'll gi'e ye a haund." He patted the revolver resting in his belt.

Holt didn't like the Scotsman and neither did his brothers. Tiorgs had run roughshod over a lot of folks over the years. He was used to having his own way, that was for certain.

"You wait here, Tiorgs. I'll get Welton and we can talk it this out," Holt said, brushing his fingers along the cardinal feather in his hatband. He placed the hat on his head.

"Dunno ye be takin' a len o'Kornican Tiorgs. I guin' wit' ye."

"I said stay here." Holt's eyes gave an even

295

stronger message and the Scotsman looked away. "And hand that gun over to Marshal Hannah."

Pushing his eyeglasses into place, Hannah motioned for him to sit down.

Frowning, the big Scotsman complied. Hannah smiled and thanked him. There was no choice but to bring in the clerk for questioning. It had seemed fairly simple. Set the two men down and work this matter out. It had to be a misunderstanding. Holt walked from the marshal's office and patted his waiting horse. It was Judge Pence's suggestion that the two lawmen always have saddled horses available. Next to it was Hannah's horse, standing three-legged, and the Scotsman's lathered mount.

The animal had been pushed hard. Too hard. Holt patted Tiorgs's horse's neck and wiped the frothy wetness against the saddle blanket. No, he wasn't going to leave Triogs's horse in this condition. With a quick yank, he loosened the cinch and pushed the saddle and blanket off the heaving animal and into the street. His own mount jumped sideways. Tiorgs's horse was bleeding where the Scotsman had savagely spurred him.

Waving at a boy running across the street, Holt untied the reins of Tiorgs's horse and waited for the youngster to come to him. He recognized him as the ten-year-old Crutchfield lad.

"How'd you like to make a dollar, son?" he asked as the boy skidded to a stop next to him.

"That would be swell, Sheriff. What do I have to do? Can I use a gun?" The boy's face was layered with freckles and his shapeless hat barely covered a long mop of brown hair.

"I want you to walk this horse to the livery. Don't let it run . . . or drink any water. None," Holt said. "Tell Mr. Littleson to brush him good and care for the cuts. Have him check that right front leg, too. I'll be down later to settle up." He reached into his pocket, past his small medicine stone, and withdrew a coin.

"Yes, sir. I'll take care of it."

"Good." Holt watched the boy lead away the weary horse, then resumed his walk to the general store with Tag at his side.

Telling the dog to wait outside, he entered the general store with mixed feelings. At least this wasn't like fighting Comanche or struggling to survive on the hot prairie without a horse. Still, having to respond to an egotistical bully like Tiorgs made him boil. He stepped inside, enjoying the range

297

of smells. Leather, tobacco, spices, gun oil, even the sweet aromas of gingham and flour reached him. Glancing at the sides of bacon hanging from the rafter, he looked around for Welton.

From the middle of the store, Henry Welton saw him and waved. The portly Welton's shiny bald head was offset by a full dark beard. His normally tailored appearance was marred by his shirttail sticking out from under his vest and his silk ascot pulled sideways. He was known as a hard worker, loyal to his employer. This wasn't going to be fun, but it had to be done.

"Good day to you, Sheriff Corrigan. How can we help you?"

Speaking softly, Holt said, "Henry, I've got to ask you to come with me to the marshal's office. Kornican Tiorgs says you stole one of his horses." He held out his hand to keep Welton from overreacting. "I know you're no horse thief, but we've got to get this straightened out."

What happened next surprised Holt. Welton drew a handgun carried in his back waistband and pointed it at him.

"N-no, S-Sheriff . . . I-I can't. I can't. Y-you c-can't arrest m-me. Y-you just can't! I didn't steal no horse. I didn't. H-he's lying," Henry Welton stammered. "I-I paid him . . . a hundred and forty dollars." His eyes blinked rapidly. "I should've known better than to trust him. He's an evil man."

The young lawman's firm, low voice walked the line between friendship and business. "Henry, hand me the gun. It's all going to work out. You don't want to turn this into something bad." His eyes locked onto the clerk's eyes. Holt held out his hand toward the agitated store clerk.

The two stood ten feet apart. Nearby, three women and a man stood frozen in fascination and fear. One woman kept putting on and taking off a new bonnet, without her eyes leaving the two men or realizing her repetitive activity.

"Look, Henry, I know you," Holt said quietly, his frown growing deeper as the clerk grew more irrational. "I know this is a misunderstanding. And I know Tiorgs. But you have to go with me. I'm sure we can get this straightened out in no time."

"If you t-take another step, I-I'll shoot you," Henry Welton stammered, his voice breaking, his shaking fist holding the cocked .44 revolver. "I swear it, H-Holt. I swear it."

The young lawman was an imposing figure even though he was only of average height. He made no attempt to draw either of his shoulder-holstered guns.

Holt took a deep breath. The man in front of him wasn't really a friend, only an acquaintance. Henry Welton wasn't the kind of man he liked to spend much time with. The store clerk was too inclined to want to talk money, or inventory, or business conditions. As far as Holt was concerned, he wasn't a horse thief, either. Far from it.

Now the situation was looking dangerous. A scared man with a gun was like a cornered panther; one never knew when or if he might strike. Holt was trying to make it easy on Welton, but the man wasn't listening. Most likely he was frightened of Tiorgs. Many were. The Scotsman's bullying ways were well-known.

Without warning, the woman playing with the hat rushed to Holt's side and grabbed his left arm. Uncontrollably, she screamed, "Do something, Sheriff! He's going to kill us all!"

Surprised by her wild challenge, Welton's gun exploded in his own emotional response and the bullet hit a table, spilling its riches of cigars, tobacco sacks, and plugs across the wood-planked floor. Holt pushed the woman away and grabbed Welton's gun, yanking it from him in one swift motion.

The clerk melted into despair. "Oh, I'm sorry. I-I'm so sorry. I wouldn't hurt . . ."

"But you almost did, Welton. Now straighten up. We're going over to the jail to talk this over with Tiorgs." Holt glared at the trembling man. "If you didn't steal his horse, you've got nothing to be afraid of."

"Ho ye, Sheriff! How ar' ye? What tae be guien' on in thar?" The big Scotsman bellowed, pawing his way through the gathering crowd around the store's opened doorway. An exasperated Hannah was twenty feet behind him, hurrying to catch up. Obviously, the Scotsman had not waited as directed.

Holt met him there. The young lawman's eyes struck the cattleman's with a coldness that would have made a lesser man weep. As it was, Tiorgs only blinked and took a half step backward in response to the deadly stare.

"What tae be happenin'? Heard a muckle o' shootin'. Wouldna thae hoss thief be comin' peaceable-like?" Tiorgs swallowed and added that someone had stolen the horse he rode into town. He seemed more surprised about it than angry.

"Your horse was taken to the livery," Holt said. "You almost killed it. No animal should be treated that way. It's getting a rubdown and some care."

"Who be doin' sech?"

301

"I did."

"Oh. What o' thae shootin'? I be comin' to help ye."

"It's nothing. Just an accident. And I don't need your help," Holt said, growing more irritated by the minute. "Go back to the marshal's office and stay there, like I told you." He looked at the curious gathering of townspeople and declared, "The rest of you get on with what you were doing. There's nothing here to see."

The broad-shouldered Scotsman was silent only for a moment, then blurted out, "Dinna' watch yerself, Sheriff, ye think I woulda come pussy-footin' tae town . . . if'n I didna have thae 'sairy proof. Weel, five years back, I woulda just hung 'im maeself. Tryin' tae do thae right thing I be." A long Scottish expression followed.

"If you had, I'd have hanged you for murder," Holt answered, unsure of what the expression meant and didn't care.

Tiorgs started to say something and decided it was best to be silent. Hannah caught up and reinforced Holt's order with his handgun. The Scotsman didn't like it, but choose to go along without arguing. Tag's fierce growl only punctuated his decision.

Back at the marshal's office, Holt ordered

both men to stand in opposite corners of the small quarters. He allowed Tiorgs, as the accuser, to go first. After listening to Tiorgs's rambling tirade, the matter was clear. Typical of his bullying style, Tiorgs thought he could coerce the clerk into paying more money by threatening him with being a horse thief. He had many horses and claimed that he was selling Welton a three-year-old bay with three white stockings and Welton took a three-year-old sorrel with two white stockings when he wasn't around.

The Scotsman snarled the clerk thought he could get away with it that way. Welton's bill of sale made no reference to the kind of horse he had bought; Holt figured this vagueness was deliberate on Tiorgs's part.

"Hold on, Tiorgs," Holt declared, pointing a finger at the Scotsman. "I thought you were supposed to be a horseman."

" 'Deed, thae best around, I be."

"Well, tell me then, how does a good horseman not know the difference between a bay with three stockings and a sorrel with two?"

Tiorgs licked his lower lip. "I dinna' be sellin' that hoss for sech wee money."

Holt turned to Welton. "Henry, did you talk to Tiorgs about a sorrel or a bay?"

"Only a sorrel. It is a fine horse . . . and I paid well for it."

"Yes, you did. Very well." Holt turned back to the fuming Scotsman.

He cocked his head. "I'll try again, Tiorgs. Where did you and Mr. Welton look at the horse you claim was stolen?"

"I donna' understand ye. Out o' thoucht." Tiorgs' face reddened and his fists clinched and unclenched.

Hannah watched him closely and casually put his hand around the butt of his revolver.

Holt continued, "Were both the bay and the sorrel standing together? Did Mr. Welton check out the horse's teeth? Which one? How about its legs? Back? Which horse's neck did he pet?"

"Ay. O' course he did."

"I asked *which* horse?" Holt's voice was gravelly as he leaned against the marshal's desk. "Meet my eyes, Tiorgs."

Welton grimaced. Would the Scotsman tell the truth? Hannah walked over to the stove, purposefully and visibly adjusted his gun in his waistband, and poured himself a new cup of coffee.

"Meet my eyes, Tiorgs. Which horse?"

Tiorgs looked away.

"Thought so." Holt said. "The next time you pull a stunt like this, Tiorgs, I'm going to arrest you for fraud. Do you understand?" He slammed his fist against the marshal's desk and papers danced in response. Hannah stood against the wall and hid his chuckle behind his hand.

"Do you, Tiorgs?"

The rancher rolled his tongue along his parched lips. "Yah, me guess so."

"You *guess* so?"

Tiorgs shook his head. "Nah. I be gittin' it." He added a Scottish phrase that Holt took for an apology.

Angrily, Holt told Tiorgs that the price was fair and that was the end of the matter; Welton had bought the horse fair and square.

After thanking Holt, Welton asked to be excused so he could get back to work.

"Just a minute, Henry. Give me your bill of sale."

"Ah, sure." Welton reached into his pocket and withdrew the folded paper.

"Give it to Tiorgs. He wants to add something to it."

"Whadda are ye sayin'?" the surprised Scotsman asked as he took the paper.

"You're going to write more detail on it," Holt declared. "Sorrel. Fifteen hands. Three years. Two white stockings." He thought a moment. "Yeah, that should do it. Tiorgs,

305

how long have you been writing bills of sale that are so vague?"

"Meself? Naw so. A guid man, I bae."

"There's a pencil on the desk. Get at it."

Tiorgs shuddered, then opened the paper, wrote slowly, then handed it back to Holt. "There. Shoulda this bae all right wit' ye?"

Holt read it, folded the paper, and handed it to Welton. "You're welcome to go now. I'll be over in a few minutes. Need some supplies for the trail."

"It'll be my honor to serve you, Sheriff."

Welton left and Holt turned to the Scotsman. "Now, about the horse you rode in," he said. "You can leave it at Littleson's for three days. Two dollars a day. Or I'll buy that horse for twenty dollars."

"How weel I be gettin' maeself back to mae place?"

CHAPTER TWENTY-FOUR

"You can rent a horse," Holt Corrigan said, folding his arms. "Then let him go when you get home. The horse will return by itself." He cocked his head.

"That be leavin' me with wee fer me fine hoss."

"You're lucky I don't arrest you for mistreating the animal."

Tiorgs reluctantly agreed to Holt's offer and accepted the money. "I suppose a bill o' sale ye bae wantin'."

"Absolutely. I wouldn't trust you with a glass of water." Holt picked up Tiorgs's gun on the desk, emptied the cartridges into his hand, and tossed the empty weapon toward the Scotsman.

Tiorgs cringed and wrote out a receipt. Satisfied, Holt directed him to the door and told him to get his saddle and bridle. Tag trotted at Holt's side.

At the livery, Jesse Littleson greeted Holt

warmly and ignored Tiorgs. It was obvious the livery operator didn't like the Scotsman. Smelling of whiskey, Littleson volunteered a similar situation involving Tiorgs two years ago. It resulted in a farmer paying two hundred dollars for one of the Scotsman's draft horses after Tiorgs said it was stolen.

Tiorgs's face erupted in crimson and he dropped the saddle gear with a thud.

"He won't pull that stunt again," Holt said, leading his packhorse from the stall.

Littleson grinned and reported on the status of the Scotsman's horse. Holt told him that he had purchased the animal and wished to leave it with him until the horse was recovered.

"I be ri't proud to do so, Sheriff," the livery operator snorted. "It'll be some weeks, I think. He was rode mighty hard."

"Tiorgs wants to rent a horse to ride back to his place," Holt said, resting his hand against a stall board. "He'll let it go."

"He be payin' in advance, I take it."

"Of course. Only a fool would trust him."

Tiorgs snorted and crossed his arms. Littleson took Tiorgs's saddle gear and headed for a back stall. "I'm going to let him ride Sadie."

Holt remembered Sadie was an older gray horse that was rarely used any more.

He turned toward Littleson. "Good choice. He won't be wearing spurs. Take 'em off, Tiorgs."

Tag growled. Holt felt the movement behind him, ducked, and spun around. Tiorgs's windmill swing of his huge right fist missed him. Holt jammed his right fist deep into the man's belly and followed it with a left into the same place. Groaning, the big man staggered backward. Thirty pounds heavier than Holt, and three inches taller, Tiorgs was a savage brawler used to winning fights by intimidation. Holt had learned his fighting from Silka and the war.

Tiorgs lunged at the young lawman and knocked off his hat. Instead of moving aside, Holt stepped closer and stopped Tiorgs's charge with a left uppercut to his chin, followed by a right jab to the Scotsman's cheek. His cheekbone split and showered blood on both men.

Yelling in pain, Tiorgs landed a thunderous right to Holt's chest that he only partially blocked. The blow took away his wind and the young lawman was dazed. Holt slammed against a stall, but catapulted from it to land both fists into Tiorgs's stomach. Tiorgs shoved him back and threw another windmill right fist that caught Holt on the side of his face, but the full force missed him. Wobbling from Holt's previous blows, the Scotsman tried to tackle Holt, but the lawman stepped aside and delivered a savage chop to Tiorgs's neck that would have made Silka proud. The Scotsman fell flat, his hands splayed to keep his face from hitting the dirt. He shook his head and managed to stand.

Tag snapped at Tiorgs and bit his right leg. Holt moved forward and his right uppercut caught the Scotsman on the chin and he flew backward. The Scotsman's head bounced on the livery floor and hay spit in every direction. He lay there, unmoving. Holt told the dog to back away and Tag reluctantly let go.

Littleson looked over from saddling the horse. "Damn, looks like this ain't his day."

"Guess not. Don't like bullies much." Holt could taste the blood in his mouth. His hands were raw and bleeding.

Littleson laughed. "I can see that."

The livery operator returned Holt's hat and said, "Better soak them hands, Sheriff. They'll swell up somethin' fierce if'n ya don't."

Without further encouragement, Holt stuck his hands into a bucket of water held by Littleson.

"Got some Epsom salts somewhar's."

"This'll be fine. Thanks."

After a few minutes, Holt dried his hands on the offered towel, then went to the barely conscious Tiorgs and pulled coins from his pocket to pay for the rental. He handed the money to the livery operator. The Scotsman's spurs were quickly unbuckled.

"Mind if I leave his spurs here?" Holt said.

"Naw. That's fine. He won't cause me no problem."

They helped the dizzy Scotsman into the saddle and slapped the horse on the rear. Sadie trotted out of the livery with Tiorgs bobbing on its back. Both watched them ride away. Shaking his head to clear it, Tiorgs gathered the reins and finally turned the horse west.

Holt slapped Littleson on the back. "I'm going to need my horse . . . and our packhorse. Going to ride the county. Introduce myself. Make sure all is quiet."

"How long you be gone, Sheriff?" Littleson brought the requested horses as they talked.

"Probably a week."

"Well, you won't want to miss the big shindig they're fixin' to hold. Finally. This Saturday, ya know."

"I'll see. But if I'm not back, you'll have to do my share of the dancing." Holt smiled as they walked toward the stabled horses.

Littleson slapped his thigh and laughed. "Sure 'nuff. 'Ceptin' no nice lady's gonna dance with the likes o' me."

Holt shook his head. "Not true, Jess. You just show up with your dancing shoes on . . . and your hair slicked back."

Grinning, Littleson growled, "Well, tell ya what. I'd like to enter that hoss race they're a'plannin'. Yes, suh, I would."

"Do it."

"Ain't got no hoss. Leastwise, nuthin' that would be fast enough."

Holt motioned toward a far stall where the second Comanche horse was stabled. "Take my other horse. He'll run like a deer."

"Really? Could I?" Littleson rubbed his hands together.

" 'Course. Ride him a few times so you guys get to know to each other." Holt adjusted the cinch on his waiting horse.

Littleson bit his lower lip. "I be in your debt."

"Just take good care of *my* new horse." Holt led his horses to the livery door. "Oh, don't wear spurs. He doesn't understand them. You won't need them anyway."

"Sure 'nuff."

Holt reached into his pocket and withdrew a gold coin. "Put this on you two, to win."

Littleson's smile cut across his wide face.

The young sheriff finished his work in the livery by gathering two canteens and his bedroll. He waved good-bye and stepped into the street. The town was busy with wagons and freighters crisscrossing the main street; mounted riders slid between them. He warned Tag to watch where he was going.

At the general store, Henry Welton was eager to help him select his supplies and settle them on the packhorse. Holt warned him about being careful with a gun and the clerk nodded sheepishly. Three-quarters of a pound of salt pork, a small sack of jerked beef, another of coffee, cans of beans and peaches, and a box of .44s. After a moment, he decided to buy three sacks of sugar, three of flour, and several copies of the latest edition of the town newspaper. As Holt was leaving, Welton hurried from the store with a fistful of cigars as a thank-you. Holt bit off the end of one, lit it, and shoved the others into his inside coat pocket. He thanked Welton. The clerk noticed Holt's bloody knuckles, but said nothing about them.

After thanking Welton, he mounted his horse and had started to pull away when he saw Allison Johnson hurrying toward him. She and Holt had been involved romantically before the war, but she had married Andrew Hamm while he was gone. Hamm had died from influenza two years ago. Holt had deliberately avoided seeing her.

Her face appeared to be frozen in time by too much rouge and powder. She was wearing an attractive dark green dress with a matching hat. The dress accented her ample bosom. Seeing her was a jolt to Holt, instantly releasing old memories. At the same moment, there was a sense of revulsion that rolled through him. He wasn't sure why.

"Holt! Holt Corrigan. I thought I'd never get to see you," she said with her best smile. "I'm living with Mrs. Yardish. I work for her, sewing."

"Didn't know that . . . Mrs. Hamm." He rolled the cigar to the other side of his mouth.

"Andrew Hamm died over two years ago," she responded. "I am a widow."

"Sorry to hear that." He tugged on his hat brim. "Well, you take care." He nudged his horse forward.

"Wait, Holt. Please."

Pulling on the reins, Holt took a deep breath.

"Can't we start over?" She stared at his face. "If I remember right, you used to like being with me." She glanced down at her breasts.

"That was a long time ago, Allison. We were just kids."

She forced a laugh. "You didn't feel like a kid."

He didn't respond.

"Will you be attending the dance Saturday?"

"Doubt it. I've got business in the county." He puffed on the cigar and wished he was elsewhere.

Fluttering her eyelashes, she asked, "Well, if you do, will you save a dance . . . for me?"

He clucked to his horse. "It's been good to see you, but I've got to get going."

"Oh, certainly." She looked down at her dress and brushed away invisible dust. "Oh, my box will have a purple bow."

She was referring to the custom of auctioning dinner boxes provided by the unmarried women. Supposedly, the boxes were kept a secret with the top-bidding man getting to have dinner with the woman.

He nodded and rode toward the marshal's office, puffing on the cigar and keeping an eye on Tag. Several men waved as he passed and he returned the greeting. Allison Johnson Hamm watched him, hoping he'd look back. He didn't, and yelled at Tag to stay close as a Dearborn wagon thundered past them, following by a shiny surrey and a buckboard.

"Holt . . . Holt Corrigan."

He knew who it was before turning. Everett Reindal. He was one of the former Rebels Holt had run with until telling them he was headed home, to his brothers' ranch. Everett looked the same, only more tired and a little thinner.

"Everett, what brings you to Wilkon?" Holt said as he turned, drawing one of his revolvers. Gripping the gun hurt his hand. "Not planning on robbing our bank, I hope. We just dealt with the last bunch. They weren't very lucky."

"You won't need that," Everett said. "I came for . . . advice." He was standing in the shadows at the entrance of an alley.

"Advice?" Holt asked without lowering his gun. "Where are the rest of the boys?"

"Don't know. We split up shortly after you left," Everett said, rubbing his unshaved chin. "Guess you made us all do some thinkin'."

Holt took several steps toward his old friend. "Good for you. All of you." He returned the gun to its holster. "Doesn't sound like you need any advice from me."

Shaking his head, the former Confederate

explained he was hoping to find a job, preferably a riding job, and had come to Holt to ask for possible ranches looking for men.

"Not a good time for that," Holt said and held out his hand as he crossed into the alley. "Roundup's over. Going to be mostly line cabin stuff. Not extra hands."

"Yeah, figured that, but I gotta try."

Reaching into his pocket, Holt withdrew some coins and held them out. "Here. You're going to need some eatin' money."

"I wasn't lookin' for a handout." Everett's face was a frown.

"Wasn't giving one," Holt said. "I think a friend can help a friend, don't you?" He paused. "Guess I thought we were friends."

Everett looked like he was going to cry. Holt stepped next to him and put his left hand on the former Confederate's shoulder while his other hand held out the coins.

"T-thanks." Everett took the money and shoved the coins into his pocket.

"Now, after you get something to eat," Holt said, stepping back and folding his arms, "I want you to ride out to the Bar 3. Big outfit. I'll give you directions." He licked his lower lip. "Ask for the foreman. Harmon Payne. Good man, even if he was a Yankee. Tell him that Captain Holt sent you."

"*Captain* Holt? Are you sure?"

"Couldn't be more certain. Harmon will understand."

Holt told him how to get to the ranch, shook his hand, and walked away.

"I won't let you down . . . *Captain.*" Everett saluted.

"Didn't figure you would." Holt returned the salute and walked on.

Entering the marshal's office, Holt went directly to the coffeepot boiling on the cranky stove and poured a cup for Hannah and then one for himself. It was scalding and he sipped it tentatively. Hannah looked for a bowl of sugar kept nearby. Tag wandered over and leaned against Holt's leg. His request for attention was rewarded with a lengthy scratch on his head.

Studying his friend, Hannah smiled. "Well. I see you and Tiorgs had more words."

"Something like that. He wouldn't take off his spurs."

They both laughed. Hannah asked if Holt wanted him to get hot water to soak his hands and Holt thought they would be all right.

"If you like balloons," Hannah said.

Holt squeezed his fists. "They're better than they look. Littleson gave me a bucket to soak them in."

"I'll bet that was clean."

"It was. Really," Holt responded and added, "Say, I told him he could ride my other horse in Saturday's big race."

"Why tell me?"

Holt chuckled. "Didn't want you to arrest him for stealing, and I bet on him."

"So now I suppose you want me to bet on him, too."

"I did. Gave him twenty dollars."

"Damn." Hannah sipped his coffee. "Just might have to check into that."

Holt followed up on his decision to tour the county, explaining he had put together supplies, and saying he should be back in a week. He planned to stop at the Rafter C after going first to the farms not far from town. Hannah told him that he had hired a deputy with the town council's approval, a young farmer in need of extra cash.

Five minutes later, Leroy Gillespie knocked on the marshal's office and entered after Hannah told him to do so. Gillespie addressed them both and turned to Holt.

"Sheriff Corrigan, I understand there was an altercation in the general store this morning," Gillespie stated. "Would you mind telling me what happened?"

Holt's first reaction was negative, but decided it was an opportunity to put the Scotsman bully in his place. He described the situation as an attempt by Tiorgs to extort more money from an innocent man.

"What about the shot that was heard?"

"A gun went off by accident. The only thing it hurt was some tobacco."

"Really?" Gillespie wrote on his ever-present pad. "I heard Mr. Welton was threatening you and others."

Holt glanced at Hannah. "Actually, he was showing me a new handgun I had expressed interest in buying. He didn't know it was loaded."

"Oh, I see."

"Eyewitnesses don't always see what really happened."

Hannah offered the editor a cup of coffee and Gillespie accepted it with thanks. It was clear they had become friends while Holt and Deed were away.

"May I ask how you hurt your hands, Sheriff?" Gillespie asking as he blew on the coffee.

"No."

Gillespie wrote another line, sipped his coffee, and asked if Holt and Hannah had heard about the special day of celebration being planned.

"Sounds like a lot of fun." Holt looked at Hannah. "That'll be good for the town."

"Yeah. Rebecca will be glad to hear about it."

Smiling, Gillespie said, "The region is most fortunate to have you as its sheriff, Mr. Corrigan, and you, James, as the town marshal. I'm doing an editorial on that."

Hannah spoke first. "No need, Leroy, it's our choice."

Holt nodded. A few minutes later, Holt excused himself, explaining he needed to head out, and left. Hannah and Gillespie continued their conversation.

CHAPTER TWENTY-FIVE

Holt Corrigan rode easily out of town. It felt good to be in the saddle again. The noise and structures of Wilkon disappeared into broken land. Thin strips of gray clouds bumped against a sky headed toward winter. A lone hawk was performing in the distance, trying to encircle a weak sun that was nearing noon. Tag bounded across the prairie, seemingly as happy to be rid of the town as his master was. Here and there, he chased a field mouse or a rabbit, catching none and not caring. The chase was the thing.

Clusters of mesquite, stubby blackjack with its gnarly roots, and post oak followed a slope of dead grass and crumbled rock. This piece of country had little to link it to the fine meadows of the Rafter C ranch to the north. He rode alongside a timid stream that wandered a few yards to the west before disappearing into the ground. The stream would reappear as a small pond near the first farm.

Two antelope stood at attention as he passed, then broke for the nearest thicket of mesquite. He smiled and studied the land. Old habits kept him alert. The only things moving were dead leaves on the blackjack. Although the land looked flat, he knew there were long ravines that could hide an entire cavalry. He hadn't forgotten the army officer's warning that a few of Achak's warriors were still on the prowl.

For the first time, it felt right to be sheriff. He patted the badge, then pulled it off and placed it into his vest pocket. It didn't make sense to give away his approach with the reflection of the metal. He had never worn anything shiny for that reason. The awful time in the prairie returning the bank's money flitted through his mind and he shook his head to push it away. The hip wound reminded him that it hadn't yet completely healed.

A few feet off the trail, a cardinal watched him pass. Holt smiled. A sign of good luck, for certain. He touched the crimson feather in his hatband. A beautiful tan female cardinal joined her mate.

"Good for you," he chuckled and his thoughts bounced to seeing Allison again after so long. Nothing there, he told himself.

Not really. Perhaps a little sadness at her situation, or was it satisfaction? The birds flew away and brought his mind back to reality. He watched Tag disappear over the frown of a small hill and reappear again, trotting toward him as if a victorious warrior. In the dog's mouth was a mouse.

"Well, that makes it easy on me for your dinner," Holt laughed.

His first stop would be a small farm. He hadn't been along this road since before the war. Way before. He wondered if it still belonged to the Halloran family. Good Irish folks. He remembered them from before the war and hoped he and Deed hadn't been ornery to them or their kids back then. Blue certainly wouldn't have.

The young lawman's thoughts slipped away to boyhood days. In his mind, the three brothers were galloping at breakneck speed out of town after buying supplies, yelling and laughing. Everything was a new competition. Another day, they raced across a big pond to determine who was the best swimmer. He was, by a stroke. They took turns breaking a wild sorrel; Deed stayed on the longest, even though he was the youngest. Hunting was always competitive. However, the first time Deed fired a rifle, it knocked him backward. Another time, the youngest Corrigan brought home an injured fawn and raised it before returning the animal to the wild. Flashes of his mother, father, and sister followed, but their faces were only blurs. Somewhere in those days, he found importance in superstition and reincarnation — and Blue found his mother's Bible. He found girls, spending a sweet afternoon with Allison Johnson. Mostly in the barn. She was as eager for him to unbutton her blouse as he was to touch her.

Their days of boyish adventure were mixed with hard work on the family ranch. But this came to an abrupt end when both parents and their sister died. Everything changed. The chance arrival of Nakashima Silka soon gave them stability and, then, confidence.

War tore into all that.

He jerked in the saddle, trying to push away the black images of that bitter conflict and the awful days after defeat. Shaking his head, he tried to clear it of yesterdays, knowing it was dangerous to daydream along this road, and most other roads within the region.

He passed a lone ash tree with its spindly branches stretching halfway across the well-traveled road. He reined his horse around them, being careful not to let any of the brittle branches touch either horse or rider. To break a branch of an ash tree was to bring much bad luck. The ash tree was known to protect against storms, witchcraft, and snakes. Studying the tree as he passed, Holt whistled for Tag and the dog appeared, his tongue hanging. Holt wondered if the dog had eaten the mouse or dropped it, not interested after the chase.

"Stay close, Tag. We're coming to our first visit."

Just ahead was a small log-and-adobe house nestled in a gentle valley. Around the farm was an expanse of plowed black land with a small pond settled around willows and cottonwoods. Holt figured the fields were already planted with corn seed for the coming year. Next to the house was an unpainted barn, a peeled-pole corral, a lean-to and two other buildings, and a stone well. A picket fence, in need of painting, surrounded the mostly bare yard. A welcoming line of smoke curled from the fireplace. He remembered the poles and sod roof with an occasional bunch of dead grass and weeds sticking up. Nothing much had changed.

After putting his badge back on, he hallooed the house as he eased his horses forward. From the doorway, a stooped figure in suspenders appeared, using his hand to shield the sun. An old pipe was clenched in his teeth. Cradled in his other arm was a double-barreled shotgun. Holt recognized Ian Halloran, even with his graying hair.

Holt reined up twenty feet from the house and declared, "I'm Holt Corrigan. I'm the county sheriff. Just riding through to introduce myself and make sure all is well." He leaned forward in the saddle. "May I get down?"

A bright smile popped onto the older man's wrinkled face. "Well, swate Jaysus, 'tis Holt Corrigan, hisself. Sheriff Holt Corrigan, indeed. Bless me soul, a fine day it be. Get down, son. Get down." The old man laid his shotgun against the door way and stepped toward the young sheriff.

Holt reined his horse forward and swung from the saddle in front of the hitching rack. A walkway of flat stones waited. After flipping the reins around the pole and telling Tag to sit, he walked toward the man and held out his hand.

"Mr. Halloran, it's good to see you again, sir."

"Aye, Holt, me lad. 'Tis good to see you." Halloran took the pipe from his mouth and grasped Holt's hand with energy. " 'Twere happy we were to hear the fine Judge Pence hisself be givin' yourself a pardon. Most deservin' it be."

"Thanks."

Halloran turned toward the inside of the house, waving the pipe in his hand, and yelled, "Greta, come here. Ye won't be believin' who be here hisself." He turned back to Holt and told him to water his horses at the trough near the well.

A round-faced woman with crow's-feet dancing around her happy green eyes came to the front door. Her graying hair was pulled back in a bun and she was wearing a soiled apron over her light blue dress.

Her hand went to her mouth and she exclaimed, "Holt Corrigan it be . . . hearin' my prayers, the good Lord be doin'. So long it's been since yourself and your fine brothers be visitin'."

"Good day to you, Mrs. Halloran," Holt said as he untied his horses.

She hurried and gave him a warm hug; her heavy breasts pushed against his stomach. Grasping his arm, she invited him inside for their noon meal. Holt was pleased. He wasn't sure what kind of welcome he might receive. Most folks around the region knew of his outlaw past. He told her that he would be pleased to join them as soon as he watered his horses. Holt rang up a bucket of cold water and splashed it into the trough. Tag was eager to drink as well.

Their home was small, but neat. A table with a red-and-white-checkered cloth was the center of attention, along with a blackened stone hearth offering a crackling fire that warmed everything. Holt was glad to see the fire was evenly orange, without any holes of blue. Smells of a venison stew reached him. On one wall were framed photographs of their family. Four sons. Two of the photographs were draped in black; Holt guessed the two sons died in the war. Holt didn't remember much of the house, but decided he probably hadn't ever been inside. The Corrigan boys, at least he and Deed, weren't likely to be asked inside such nice homes.

Mrs. Halloran brought Holt and her husband steaming cups of coffee. It was freshly brewed, hot, and delicious. He said so. The Hallorans were eager to learn of news around town. They had heard about the bank robbery and the successful return of the posse, but wanted details. He mentioned having copies of the latest edition of the town newspaper in his gear and would leave one with them. He told about the upcoming celebration of activities and said he thought Mrs. Halloran would want to enter the cake contest. Her shy smile was her only response, but her eyes glowed with happy anticipation.

A tall young man of eighteen with light brown hair nearly covering his ears entered the room. The Hallorans' youngest son, Doolin, had been in the barn. Holt introduced himself and the boy smiled, saying everyone knew who he was. Ian laid his pipe beside his plate, part of his mealtime routine.

After Greta added another chair and tableware, they sat down at the table and Mrs. Halloran asked Holt to say grace. He was thankful for listening to Blue's prayers over a meal, and nodded and recited, " 'God is great. God is good. Him we thank for our daily food. By his hand, we all are fed. By his love, we all are led. Amen.' " He couldn't resist a grin in remembering never having said grace before. It was always Blue's duty and, during the war, it wasn't done. At least not where he ate.

"Thank you, Holt," Greta said and passed him the bowl of stew, followed by a large plate of fresh biscuits. "Not be happy with these biscuits meself. Sure an' it be this day that they disappoint me."

"I'm sure they're great, ma'am," Holt

said, helping himself to the stew. "You are most kind to invite me to your table. I am honored." He took a biscuit and was handed a bowl of butter and another of jam.

"It be the Hallorans who be honored with the presence of the fine sheriff of this county," Greta said and smiled.

Ian patted Holt on the back. "A rider be comin' through last week. Said ye and yer brothers be bringin' back the bank's money." He crossed his arms. "Said ye had killed that Comanche from hell. And some o' his men, I be told."

"Yes, Achak. We lost two fine men, though. Malcolm Rose and Ira McDugal. Brave men."

"Heard that, too. Real shame."

"A cavalry unit is hunting down the rest of them. You'd best stay alert."

"By the grace o' God, we do. Thank ye."

Like most Western people, they ate in silence, and then Ian Halloran proudly pronounced that they had just purchased a new two-bottom sulky plow pulled by three horses while a man rode. Much faster than the older single plow pulled by two oxen or mules. Doolin added that he did the riding. Holt made appropriate comments, realizing how little he knew about farming.

"Doolin, me boy, yourself be eating with

one of the heroes themselves who stopped all those Yankees at Sabine Pass. Aye, just forty-three Confederates with rifles and six small cannon stopped a whole fleet of fifteen thousand federals who be tryin' to land. Aye, that they did."

Holt shrugged.

"Our boys be sinking a gunboat, capturing more, and turning away the rest of that whole fleet sure as you please. Be taking four hundred prisoners. Best of it be, they dinna' lose a man." Ian shook his head. "Heard that meself direct from one who were there."

"We were lucky that day," Holt managed to say.

"Aye, an' our two oldest, Killian and Aiden, not be so. We lost them to that awful war." Ian turned his head. His next word was barely a whisper. "Gettysburg." His right hand reached for his dead pipe, then pulled back.

Greta wiped her eyes with her apron and managed to change the subject a little. "Our third son, Patrick, did come home. A captain, hisself be." She swallowed and continued, "Now he be livin' in Dallas with his sweet wife and two children. Theirselves be joinin' us for Thanksgiving." She motioned toward Doolin. "Our youngest is, of course, with us. A mighty big help, he be."

"Thanksgiving'll be a grand time, I'm sure," Holt said and sipped his coffee, deciding not to comment on their loss of two sons. Greta gathered the empty dishes and disappeared into the kitchen.

Doolin selected another biscuit, plastered it with butter and jam, and took a large bite. With his mouth full, as if to give him confidence, he asked about Holt's days as an outlaw after the war.

Ian's response was immediate and harsh. "Doolin, what be ye thinkin'? That be no way to be talkin'."

Holt set down his cup and said, "That's all right, Mr. Halloran. He . . . and you deserve to know." He licked his lower lip. "Back then, I couldn't bring myself to admit the South had lost. I just couldn't. There were others like me. We started hitting Union payrolls and the like. Guess we thought it would bring back the South." He looked at Ian Halloran. "It didn't. Just made me a wanted man. Nobody's fault but mine."

Leaning forward on his elbows, Doolin said, "Sounded like you were . . . everywhere."

Holt nodded. "Yeah, we started getting blamed for every bank robbery and stage holdup around. I'd love to have the horse I was supposed to be riding everywhere. He'd be magical. Anyway, you can't believe everything you hear or read. I was lucky that Judge Pence decided I deserved a second chance."

He looked up as Greta, returning from the kitchen, placed a plate of oatmeal cookies in front of him, touched his shoulder, and quietly said, "Help yourself, Holt."

"What about the other Rebels . . . the ones who rode with you?" Doolin asked and shoved the rest of the biscuit into his mouth and grabbed two cookies in one continuous motion.

"That's a good question, Doolin," Holt said, munching on a cookie. "These are wonderful, Mrs. Halloran. Best I've ever had."

She blushed and curtseyed, returned to the kitchen, and came back with the coffeepot. Holt returned his attention to the youngest Halloran as she refilled all their cups and sat down again.

"Since I was the only Rebel identified, they were free to return to their homes and begin again. I told them to do so."

"Did they?"

"Don't know." Holt decided not to mention seeing Everett Reindal.

Wiping cookie crumbs from his mouth, Doolin asked if the amnesty was forever. Holt responded simply that it dealt only with past deeds. Like all citizens, he was expected to obey the law.

"Aye, an' a fine job ye be doin'." Ian picked up his pipe, checked the load of tobacco, and lit it with a match from his shirt pocket. An intense glare at his son followed. But Doolin mistook it for approval to keep asking questions.

Warming to his interest, Doolin asked about the story of Deed taking on three bank robbers. The first robber had shoved a gun into Deed's belly and so Deed took him down with only his hands, then grabbed the outlaw's gun, killed the second outlaw, and wounded the third. Doolin had heard the story on a visit to town for supplies.

"That's quite true."

"I also heard your brother Deed whipped Sear Georgian with his bare hands. An' Deed being weak from being wounded an' all. Your brother was protecting one of the Sanchez men. That true?"

"That's true. Deed can fight well with his hands, his feet, anything, I suppose." Holt pushed back his chair to end the discussion. "Folks, I appreciate very much your hospitality, but I must be riding. Got a few other places to visit before nightfall."

"Of course," Ian said, visibly relieved to have his son's questioning stopped.

Outside of the home, Holt got into his pack, pulled out the newspaper and a sack of sugar, another of flour, and one of coffee.

"I figured this time of year, you might be needing some extra." He smiled and handed the sacks and paper to the pleased couple. Smiling, Mrs. Halloran turned to her husband and whispered to him.

"We thank ye kindly, Holt Corrigan. Ye be comin' back soon."

They stood waving as he rode away and headed for the second farm in the county. He couldn't remember who lived there.

Chapter Twenty-Six

After riding a few minutes, Holt remembered the cigars in his coat pocket and pulled one free. He wished that he had remembered them while at the Hallorans; he could have given a smoke to the men. For an instant, he considered going back, but decided against the idea.

He bit off the end and lit the black cigar, watching Tag as they rode. The dog was enjoying a piece of jerky Holt had given him. The road wasn't as well traveled as earlier and followed the slope of an uneven hillside. He dipped into a long, narrow draw, crossed a sometime stream, and headed across broken land mixed with rock, mesquite thickets, prickly pear, willows, and a line of cottonwoods. They rode silently, dipping into a shallow draw and following it. He crossed a dried creek bed and stopped on the frown of a hillside.

Ahead, he saw the next farm with its

cultivated land and freshly painted barn and outbuildings. From here, he could see chickens exploring the main yard and a dog trying to act like he was in charge. Holt was certain that he didn't know who lived here. Rubbing out his cigar on his saddle horn, he looked down to see that his badge was still attached to his vest. As he neared the house, he yelled his advance.

A tall man wearing an ill-shaped hat and holding a Henry came from the barn. He studied Holt for a long minute and said nothing. His nose was pointed and his cheeks were sunken, with a firm chin. His overalls showed signs of long wear and his shirt had once been red.

"Afternoon, sir. I'm Holt Corrigan, county sheriff. Just left the Hallorans," Holt declared, keeping his hands on the saddle horn. "I'm just riding through the county to introduce myself and see if all is right. May I come closer?"

The man cocked his head to the side. "You that Rebel outlaw?"

"I was. Riding for the law now."

"How's that work?" The man adjusted his rifle, but it remained pointed in Holt's direction.

Holt tried to smile. "Judge Pence awarded me full amnesty. In exchange for taking this job." He nodded. "I took it."

The man walked toward Holt, still not lowering his rifle. "The last time the county lawman came visiting, he told me that I owed him a hundred dollars. For protection."

Holt leaned forward in his saddle. "That would've been Shields. He's dead. The others are on the way to prison."

"Good for you."

Holt smiled. "Did you pay him?"

"Nope. Didn't have the money in the first place. Told him if he ever came around again, I'd put a hundred dollars' worth of lead in his belly."

Holt returned the man's just-used phrase. "Good for you."

It was the farmer's turn to smile. "Sheriff, I'm Logan Wheeler. Bought this place five years back from the Bucknells." He wiped his nose with his hand, letting the gun drop to his side. "My Lillian up an' died on me last year. January, it was. The twenty-third." He turned his head away for a moment. "Now it's just me an' my two kids."

"Sorry to hear that, Mr. Wheeler."

"Yeah, it's hard. Real hard. But we'll make it. Just need a good crop or two, that's all."

"I'm sure you're right. Anything I can do for you?"

Wheeler motioned toward the house. "Well, you could have coffee with me. Don't get many visitors. And call me Logan."

"I'd like that, Logan," the young lawman replied. "Please call me Holt."

"You got it . . . Holt."

The middle Corrigan swung down from his horse and tied both mounts to the hitch post next to the front porch. Tag discovered a mangy black dog with a white spot on its back and the two wandered off together.

Inside the farmhouse, Holt saw and felt the lack of a woman's touch to the simple surroundings. The bare floor was only partially swept and the stone fireplace was strewn with ashes and pieces of burnt wood. Only a tiny flame struggled to remain alive.

From the bedroom, separated from the main room by a hung blanket, came two children dressed in handmade clothes. Wheeler introduced the fourteen-year-old boy as Lloyd, and the seven-year-old girl as Josie. Both were family names, he explained, on their late mother's side.

Lloyd stepped up to Holt and held out his hand. "Are you a lawman, mister?"

Shaking the boy's hand, Holt replied, "I am the county sheriff and I'm glad to meet you."

The boy's shirt was too large for him and

Holt made a mental note to see if Blue had any clothes his children had outgrown.

Josie's golden hair fell to her shoulders and flipped as she talked, which was constantly. She reminded Holt of a teacher he'd known as a child.

"My father chased off the last sheriff that came here. You'd better watch your step." She finished her statement by putting her hands on her hips.

Grinning, Holt said, "I will. Thanks for the warning."

Without further encouragement, she told him that her full name was Josephine, then about their late mother and their farm in greater detail than anyone would want to know, including how many chickens they had and the names she had given them.

"That's enough, Josie."

"Well, I thought he should know."

Pushing his hat back from his forehead, Holt said, "I appreciated hearing about all of you."

Shrugging his shoulders, Wheeler apologized for her verbosity and explained that she took after her mother. A weak smile trailed his words. The tall man with the weathered face and firm chin invited Holt to sit at the table in the center of the room. A long scar on its surface was only partially hidden by a vase with dead flowers.

Lloyd held a small chalkboard, as did Josie. On both were scribblings in chalk that Holt couldn't read from where he stood.

"Lloyd, did you finish your words?" Wheeler asked as he returned from the kitchen with a coffeepot and two cups.

The boy nodded, but made no attempt to hold up the board for his father's inspection.

"And Josie, how about you? Where are you with the alphabet?"

Proudly holding up her chalkboard to show her writing, she declared, "I've written them all the way through 'P' . . . capitals and lower."

"Good," Wheeler said and turned to Holt before Josie could continue. "Kinda worried about school. Miss Temple left town."

Smiling, Holt was glad to tell him that the town marshal's wife was going to step in and teach until a new permanent teacher could be secured. Wheeler's eyes brightened.

"That's great news, Holt. It really is."

"Yeah, I think she's starting on Monday."

As they drank coffee, very hot and very bitter, Holt told him about the town's happenings and the planned celebration. Both children were eager to hear about the scheduled fun, especially Josie. She told him about the Fourth of July celebration at the church last summer, pointing out that a woman had been nice to her father.

Wheeler blushed slightly, but said nothing.

Her eyes bright with sharing, Josie said the preacher that day had only one arm.

"That was my brother Blue. He and Deed, my other brother, and I have a ranch north of here, the Rafter C."

Lloyd sat with his hands folded over his chalkboard. Finally he could keep quiet no longer.

"Do you always carry two guns?"

Holt sipped his coffee, then blew on it and sipped again. "Have for a long time."

"Don't think I've ever seen anyone wear holsters like that." Lloyd pointed at Holt's rig under his opened coat.

Bored with the subject, Josie left the table and disappeared behind the blanket separation.

Holt tried his coffee again, uneasy about the conversation.

"Those guns look mighty fancy."

"A friend gave them to me." Holt was eager to change the subject and glanced at Wheeler.

Licking his lower lip, Wheeler said, "Lloyd,

better go check on the dogs. Who knows what they might've gotten into."

Reluctantly, the boy stood and walked outside.

After watching him leave, the young sheriff said, "Thanks, Logan. Wasn't sure how to handle that."

"None needed. He's at that age where guns make quite an attraction." Wheeler finished his coffee. "Actually he's a pretty good shot. Got us a deer two days ago."

"What about us going outside," Holt asked, "and let him shoot one of my Russians?"

"He'll think that's as good as it gets."

"Let's do it then."

As they walked toward the door, Wheeler told him the previous sheriff had advised him to leave, that Bordner was taking over the entire region. Holt simply added that Bordner wasn't as good as he thought.

"Damn glad o' that," Wheeler pronounced. "Ya sure you got all o' them?"

"No. Not for sure. We'll just have to keep working on it."

Outside, Lloyd was pouring a bucket of water into the trough for the two panting dogs.

"Looks like they're buddies for life." Wheeler chuckled.

"What's your dog's name?" Lloyd asked as he returned the bucket to its position atop the side of the well.

Holt walked over and patted both dogs. "Well, his full name's Tag Along. I call him Tag most of the time." He explained the reason for the moniker.

"Tag. I like that." Lloyd held his arms. "Our dog is named Blackie. 'Cause he's black."

"Good-looking dog."

"He keeps the coyotes away from the chickens. Most of the time."

Holt glanced at Wheeler and asked Lloyd if he would like to shoot one of his revolvers. The boy's eyes lit up and his whole body shook with excitement.

"Really? Me?" Lloyd looked at his father, who smiled and nodded. "I sure would."

Together, the two men and the boy walked back toward the barn. Pecking their way through the dirt, chickens greeted them with squawks and flapping wings. Where the land crossed from dead grass to plowed ground, Holt pointed at a large dirt clod unearthed by Wheeler's plow.

"I want you to shoot that." Holt drew his right-shoulder-holstered gun. "This is a Russian Smith & Wesson .44. Some think it's the finest gun made." He handed the weapon, butt first, to the boy and showed him how to hold it with both hands.

"The best way to shoot a revolver is to think like you're pointed your finger," Holt said. "Keep the gun pointed at the ground for now. Always figure a gun is loaded, no matter who says different. Until you check it yourself." He shook his head. "Lots of folks have been killed by guns that weren't supposed to have any bullets. I keep five bullets in each gun, leaving the cylinder under the hammer empty. For safety."

"You sound like my pa."

"Glad to hear it," Holt responded. "Now I'm going to cock it, then you point at that clod, take a deep breath, and hold it. Squeeze the trigger when you're ready." He looked at the boy's serious face. "Remember, this trigger is like a butterfly. Touch it and the gun'll shoot."

After Holt cocked the hammer, Lloyd lifted the weapon as he had been told. The roar of the gun was intense; the bullet spat into the dirt a foot from the clod. Lloyd was jolted backward a step.

"That's good for your first time." Holt said. "Let's try again."

In short order, Lloyd fired four more times, emptying the gun, and finally clipped the top edge of the dirt chunk. Holt reloaded the gun with cartridges from his coat pocket, spun it in his hand, and fired three times so fast they sounded like one roll of thunder. All three shots tore into the clod, splitting it into little pieces.

"Wow, mister . . . Sheriff. That was something!"

"Just practice, Lloyd. No different than learning to plow a straight line. Only plowing'll make good things happen."

"Have you killed a lot of men?"

Holt hesitated as he reloaded the gun. "Only those who were trying to kill me or my family." He slipped the gun into its holster.

Biting his lower lip, Lloyd asked, "What are those . . . on the handles? They look like mountain lions."

"Yeah. A friend called me 'El Jaguar' for some reason and had those handles made."

"El Jaguar. Wow!"

From the house came Josie carrying a small doll in a dress that matched her own. "There you are. I've been looking all over for you. I wanted to show you Little Anne. My mother made it for me before . . ."

Holt knelt and examined the doll. "Little Anne is beautiful. Just like you."

"Aw, it's just a doll. Doesn't really have a name," Lloyd blurted.

"Thank you for showing Little Anne to me," Holt said softly and stroked the doll's head.

"That's enough, Lloyd," Wheeler admonished and turned to Holt. "Won't you stay for supper? Got some good venison stew, thanks to Lloyd."

"Well, I'd like that, but I'm expected at the ranch," Holt said. "Next time?"

"We'd like that." Wheeler grinned.

Holt went to his mount, then moved to his packhorse and removed sacks of flour, beans, coffee, and sugar. Laying them on the porch, he said, "Thought you might have use for these."

"Do we look like we need a handout?" Wheeler pouted.

"No, but I needed to say thank you for your friendship." Holt strode over to the farmer and they shook hands.

The threesome waved as the young sheriff rode away. Reaching the hillside, he turned and waved back. In minutes, the farm was out of sight. Tag was dropping behind.

CHAPTER TWENTY-SEVEN

Now that they were out of sight of the Wheelers, Holt Corrigan reined up, dismounted, and led his horses back to the resting dog. A cold wind had found its feet and was working its way across the land.

"Wore yourself out, did you?" he grinned. "Yeah, I liked them, too."

Lifting the dog, he placed him onto the greatly depleted packhorse, then covered him with his saddle blanket and gave Tag a piece of jerky. Holt pulled on his own long coat, remounted, and rode on.

The uneven land was scattered with mesquite and cactus. Off to his right was a small pond, more of a seep. Tracks around the water were a clear indication that prairie animals used it often. He passed two burned-out farms, their blackened timbers pointing toward the graying sky. Silent reminders of how close Comanche destruction waited. Instinctively, he drew his carbine from its saddle boot and laid the gun across his saddle.

A path wandered away from the main road, heading for Tiorgs's horse ranch. There was no reason to see the Scotsman again; Tiorgs knew who the sheriff was. Holt smiled and reined his horse to stay on the main trail. It led to the farm of Judd and Mary Johnson, Allison's parents. Every bush seemed familiar, even though he hadn't been along this path since before the war. Strangely, his mind didn't seek old memories of his times with Allison.

The trail had become lined with small cottonwoods, elms, and ash trees, some little more than whips. Ahead he saw that the Johnson farm looked like it had been freshly painted. Judd Johnson was a most successful farmer. During the war, he sold his crops to the Union army for gold. It wasn't a popular move, but he didn't care.

As he rode, Holt tried to recall how many children the Johnsons had. A son and daughter older than Allison, for sure. There was a younger son who would be about eighteen now, he thought. He vaguely recalled a daughter who died when he was seeing Allison; the girl had been six.

Ahead on the left side of the road, an old-shaped tree caught his attention. It was almost bent over into a half circle. He and Allison had chased each other around it before getting going on to other things. He nodded to himself and pulled his collar up around his ears.

Mrs. Johnson was flipping a blanket off the side of the porch as Holt rode up. She was humming to herself, well into a daydream, and didn't hear his advance.

"Afternoon, Mrs. Johnson . . . Holt Corrigan," he said, "I'm the county sheriff, just making the rounds."

She jerked into today. Her eyes widened as the significance of his statement soaked in. Her blanket fell to the porch.

"Hol . . . Holt? Oh my goodness, how wonderful!" she exclaimed. "Why didn't you bring Allison with you?"

The question wasn't what he expected, or wanted to hear. His hand gripped the carbine. Out of the corner of his eyes, he saw a young man bringing in cows for milking.

She hurried to Holt's horse and looked up, hesitating to touch his leg. "Oh, it's so good to see you again, Holt. Allison has been telling us about the two of you getting reacquainted. Picnics and rides." Her smile cut her face in two and that's when he saw the redness on her right cheek was in the early stage of bruising. "We're hoping for something special this time." For an instant, he thought she appeared not right in the head.

Holt studied for face for a moment. Time and unending work had been hard on her. Crow's-feet lined her eyes and several stretched downward across her face. Gray had taken over much of her hair. Still, she was an attractive woman, full figured and sweet, but her eyes were troubled and wouldn't meet his. There was something more here. Mrs. Johnson was an abused woman. Why hadn't he seen it before? Probably because of his lust for her daughter.

"Mrs. Johnson, I'm sorry to tell you this, but the first time I saw Allison since the war was this morning. I was packing supplies in front of the general store when she walked over." He paused and swallowed. "We're not seeing each other, ma'am . . . and don't intend to. That was long ago. I'm sure she'll find a good man."

The woman looked like she was going to vomit. She spun away from his horse as if she'd been told of a death and yelled, "Judd! Judd! Come out. We have a visitor, someone you know." She didn't look at Holt again and walked back onto the porch, touched her reddening cheek, picked up her blanket, and began folding it.

A large man dressed in dirty overalls appeared in the doorway, nearly filling it. His longish brown hair indicated he had been sleeping. Even from a distance, Holt knew Judd had been drinking. He had always been a mean man, used to having his own way with his wife and their children. Somewhere in his mind was the recollection of Mrs. Johnson having bruises on her face and arms, and saying that Judd had hit her, but that she deserved it. He wished he had just ridden on. His sweet memories were becoming a nightmare.

Judd Johnson blinked as he stood in the doorway. He held a double-barreled shotgun in one huge hand. It looked like a toy.

"Wha . . . ?" He growled.

"It's Holt Corrigan, honey. He's the county sheriff, you know," Mrs. Johnson cooed. "Just rode in to say hello. He's making a tour of the county, meeting folks. Isn't that nice?"

Judd glanced at her, frowned, and bellowed, "Whar's my daughter? From the sound of it, you two are gittin' together all the time."

"That's not so, Mr. Johnson. I saw her for the first time this morning, since the war. She came up to me while I was packing my horse." Holt stared at the man. "We are definitely not together . . . and won't be."

Straightening his back, Judd's wild eyebrows nearly met in a fierce frown. "Not good 'nuff fer ya, huh." His hands tightened around the shotgun.

Mrs. Johnson shivered against the house. "Didn't say that, Mr. Johnson. Allison and I were just kids back then."

"What's that got to do with it? I married the missus when she were but thirteen."

Holt noticed the young man who had brought in the cows was sneaking along the side of the house toward them. In his hands was a Henry.

"Didn't mean to upset you folks. I just stopped by to say hello," Holt said. "Sounds like you need to talk with your daughter. Maybe she's afraid to tell you the truth."

Judd took two steps forward onto the porch. "What's that mean, Corrigan?"

"That means, Mr. Johnson, that she has a life. A real life. You need to hear it." Holt was fighting to keep his temper. "Maybe she could use a little help."

"Well, you sonvuabitch, I suppose yur gonna git hitched to one o' them red niggers like yur brother," Judd snarled, waving his shotgun.

Twisting in his saddle, Holt raised his rifle

and levered it. "Mr. Johnson, I'll let your insult to me pass . . . for now, but you're not going to talk that way about my brother's wife. Apologize. Now."

Waving the shotgun, Judd laughed. "Or what?"

"First, I'll put a bullet in your kneecap, then we'll see if you're interested in being polite," Holt snapped. "If not, I'll take out the other one." He aimed his rifle.

"I didna mean nuthin'. I'm, I'm sorry." Judd waved his right hand, holding the shotgun with his left.

Holt glanced at Mrs. Johnson cowering against the side of the house. "Mrs. Johnson, what's your youngest boy's name?"

"O-Oliver. Why?"

"Tell him to come up and drop his rifle, because I'll be putting a bullet in him next. He's going to get himself hurt for nothing."

The woman complied and the gangly young man strode toward the porch and laid his rifle on the wooden planks. Holt didn't lower his gun, nor relax. Judd Johnson was crazy enough, and drunk enough, to rush him.

"Now, Oliver, take the shotgun from your pa's hands and bring it to me." Holt motioned with the gun. "You'll be doing him a favor, son."

Judd stared at his son, started to pull away as the boy reached for the weapon, then released it. The big man glared at Holt, clenching and unclenching his fists.

"Bring me both guns," Holt said.

The young man, looking much like his mother only with an elongated face, walked over to Holt, carrying both weapons in his arms. Oliver's determination was carrying him now.

"Lay them on the pack, beside my dog," Holt glanced toward the packhorse. "Tag, play nice."

"Now what, Sheriff?" Oliver laid the guns beside Tag.

Holt said, "I'm going to ride out of here, but I don't want to have to dodge gunfire doing it, so I'm going to leave these out by the road. You can get them there."

Oliver nodded. "I heard you all talkin'. My ma made up all that about Allison. Ma's afeared o' Pa. He gits real mean when he drinks. Beats her . . . bad." He lowered his eyes. "I'm afraid o' him, too."

"Listen to me and listen good," Holt said, almost in a whisper. "Your mother's too good a woman to get beaten up by . . . him. And you know it. Now you must help. You must stand up to him . . . or watch your mother get hurt. You've got a buckboard?"

"Yas, suh."

"I'm going to wait for you to hitch up a team. Take her to town to see your sister. Do it now. Have you seen Allison recently?"

"Uh, no, suh. I hasn't. Bin too busy doin' chores."

"You're a good son, but do what I say, all right? You stay in town with them for a few days. 'Til this gets straightened out."

"Yas, suh, I will." Oliver's back straightened, then he glanced at this glaring father and shivered.

Shaking off his fear, the young man turned and ran toward the barn. Judd watched him go, seemingly puzzled.

"Mrs. Johnson, your son is getting a buckboard, going to take you to town to see Allison," Holt said, staring at Judd.

Mrs. Johnson glanced at her husband and walked to the front of the porch. There was a brightness in her eyes he hadn't seen before.

"I will do that," she said.

"Ya ain't goin' nowhar I don' say ya can, woman." Judd grabbed her arm and pulled the distraught woman toward him. His fist swung at her face, but she managed to deflect the main force of the blow. Still, it landed hard on her cheek, drawing blood from her mouth.

Holt jumped down from his horse, flipped the reins over the hitch rack, and flew toward them. Dazed, Mrs. Johnson struggled to break free of his tenacious grip, but was losing the effort.

The young sheriff jammed the nose of his rifle into Judd's stomach. The blow drove the wind from the larger man and he let go of Mrs. Johnson to grab his stomach and bent over. In a continuing motion, Holt drove his rifle butt up and into Judd's chin, snapping back the man's head. The unbalanced farmer collapsed on the porch.

Both Mrs. Johnson and Holt stood over the unconscious man for a long, silent moment.

Finally, she looked up at him and smiled. "I think I'll help Oliver. Get some things."

"Certainly, ma'am."

She touched his cheek. "Thank you, Holt Corrigan. You would have been a wonderful son-in-law."

"You're welcome."

In a few minutes, Oliver and Mrs. Johnson drove away from the farm, waving at Holt. He had told them to find Marshal Hannah and he would help them. He knew this wasn't the end of the matter, but it was a beginning. Maybe Mrs. Johnson was strong enough. Maybe. At least, she would be with

Allison. His gaze took in Judd Johnson, who was stirring. How the man reacted would be anybody's guess. But at least Mrs. Johnson was free for the moment. The rest would be up to them, and Allison.

Walking back to his horses, he looked back at Tag lying on the packhorse. "Come on, Tag. I've never wanted to be away from a place so much in my whole life." Mounting, Holt nudged his horse into a trot and looked back to make certain Tag was settled onto the pack. If he pushed it, they could reach the ranch tonight. Late, but home.

No matter, this didn't feel right. He couldn't leave these people right now. He just couldn't. If he hadn't come by, nothing would have happened. Nothing new, anyway. Judd Johnson would have continued terrorizing his wife and son. But now, he knew.

No, he would ride with them back to town get them settled somewhere. If necessary, they could to stay in his small sheriff's quarters for the night and he would sleep in the jail. Spinning his horses around, he yelled at Tag.

"Tag, we've got to help these folks." Holt ran his fingers along the cardinal feather in his hat for luck.

As they rode back past the Johnson's

farmhouse, Judd was standing on the porch, looking inside. Tag growled.

CHAPTER TWENTY-EIGHT

Farther south and west of Wilkon, the prisoner wagon and the Ranger escort were stopped for the night. The last red spears cut across the dying horizon and the night was already cold. Their camp was a frequent one for travelers headed for and from Austin. A small, deep pond offered fresh water most of the time. The next water was a day's ride away at the rate the wagon was going.

The camp itself lay on an elevated shelf west of the pond and had been used for this purpose many times, judging from the old fires. A campfire was dying into red embers. Around them night sounds were surprisingly absent. The outrider horses and wagon mules were watered and picketed with oat bags. The prisoners had been fed beans, jerky, and coffee, allowed to relieve themselves, and locked into the wagon for the night. Each was given an old army blanket.

The half-breed, Pickles, asked if the Rangers had any pickles and was told they didn't. Rhey Selmon, in his traditional bearskin coat, told him to shut up. Pickles fumbled in his pockets and was quiet.

Ranger Captain Palerns rolled his stiffened back, checked his Winchester, and stepped to the campfire for a last cup of coffee. He would take the first watch. One of the first things he did when they stopped was find a good place to watch the land. An old habit.

Watching him, Ranger Rice lit a cigar off a small stick from the fire, stomped his boots, and decided the fire needed building up. His rifle was propped against the wagon behind him. He shivered and pulled his long coat closer. Breath-smoke hovered around his face. He was tired and looking forward to a few hours of rest. A señorita was missing him in Austin. He smiled and exhaled cigar smoke to join his chilled breath. Cradling his Winchester in his arms, Captain Palerns stepped toward the younger Ranger. "Wouldn't be smoking if I were you, Ranger. Makes a good target. So does standing next to a fire."

Chuckling, Rice said, "Who the hell would be out here tonight? My ass is half froze."

"Your decision. I'll take the first watch. Williams has the second. Put out the fire." The captain walked away.

Ranger Williams was spread out under the wagon. So was the driver, snoring loudly. Glancing at the noise, Rice pushed his hat back on his forehead and reached for the coffeepot. He jiggled it. Enough for another cup. Maybe later. The lanky lawman took another drag on his cigar, grabbed a small log from the gathered wood, and added it to the struggling flames. Quickly, its hot fingers brought warmth to his body. Man, that felt good. So good.

He was alert. What did he hear? Over where the captain just went? A gurgle? Couldn't be. He was imaging things. The captain had made him jumpy. No one would be out on a night like this, he reminded himself. Especially not Indians. He hesitated, tossed the cigar, then went for his rifle anyway. Cradling the weapon, he turned and peered into the darkness.

A silhouette strutted from where Captain Palerns had gone.

"Oh . . . is that you, Captain? I thought I heard . . ."

An orange flame erupted from the silhouette. Then two more. Rice stumbled sideways and fell headfirst into the fire. Groaned and was still. Ranger Williams woke up with a start and was driven back by three more bullets. Two additional shots stopped the driver's snoring.

Silence again took over the camp. A short man with blond hair and a green sash stepped closer into the uneven light from the fire. Pearl-handled revolvers reflected the flames. His light green eyes studied the death camp under his wide-brimmed black hat. He kicked Rice's body and shot into it.

Satisfied, he walked back to where the captain lay, his throat cut. He pulled clear the knife, cleaned it on the dead grass, and returned the blade to its sheath at his hip. It took a few seconds to find a set of keys within the captain's coat. He walked casually to the back of the wagon. The gunman, known as Lorat, was in total control and enjoyed the moment.

He burst into song, a Civil War tune that used the melody of the "Yellow Rose of Texas."

" 'Tis joy to be a Ranger! To fight for dear Southland! 'Tis joy to follow Wharton, with his gallant trusty band! 'Tis joy to see our Harrison plunge, like a meteor bright, into the thickest fray, and deal his deadly might. O! who'd not be a Ranger and follow Wharton's cry! And battle for his country, and, if needs be, die?"

He stopped at the back of the prisoner wagon and yelled, "Rhey, are you in there?"

"Dammit, little brother, where'd you think I'd be? You took long enough," came a sarcastic response from Rhey Selmon.

"Get away from the door. I found all the keys, except the door key," the short man responded. "I'm going to blast off that lock."

"Get at it."

Minutes later, Rhey Selmon, Sear Georgian, Willard Hixon, Pickles, an eye-patched outlaw known only as Bear, and the additional Bordner outlaw called Billy Joe poured out of the wagon. Hixon and Georgian sought the dead Rangers' long coats while Rhey and Bear eagerly strapped on the Ranger handguns given to them. One at a time, Lorat removed their hand and leg irons with the keys from the dead Ranger captain.

He licked his lower lip. "Oh yeah, get all of the Ranger badges. Who knows, we might want them."

Rhey looked at the waiting Ranger horses and mules. "What are we doing with their stock?"

"Cut them loose. We don't need them. Got horses waiting."

Rhey released the animals from their pickets, but decided not to make them run. It didn't matter what they did.

Georgian made a point of urinating on

the dead Ranger captain's body after taking his coat and rifle. Hixon drank the rest of the coffee from the pot. As soon as the camp was stripped of guns, ammunition, supplies, and coats, Lorat led his half-brother and the other Bordner outlaws down a long draw. A quarter of a mile away was a string of saddled horses. One of the Ranger horses followed on its own.

"Couldn't ya have left the hosses closer?" Sear Georgian grumbled as they walked through the night.

Lorat looked at Rhey. "Do you want to tell the big idiot about horses whinnying . . . or should I?"

The big-shouldered Georgian fumed and sputtered, "I know. I know. Je's makin' talk. It's cold out here, ya know."

Lorat's eyes blinked quickly. He snapped, "I've been watching those Rangers stand around a warm fire for two hours. Just to get you loose." Cold breath covered his face. "So tell me about being cold, big boy."

Georgian's teeth clenched, but he said nothing. Rhey's glare was enough to keep him quiet.

Paying no further attention to the large outlaw, Lorat explained they would ride about two miles to a small farm in a narrow canyon. He pointed at twin mesas barely visible in the night sky and indicated that the hideout sat between them. He had killed the farmer and his wife earlier in the day.

"We'll spend a couple of days there. Got plenty of food. You guys can get rested up," Lorat said as they walked. "We'll ride into Wilkon early Saturday morning, kill the sheriff, and take back the money."

"Anything's better than bouncing in that damn wagon," Hixon exclaimed and adjusted Ranger Williams's gun belt around his waist. "Don't like the way the Ranger's rig fits me. Just doesn't feel right." He stubbed his toe against a mesquite root and nearly fell.

"Be glad you've got a gun," Rhey said. "And watch where you're going." He chuckled.

The lithe half-breed ran up to Lorat. "You have pickle?"

Nodding, the gunman told him a full jug of pickles awaited. Pickles giggled and skipped ahead. Laughter cut through the darkness.

A dark row of mesquite trees greeted them, and was accompanied by the sounds of stomping hooves, creaking leather, and curious whinnies.

"This sorrel is for you, big brother," Lorat said as they reached the string of mounts.

"It matches mine. Mother would like that."

"Mother was a whore."

"That she was. So what?"

"Where'd you get all these horses?" Hixon asked as he adjusted the cinch on a tall bay.

"Got 'em from some Mexicans. South of here. They didn't seem to mind. Didn't say anything anyway." Lorat's evil chuckle made even Rhey shiver.

The band of outlaws headed east with Lorat leading the way. Turning in the saddle, Lorat said, "There's a trail around this thicket and through the shallow creek ahead. We'll water the horses there and then we'll move on to the farm."

No one spoke until they reached the creek. Lorat smiled and shared more of his plan. "We'll slip into town Saturday morning when everyone is gathering for their big celebration." He chuckled. "To celebrate getting the town's money back."

"Some of us are known in town," Hixon declared. "All of us, I guess."

"Right. That's why we'll be wearing disguises. Nobody will pay any attention to us until it's too late." His laugh was shrill and evil.

"What about Ranger headquarters?" Rhey pulled his horse from the creek.

"It'll be days before they know what happened. We'll be long gone by the time any Rangers can get here."

The group continued riding in a small bunches of twos and threes, following the creek bed. After a handful of minutes, Hixon blurted, "What about Holt Corrigan and that gunslick friend of his . . . James Hannah?"

Lorat looked back and grinned. "You aren't the first to think about them." He glanced across at Rhey's sorrel and added, "We've got some surprises for them. Real special surprises."

Georgian wasn't convinced. "If it's such a big day, don't you think Deed Corrigan and his Jap friend will be there, too?"

"I certainly hope so." Lorat began to sing his strange Civil War Ranger song again.

CHAPTER TWENTY-NINE

Dawn had not arrived Saturday morning and two separate groups, unknown to each other, were already on the move.

Deed Corrigan was on the way back from the stage station to the family ranch with Atlee and her children so they could enjoy Wilkon's celebration. The Beinrigts would manage the station, even though no stages were expected until Monday. Deed and Atlee would meet with Blue, Bina, and their children and all go into town together. All were excited about the day.

Back on the hidden farm, Lorat and the Bordner outlaws were ready to head for Wilkon. Lorat, Rhey, Billy Joe, and Hixon were dressed as women, their heads and most of their faces covered by large, tied-down hats. All wore wigs as well, except for Lorat, whose long blond hair served the same purpose. Lorat actually made a pretty woman and made a point of saying so. Each man disguised as a woman carried a large purse containing two pistols each

Georgian, Bear, and Billy Joe were dressed as farmers and wore fake beards; handguns were shoved into overall pockets. It was decided that Bear's eye patch wasn't that distinctive, particularly if he kept a a full-brimmed hat pulled down. But Pickles himself would be too easily spotted. Lorat decreed that the half-breed would hold all of the getaway horses outside of town. Lorat and Bear were riding together in a carriage as husband and wife; Rhey and Georgian were in a buckboard as another married couple. Hixon and Billy Joe rode in a carriage. Their arrivals into town would be staggered so no one would pay any attention to them. The rest of Lorat's strategy was quite specific. Bear and Georgian would hit the bank with Billy Joe and Hixon waiting outside. Rhey and Lorat had the assignments of killing Holt Corrigan and James Hannah. All were excited about the day.

Deed and Atlee talked and laughed as they rode through the early morning. Streaks of rose and gold were turning the land into a rich presentation of the coming day. In the back of the buckboard, Benjamin was watching his tied, saddled horse. The mount was Chester, the older horse Deed had given the boy. Benjamin was going to compete in the boy's gymkhana. Elizabeth held her doll, Jessica, and sang a song only she knew.

Nestled against the wagon was Atlee's packed supper of fried chicken, complete with a pink bow, for the women's supper raffle. All of the money raised would go to improving the school. The wives went along with the fun, but the real emphasis was on the single men trying to guess which box belonged to which single woman. Mrs. Beinrigt had sent along a German chocolate cake to go into the cake contest. Atlee read aloud from the latest *Wilkon Epitaph* newspaper Deed brought, sharing all of the day's activities. In addition to the gymkhana and horse race, cake contest, and box-supper raffle, there would be a Mexican band, a band from the fort, horseshoes, and special activities for children. Homemade ice cream would be ready in the afternoon.

"Gosh, I can hardly wait!" Benjamin exclaimed. "How do you think I will do at the gymkhana?"

"You'll do great," Deed said, smiling. "Chester may be old, but he's one savvy fellow."

"Do you know what all they'll make us do?"

Deed shook his head. "No. That's a surprise."

"What if they make us jump?"

Atlee glanced at Deed, frowning.

"Haven't you and Chester jumped over a log?"

Benjamin nodded. "Oh yeah, lots of times."

"Well, then, you're ready. Just give Chester his head."

The Rafter C ranch came into sight and stopped Benjamin's concerns. Waiting for them at the entrance was Blue's family and Silka. The ranch would be protected by their regular hands, with the promise of a big steak dinner cooked by the ranch cook, Too Tall, a short, quick-tempered man with a flair for fixing good food.

No one thought the former samurai would be strong enough to go, but if he did, it would be in Blue's wagon. Silka would have none of it, insisting on riding his own horse.

Jeremy, Matthew, and Mary Jo were excited to meet Benjamin and Elizabeth, and it was quickly decided the children would all ride in Blue's buckboard.

Deed's fast-running Warrior was tied to the back of Blue's wagon; he planned to enter him in the race. The black-and-white horse had been rounded up last year in a group of mustangs. It was a Comanche warhorse that had taken to Deed and become a fine cow horse.

"How good to see you again, Atlee," Blue said and held out his hand.

"Oh, the pleasure is all mine, Blue. Your family is beautiful."

"Atlee, you remember my wife, Bina."

The two women were soon talking like old friends. Soon the joyful band was on the way again. A beautiful October day welcomed them. Wilkon was filling with people as their two wagons headed for the livery. Signs indicating where the various events were to be held highlighted most of the main street and the adjacent park.

Deed and Benjamin took their horses to the areas marked for them. The gymkhana was scheduled for the morning; the horse race would cap the day's activities. The baseball game between a town Red team and a town Green team was already under way. The boy asked if he could stay and watch the course be set up and Deed agreed, saying he would return shortly. Silka seemed to become more perky the closer they got to town. Quietly, Silka told Deed he was going to the barbershop and grinned.

The young gunfighter remembered the Chinese woman and smiled.

Bina and Atlee dropped off their supper boxes at the long table set up for that occasion and two smiling women accepted them and wrote down their names on the list of participants. Bina's box was wrapped with a blue ribbon, Atlee's with a pink one.

After dropping off Olivia Beinrigt's cake at the cake competition table, the two women guided the younger children to an area near the school where Rebecca Hannah and three other women were waiting. One was the new schoolteacher, Claire Baldwin. She had arrived yesterday, thanks to Billy Lee Montez bringing her in a buckboard to town from the station. Her blond hair was pulled back in a bun and she was filled with energy. The other two women were volunteers from town. They would be in charge of the children's activities, including a spelling bee for all ages.

Blue and Deed excused themselves and headed for the marshal's office to see Holt and James Hannah. In the alley next to the general store several men were beginning to work on making ice cream. Fiddle music filled the town with a lively sense of celebration. Later, a dance would be held in the street.

Holt greeted them at the doorway, holding a cup of coffee. "Hey, look here, it's my two favorite brothers! Come on in!"

They shook hands and Holt welcomed them inside. "Strongest thing I've got is hot coffee. But it's fresh."

"Sounds good to me," Deed countered. "Say, where's Tag?"

"Oh, he and a buddy hooked up to explore the town."

After pouring coffee for them and a few minutes of catch-up, Blue briefed him on the status of their ranch and the Bar 3. Both spreads were in good shape for the coming winter, with plenty of cut hay stored and the line cabins occupied. Most of the washes had been damned up to hold any water and all the regular water holes had been cleaned. New calves were being branded on both ranches as soon as they were spotted. The coolness of fall had driven away any signs of disease, no screwworm or black fly infections.

Shaking his head, Holt told them about his unfinished tour of the county, seeing the Hallorans again, meeting Logan Wheeler and his two children, and seeing the Johnsons once more. He told them about Judd and that his wife and son were staying in the hotel for now. Deed asked if he was interested in Allison and Holt shook his head, but said he couldn't leave them with Judd. He said the Hallorans had come by earlier this morning, and he hoped the Wheeler family would attend the day's festivities.

Blue asked if he had met the new teacher and Holt was surprised to hear she had arrived, then realized she had come when he was out of town.

"Say, where's Hannah? Sleeping in?" Deed asked, changing the subject.

"No. He's at the bank. In it, actually," Holt answered. "Been there since last night. We decided this would be a good day to rob the bank. What with everything going on." He blew on his coffee.

"Makes sense." Blue walked over to the window, sipped his coffee, and watched the street. "Don't think I've ever seen the town this busy." He glanced back at Holt. "We could've kept the bank closed, you know."

"Thought about that, but there are a lot of folks who'll want some money today. Good for business," Holt responded. "How's Silka?"

Deed chuckled and told him the samurai had ridden into town with them and had immediately gone to see a certain Chinese woman at the barbershop. He sat on the edge of the marshal's desk and tried his coffee. Very hot. He blew on its surface and tried another sip.

Finally finishing his coffee, he laid the empty cup on the desk. "I need to get back to the gymkhana. Atlee's boy is entering."

"You should be there . . . *dad,*" Holt teased.

Deed's neck reddened, but he grinned.

Blue put his cup down on the desk. "Yeah, we'd better catch up with the womenfolk."

"Sure," Holt said. "By the way, your Warrior will be going up against one of my Comanche horses. Littleson is going to ride him. Best I stay out of it."

"Hey, that'll be fun. Want to make a side bet?"

"Of course."

The three brothers laughed. Blue agreed to hold the wager and the other two brothers handed over their money. Blue and Deed headed for the door.

"We'll see you later," Deed said and left with his brother ahead of him.

"Looking forward to it."

Holt strolled over to the stove where the coffeepot sat. It was nearly empty, so he decided to make more now. A bark at the door told him Tag had completed his adventure. He opened the door and animal and

378

man greeted each other enthusiastically.

"Making some coffee, Tag," Holt said and returned to the stove. "Want some?" He chuckled.

After filling the pot with water from the big pitcher and filling a water dish for Tag, he went to the cupboard beside the stove to get the coffee sack.

Another knock on the door. Being sheriff meant being available. At the door were Allison and her mother and brother.

"Good morning, Sheriff," Allison cooed. "We just dropped by to see you . . . Thank you again for helping Mom."

It was awkward, but he had to be cordial. He invited them in and apologized for not having any coffee. Mrs. Johnson said they didn't intend to stay, just wanted to greet him. Oliver proudly told him that he had a job at the hotel, cleaning rooms, helping out at the front desk, in exchange for their room.

Allison tried to flirt with him and it had annoyed him. He had finally asked them to leave because he had work that needed doing.

Nodding, Mrs. Johnson said, "Oh, of course. How silly of us. I'm sure you're very busy. Come along, Allison. Oliver." She headed for the door.

At the door way, Allison mentioned the dance scheduled later and reminded him that her supper box was tied with a purple ribbon. After they left, he wished he had told her that he would be on duty. Instead, he had only muttered that it sounded like fun. He growled to himself and reached for the half-used sack of coffee. Tag rubbed against his leg.

"Yeah, I'll get you something to eat, too." He looked again in the cupboard and produced a piece of jerky for the dog.

From down the street came two quick booms! Hannah! Holt dropped the sack, grabbed a Winchester from the rack, and hurried out the door. He thundered down the boardwalk with townspeople jumping out of his way, unsure of what was happening at the bank. Others realized the shots were coming from the bank and ran for cover. The music stopped as if on cue. Tag barked and kept with him stride for stride. A carriage with an older couple skirted down the crowded street, somehow avoiding hitting anyone.

Outside the bank, Billy Joe and Hixon sat in the buckboard as planned and were uncertain what to do. From the commotion inside the bank, it was clear Marshal Hannah had been waiting. No one expected that.

"Let's make a break for it. Nobody'll figure we're part of this," Hixon said and unwrapped the reins from the brake.

"No, wait. Here comes Holt Corrigan. We'll get him. That'll spook that gunman marshal friend of his. We can still get the money. It'll be easy. Nobody else is gonna stop us," Billy Joe growled and put his hand on the reins to stop Hixon's retreat. "It'll be easy. Just let him turn his back to us."

Hixon swallowed. "A-all right." He drew a short-barreled revolver from his overalls pocket and held it at his side. Billy Joe was already holding a Winchester in his lap.

Holt hurried past him and into the bank, Tag at his side. From up the street, Blue and Deed ran toward the bank, coming as soon as they heard the shots, and saw what was happening. Both Hixon and Billy Joe aimed at Holt as he entered the bank.

"Those two in the buckboard are part of it." Deed knelt on one knee in the center of the now-vacant street, aimed, and fired his Remington.

"Look out, Holt!" Blue yelled.

Two steps behind, he drew his Walch Navy 12-shot revolver and fired in one motion, then fired again. Deed's shot struck Billy Joe in the temple and he collapsed against the front of the buckboard. His rifle looped in the air and thudded on the boardwalk. Hixon grabbed his leg as Blue's second shot drove into his right thigh. From inside the bank, Holt's two rifle shots sounded like one and Hixon stood in the wagon, staggered backward, and fell.

Resuming their rush to the bank, Deed and Blue hurried to the two downed outlaws.

"That's fine shooting, Deed," Blue said, looking at the black hole in the side of Billy Joe's head. His wig had dislodged from his scalp, along with the large bonnet, and lay in a pool of blood.

"Hell, Blue, I was aiming for his gut," Deed responded. "Holt, you all right in there?"

Tag wandered from the bank and stood as if on guard.

"Yes, but take a close look at those two," an unseen Holt yelled. "They're part of the Bordner bunch the Rangers took away.

Deed stared again at the bodies of Hixon and Billy Joe. "Of course. This is Willard Hixon." He pulled the unmoving body of Billy Joe aside so he could see his face. "And this is that scumbag they called Billy Joe. Tried to ambush us in the livery."

From across the street, inside the general store, a woman turned to her husband and proclaimed, "My God, Henry, they shot a woman. A woman!"

Hannah came from the bank, pushing Georgian ahead of him with the nose of his shotgun. "The other one's dead. Bear's what they called him. That means there's more somewhere in town."

"Yeah, plus whoever helped them get away from the Rangers." Deed shoved a new cartridge into his Remington.

"Wait, James," Holt said. "This is Georgian. He's a smart man. He'll tell us what happened. Might save his neck."

"Go to hell."

"Bad answer, asshole." Deed stepped against the outlaw and pressed his Remington against Georgian's stomach. "Remember, I'm not a lawman. It doesn't matter to me or anyone else if you make it back to the jail or not. Talk. Do it now. Actually don't. I'd much rather blow you apart."

The big outlaw tightened his mouth and Deed slapped him across the face with the nose of his gun. "Last chance."

"I-I . . . Rhey's half-brother broke us out. Lorat. He's crazy. Killed the Rangers, all of t-them. Caught them sleeping at Make-Camp Pond." Georgian stammered. "P-please . . . I didn't do it. Lorat and Rhey set all this up. I-I . . ."

"Of course, you were just an honest man caught up in a bad situation," Deed growled.

"P-please . . . don't shoot."

Deed spun away from the man. "That means there are three left."

Blue was outside, staring up the street. "I think we just found out where two of them are. They've got Bina and Atlee."

"What?" Deed began running toward the jail. Blue was a few steps behind him. Holt was standing beside the bank, talking to Hannah.

In the street, Rhey held Bina in one arm and Lorat held Atlee.

"Stop right there, boys . . . or your womenfolk die," Rhey commanded and pointed his pistol at Bina's head, then turned it back at the oncoming brothers. "We'll blow their brains all over this street."

Blue stopped, but Deed kept advancing. Across the street, he glimpsed a nervous man cowering behind a horse trough. He would be no worry. But leaning against the post outside the Blue Dog saloon was a well-dressed stranger. The tall man wore knee-high tan boots with his striped pants tucked inside them. A tailored vest and silk cravat set off a buckskin jacket with fringe. His short-brimmed fedora covered brown hair. He lit a black cheroot and watched the situation with no apparent inclination to get involved.

Deed decided the man was not a threat and turned his full attention back to the outlaws in the street.

Sneering, Lorat added his own command and pointed his pistol at Deed. "Bring up that buckboard, tied at the bank. When we're safe out of town, we'll leave these two lovely ladies." His forearm clasped Atlee's neck. "Maybe they'll be alive if you're quick about it . . . and they're nice to us." His laugh was taunting.

With his heavy pistol at his side, Blue turned toward Holt, still at the bank. "Holt, bring that buckboard up here. Hurry."

"That's a good boy." Lorat grinned. "Don't try coming any closer, Deed. I know your tricks. Both of you, drop your guns or we'll shoot. Got it?"

Deed took two more steps toward the two outlaws and stopped.

"I told you not to come closer . . . and I told you to drop your guns. You want me to shoot?" Lorat's voice was shrill and agitated.

Deed took another step closer; he was now fifteen feet from them. His Remington was at his side. "I get this, Lorat. You harm either of those women and I'll hunt you down and kill you like the dogs you are. It doesn't matter where you go, or what you try to do. Now . . . do you get it?"

Lorat's eyes widened and he blinked several times. "I said drop your gun."

Deed leaned over and laid his revolver on the ground in front of him.

"Stupid fool," Lorat sneered and pointed his gun at Deed.

From the schoolhouse area, Logan Wheeler came running. In his hands was his Henry. He skidded to a stop, knelt, and yelled, "Put down your guns. You're surrounded."

Both Lorat and Rhey glanced in the direction of the farmer. Glancing first at Deed, Atlee swung her purse directly up and into Lorat's face and spun away from his grasp. Almost at the same moment, Bina jammed a pair of scissors from her purse into Rhey's stomach. She, too, jerked away, diving to the ground.

Lorat screamed like a wild animal and aimed his gun to shoot at Wheeler. The farmer fired and missed. So did Lorat. Deed grabbed the throwing knife carried in a sheath behind his back, on the rawhide that also held the *bushido* brass circle. His throw was hard and direct, catching Lorat in his throat, up to the hilt. The outlaw seized the

386

knife to pull it free. Deed re-grabbed his Remington and fired in one motion.

"I'll kill you!" a wild-eyed Lorat gasped, blood spurting from his neck. Holding the knife in one hand, he tried to raise his gun.

Wheeler levered his Henry again and fired.

Lorat jerked sideways as both bullets hit him. Moving forward, Deed fired three more times into the blond outlaw.

Next to him, Rhey sat down in the street, holding his stomach with one hand, where a red spot was growing, and his gun in the other. Bina's scissors lay a few inches away. Wheeler ran over to Rhey and held his rifle on the downed outlaw.

"You sonuvabitch, you threatened my brother's wife and . . . the woman I love!" Deed screamed. His gun clicked on an empty chamber.

Wheeler forced Rhey to drop his gun and the farmer picked it up. Blue came to his brother, holding Bina with his lone arm. "It's over, Deed. He's dead."

Deed stared at Blue, then at Bina, blinked, and hurried to where Atlee stood. "Oh my God, are you all right?" He took her in his arms.

"Y-yes. Thanks to you."

He kissed her cheek.

A few feet away, Blue and Bina exchanged

quiet words. Holt wheeled the buckboard alongside his brothers and their women. Beside him on the bench was one of his black-handled Russian Smith & Wesson revolvers. Next to it was his medicine stone. His second handgun was propped out of sight, against his right leg, for easy reach. Tag was in the back, as if standing guard.

Stepping next to the buckboard, Deed studied the readied weapons and the special rock. "You weren't planning on giving them the buckboard, were you, big brother?"

"Seemed like a good idea."

Running from the bathhouse came a shirtless Silka. In one hand was his large sword. In the other, its sheath. The wounded Rhey Selmon saw the former samurai advancing, pointed at Silka, and yelled, "Keep that crazy bastard away from me! I'll tell you anything you want."

Chuckling, Deed yelled to Silka. "Thanks, old friend, but it's over. You can return to your . . . business."

Silka stutter-stepped to a stop, not yet believing or wanting to believe the fighting was over. He looked at Rhey, then the three brothers and Wheeler.

From the general store, the woman again declared that the Corrigans had killed two more women. This time, her husband told her that they were outlaws disguised as women. She wasn't certain. Another customer reinforced his assessment.

"I know him. Bear-coat man," the Japanese warrior declared. "Holt bring him in once before. Judge Pence praise."

"Yeah, I sure did," Holt said and clucked to the buckboard team to return them to the bank hitching rack and out of the street. Tag was now sitting beside him. Silka saluted and went back to the bathhouse.

All around the town, people were beginning to believe the shooting was over and coming out again. Claude Gausage, undertaker, had surfaced and was going about his business, dealing with the dead outlaws.

A merchant across the street yelled, "Sheriff Corrigan, is it safe again?"

Holt's voice was clear. "Yes, Wilkon is safe . . . again. Let's get on with our celebration."

Somewhere a cheer went up, then another. An older woman strutted out onto the boardwalk from the general store. She smiled brightly and cheered, "You saved our bank . . . again! Let's celebrate!"

Cheers began popping up throughout the town.

Hannah joined them, pushing Georgian ahead of him. "Keep moving. Remember, it would be easier for me to blow you away then to mess with you in my jail." Shifting his shotgun to his right hand, he waved at the Corrigan brothers and yelled, "Riders coming. Far end of town. Some of Taol's men and your Bar 3 hands." He pointed toward the south. "They're bringing something that'll make you smile. They've got that half-breed. That's the last of them."

"Yep. It's over."

Taking Atlee by the hand, Deed walked down the street. Men slapped him on the back as they passed; women smiled and thanked him. Near the bank, he met the oncoming band of men — ten vaqueros led by Taol Sanchez, and another eight riders from the Bar 3 led by Harmon. In front of the armed group was Pickles on a horse with his hands tied behind his back. He was sullen; his face carried marks of being hit.

"Taol and Harmon, you don't know how great it is to see you." Deed waved at the approaching riders. "And especially with your gift here."

Taol Sanchez broke away from the group and rode over to Deed on a magnificent black horse. They shook hands. Deed reminded him that he had met Atlee earlier and Taol took off his sombrero and bowed graciously.

"How'd you come across this guy?"

Taol told him that two Bar 3 cowhands were checking cattle on their far range when they spotted the empty prisoner wagon. The Bar 3 foreman, Harmon Payne, rode over to the Lazy S and the combined riders began backtracking the escaped outlaws. They found the deserted farm, the murdered farmer, and his wife. On the way to town, following the outlaws, they found the Bordner half-breed holding getaway horses.

"Well, it is good you are here," Deed continued. "The celebration will be twice as sweet." He glanced at the vaqueros. "You didn't bring your sisters?"

Taol's eyes twinkled. "*Sí*. They is come in the carriage. With mother and father. They knew they would be welcome with you Corrigans here."

Deed frowned. "If they aren't, no one is." He walked over to Harmon Payne, sitting on his horse with a rifle across his saddle. Not far away from Harmon was his Confederate friend, Everett.

"Awfully glad you're all right," Harmon said. "I was worried. That's one mean bunch and they had a big lead."

"Not mean enough, I guess," Deed said and introduced Atlee.

"Mighty glad to meet you, ma'am." Harmon touched his hand to his hat brim. "We were wondering what the boss found so fascinating about stagecoaches. Now we know." He smiled broadly.

Atlee returned the greeting.

Deed laughed and recited, " 'And this stern joy which warriors feel . . . In foemen worthy of their steel.' "

Harmon smiled. His love of Sir Walter Scott and Tennyson were well known by the Corrigan brothers. "You remembered. Sir Walter Scott's 'Canto V.' "

"Of course. After you drop off these two at the jail, I'll stand drinks for all of you."

"Sounds good to me, boss," the well-educated foreman said. "Then we're heading back. So are the Lazy S men. Don't feel comfortable leaving our range unprotected. Not if there might be more of these bastards around." He straightened his back. "Besides, R.J. is cooking them a big steak supper. Like Too Tall's doing."

"Take along some bottles of good whiskey when you go. They earned it." Deed walked over to Everett and introduced him to Atlee. "This is one of my best friends from . . . after the war."

Everett smiled widely and leaned over his saddle to take her offered hand.

CHAPTER THIRTY

Finally the day got back on track. Music once again filled the town. Holt wired Ranger headquarters providing an update of the situation. The return wire was immediate and thankful. Benjamin and Chester did well in the gymkhana, taking third place. A young clerk won the footrace, as he had for three years in a row. The Red team beat the Green team 8 to 3. Mrs. Beinrigt's cake took second in the cake-baking contest and Deed bought it in the auction that followed.

The big horse race drew significant competitors. In addition to Deed riding one of Holt's bay Indian ponies, Taol entered with his black horse, Kornican Tiorgs brought a fine sorrel, and the stranger Deed had seen earlier brought over a white Arabian. A clerk decided to compete with his own horse, a short-coupled bay mustang. At the last minute, Mayor Patterson Cooke decided to enter a steel-gray horse, to be ridden by his twenty-year-old son. Around the starting line, heavy betting was underway.

Deed left his gun belt with Blue. His saddle was already free of its saddle gun. Holt stood near the starting line, smoking a cigar. He walked over to his younger brother, checking his cinch.

"Ride well, little brother. I hope you come in second." He laughed and so did Deed. The youngest Corrigan didn't see his older brother slip the cardinal feather from his hatband between Deed's saddle and saddle blanket.

After mounting, Deed leaned close to Warrior's neck and whispered a Comanche phrase Bina had given him earlier, blessing the horse and asking it to run like the wind. Bina herself left the other spectators and came over. Without saying a word, she tied an eagle feather to its headband, whispered something to the powerfully built paint horse, and returned. Deed's gaze found Atlee's and their eyes made love.

Beside her was Silka, smiling proudly. He touched the brass circle at his neck and Deed returned the tribute.

Six horses were now officially entered and standing at the starting line. The race would be a mile long, out north of town and back.

Four judges on horseback were stationed along the course, so no competitor could turn early or foul other riders. The turn-around point was an old elm, white and gnarly against the gray sky. The tree had to be circled. Off to the side, several boys had been secured to hold town dogs away from the running horses. Holt had Tag in his arms.

"Riders to the ready," the starter yelled and cocked his starter gun. "Get set. Go!" He fired into the air.

The horses broke as one and galloped smoothly away. Tiorgs's big sorrel took the early lead but Deed held Warrior to an easy ground-eating stride three horses back. Taol's black horse was right beside him. The cheers and yells of the crowd were lost in the thundering hooves. The course initially followed a narrow creek bed, crossed a wide strip of sand and cactus, and followed an uneven line of oak and pecan trees, then opened into a wide expanse clotted with mesquite and offering some surprising gullies.

With the horses spreading out some, Warrior was the third to reach the sand. Fine sprays of gravel peppered against Deed's face as they ran through this ragged piece of the race.

"Stay steady, Warrior. Your time will come. Steady now."

Tiorgs's horse was tiring and soon the stranger's white Arabian took the lead. Tiorgs's horse was slipping fast. Deed and Warrior settled into fourth, behind Taol, Littleson, and the stranger. The clerk pulled up with his horse limping. Oak and pecan branches slapped at all their faces, but with little effect.

The turning point elm was soon reached and left behind. The white horse had opened a two-length lead with Taol in second and Littleson's borrowed horse from Holt, third. Tiorgs was fourth. Deed and the mayor were in the rear.

Five hundred yards from the finish line, Deed slapped Warrior on the withers with his reins. "Now, Warrior!"

As if waiting for the okay, the big horse began to run as if the other horses were standing still. The eagle feather flattened against his neck. Deed's hat flew off, held at his neck by its stampede string. They closed in on Tiorgs and the Scotsman reached down and grabbed at Deed's cinch, popping it loose, as Warrior ran past him. He laughed wickedly.

Deed realized what had happened. His saddle was now loose, simply resting on

Warrior's back with nothing holding it in place. All he could do was to keep balanced and keep Warrior running. Trying to retie the cinch would be next to impossible and likely to cause him to fall off. The best thing he had going for him was that the horse was used to all kinds of saddles.

"Come on, Warrior! I'll stay on. You win this thing," Deed whispered, leaning forward. If the saddle slipped, he would try to jump up and stay on the horse.

Deed and Warrior passed Littleson's Indian pony, then Taol's, and ran by the stranger's Arabian with twenty yards to go.

"You are the wind, *amigo*," Taol yelled as Warrior thundered past the Mexican's horse. "Ride, *amigo*, ride!" The Mexican saw the loosened cinch and bit his lip.

Warrior and Deed crossed the finish line to the cheers of the Corrigans and some others. In second came Taol, followed by the stranger's Arabian. Littleson was fourth and Tiorgs and the mayor's mount tied for last. Benjamin was first to reach Deed as he slowed the horse to a trot, then a walk. Finally, he jumped down and the saddle came with him.

"I knew you'd do it, Deed. I knew it!" the boy beamed.

"Thank you, son. He's quite a horse. I just

had to sit on him."

Carrying the saddle over his shoulder, Deed began walking Warrior to cool him down. He and Benjamin headed toward the buckboard where Deed tossed the saddle into the back and tied up the heavily sweating horse. A bedraggled red feather fell on the ground. Deed glanced at it, then took two big towels from the wagon and began rubbing Warrior's back. Blue came over and congratulated him, giving him the earlier side bet. Holt joined in, looking surprisingly happy.

"Wow! Got beat by a tornado. That was something," he said and slapped Deed on the back. "By the way, I did well." He grinned. "Bet on you to win. Put one down for you, too." He grinned and looked at the ground. "Actually, I just came over to get this back." He bent over and picked up the ruffled cardinal feather, stroked it with his fingers, and returned the small plume to his hatband, grinning like a cat who'd just emptied a bowl of cream. "You won't need it anymore."

Deed nodded. "I see. Glad it was with me."

"Probably kept you from falling. What happened with your saddle? I saw the cinch flapping."

"More likely it was my two legs." Deed told him what Tiorgs had done.

"That sonuvabitch! I'm going to arrest him."

Deed smiled. "I'll take care of it. You just be your wonderful gentle self." He shook his head. "Who's at the jail?"

"Well, Hannah's there . . . and his new deputy. Logan Wheeler replaced the wounded one when Bordner's boys first came to town," Holt said, walking with them.

"Glad to hear it. He'll make a good one," Deed said, continuing to dry off Warrior. "What's he going to do with his kids while he's working?"

"Rebecca's going to watch them. She loves children."

One by one, the other riders came by with their congratulations. Taol was first and the most gracious. Littleson was impressed that Holt's Comanche pony had been beaten by another Comanche horse. Mayor Cooke stomped his boots and brushed his shirt before coming up to Deed. His son had disappeared into the crowd.

"*Ja,* I am better stick to *mein* business." Cooke held out his hand to Deed. "Should haff known myself better than to ride against a Corrigan." That was followed with a German expression of praise and a sub-mission of the cash prize for winning the race.

"Thanks. It was great fun. You've got a fine horse there . . . and your son rides very well." Deed accepted the money, then handed it back. "Here, put it with your fund for the town."

"Danke."

Behind them, boys were walking the weary horses to cool them down. Only the clerk and his horse were absent. Deed guessed he had taken the animal into the livery to care for it.

Tiorgs stomped past him, leading his horse and hoping to avoid Deed's stare. "Naethin' guid ta come from this day. I shoulda known."

Deed stepped in front of him. "You and I need to settle something, Tiorgs."

The Scotsman tensed. "What are ye speakin' of?"

"My cinch."

"Nay, I dinna' know what ye be speakin'."

Deed put his hand on the Scotsman's shoulder. "Usually I wouldn't give a man who tried to kill me a second chance. But I'm feeling real charitable today, Tiorgs." He pushed the Scotsman backward. "I don't want to see you again. Ever. If I do, you will die. No one does that. You're a piece of crap."

"I dinna' wear a gun."

"Won't matter. Get out of here before I change my mind about waiting."

Watching him pass, Holt said, "Be sure you take care of that fine horse, Tiorgs. You didn't do too well with the last one you ran hard."

The Scotsman gave him a hard look, uttered a Scottish curse, but kept moving.

"Easy now, Tiorgs. We don't allow cussing in public, you know," Holt snapped.

Tiorgs humphed and pulled on his horse to move faster.

Behind them came heavy footsteps. Deed turned to see the stranger. He was smiling.

"That was some ride, friend," the stranger said. "Didn't think anyone could catch my Arabian." He held out his hand. "Meden Taliff. Just came to town two days ago. I'm an attorney." His handsome face met Deed's. "Kinda like the way Wilkon is growing."

"Glad to meet you, Meden. I'm Deed. Deed Corrigan," the youngest Corrigan brother said. "These are my brothers, Blue . . . and Holt."

Blue and Holt shook Taliff's hand. Deed then introduced Benjamin and praised the boy's performance in the gymkhana.

"Think you were out of town on business when I came in, Sheriff," Taliff said. "Glad to make your acquaintance. You Corrigan boys have quite a reputation, you know."

Holt said, "I'm sure Judge Pence will be eager to meet a fellow of the court. He's the federal circuit judge. Thought he'd make it for today's celebration, but I guess he got tied up."

"Heard the name. Looking forward to meeting him," Taliff said. "The mayor asked me to become justice of the peace and I accepted. So I'm sure we'll be working together. Saw you boys in action earlier. You don't mess around."

"Didn't have much choice," Deed responded and asked Benjamin to walk Warrior again. "Don't let him drink. Yet."

The boy beamed at being given this responsibility and led the big animal away proudly. Taliff lit a black cheroot and asked, "Will there be a trial for the men you arrested today? Here?"

"Whenever Pence gets here. His call. We just arrest them," Holt responded.

Taliff's eyes narrowed for an instant. "Maybe I'll see if they need legal counsel. From what I've heard, there were no witnesses to this Ranger breakout."

If either Holt or Deed were surprised, they didn't show it.

"Every rat bastard deserves a fair trail. Have at it, but it's pretty hard to deny an attempted bank robbery . . . and attempted murder of two women," Deed growled. "Not to mention attempting to kill the sheriff. I don't think you'll make much of an impression defending them in Wilkon. Your decision." He saw Atlee working through the crowd. "You'll excuse me, Mr. Taliff . . . Holt. Got a pretty lady coming my way."

"Of course. Talk to you later, Deed," Taliff said, turning to Holt. "You might like to know I am of the Southern persuasion. Some of us hoped you wouldn't accept the amnesty."

Holt's face froze in anger. "Interesting. Well, there's nothing keeping your friends and you from trying to resurrect Dixie."

"That's not what I meant."

"Yeah, that's what's sad." Holt said. "Excuse me, but I've got to collect on some bets." He walked away without another word.

Atlee hurried next to Deed. "Oh, you were magnificent."

"I had a great horse. Let's go check on him."

With Atlee at his side, Deed went to Benjamin and Warrior. The fine paint horse was cooled and ready for water. After watering him, Deed tied his lead rope to the buckboard and gave the horse a nosebag of oats. Then the happy threesome went over to the box supper raffle.

Holt gathered his personal winnings and looked around to see where Deed was walking to give him his personal winnings. From across the open field, he saw the mayor, Taliff, and the new schoolteacher walking. When he saw her face, he was stunned. This woman. This woman. Where had he been with her before? Another life? He couldn't remember feeling this way about a woman. He was sweating. And cold. At the same time. She glanced his way and their eyes met for an instant. For Holt, it was like getting hit in the stomach. She quickly turned her attention to Taliff and laughed gaily at something he said.

All Holt could think of was to get away. He needed to be alone. To think. He went to the jail and told Hannah and Wheeler to go enjoy the box supper. He would watch the prisoners. Both men were glad to have the opportunity.

The box supper auction was lively. Blue and Deed bought their women's offerings for five dollars each. Allison tried to find Holt to remind him which box was hers. She gave up and Logan Wheeler bought it for two dollars. Behesba Miller also looked briefly for Holt, but was just as happy to have her offering bought by one of the town's leading men. Hannah bought his wife's supper for two dollars as well.

Everyone spread out to eat, and the Corrigans went inside the schoolhouse as the day was cooling. After a dinner of fried chicken and biscuits, Blue and Bina headed home with their children, deciding to leave the dancing to the townsfolk. Silka rode with them, weary but happy.

Deed, Atlee, Benjamin, and Elizabeth were close behind. A warm blanket covered the children and another was wrapped around the adults' legs in front. Elizabeth wore a paper crown displaying "Bee – 6" to show she had won her spelling-bee age group. Benjamin chattered about the day for a long time before falling asleep. At the stage station, Deed lifted the boy and carried him to his bed; Atlee carried Elizabeth.

Standing beside the rejuvenated fire, Atlee and Deed held each other. She stared into his eyes. "Deed Corrigan, I asked you to wait for me."

"I will wait for you . . . forever."

"I want to marry you now."

CHAPTER THIRTY-ONE

The next day was both bright . . . and ugly. It was bright at the Rafter C, where plans were being made for a wedding on Thanksgiving day, a traditional gathering for the Corrigans and their friends as Deed and Atlee shared the news. Silka was easily the most excited and kept proclaiming that the ceremony should include some traditional Japanese aspects. Deed thought it would be fun to do; Atlee wasn't so sure.

In town, however, the day began ugly.

Before dawn, Judd Johnson, drunk and vicious, tried to find his wife and children, going from saloon to saloon, yelling and making threats. In the Trail Dog, he made the mistake of getting into an argument with a freighter who was starting his day with some whiskey. In the ensuing fistfight, Judd hit his head against the bar and died. Deputy Wheeler was the only lawman on duty at the time, so he couldn't leave the jail. The bartender handled the situation, getting Gausage out of bed. Both made the decision that the death was an accident, due to self-defense. Mrs. Johnson, Allison, and Oliver were the only people to come to the undertaker. It was said none of them cried.

With Tag at his side, Holt walked along the quiet boardwalk from his sheriff's living quarters to the jail. He had laid down in his clothes, but had barely slept, and finally got up, shaved, and fed Tag. Here and there were left-behinds from yesterday's celebration. He stepped over a drunk asleep propped against a building. Somebody had left his fiddle and Holt picked it up.

"We'd better keep this so it doesn't get broken."

Tag smelled the instrument and woofed. The drunk stirred, smiled, and mumbled, "That's my favorite, Jimmy."

They walked on, passing several empty supper boxes. He would talk to Hannah about getting three or four boys to make a run through the town, picking up trash. Maybe Wheeler's boy would like to make a couple of extra dollars. His mind drifted once again to yesterday. Seeing Claire Baldwin was like a strange dream. Almost like he had been drunk.

On the way, he saw a crow perched on the

corner of an overhanging roof. A sign of bad luck, he told himself. Damn. He reached into his pocket and felt for the reassurance of his medicine stone.

At the jail, he thanked Wheeler, and the tired farmer was glad to get to get some rest. He and his children were staying in the hotel. Before leaving, Wheeler suggested putting the fiddle on top of the small cabinet so it would be out of the way. Then he told Holt the prisoners had been fed their breakfast and taken out back to relieve themselves.

Rhey Selmon was the only prisoner awake as Holt placed the fiddle on top of the cabinet and made certain it wouldn't fall.

"Corrigan! Why don't you start your day real nice and let us go. I promise we'll ride out of here and never come back. The whole town's asleep. You can say we busted out during the night."

Holt told him that he was in no mood for jokes.

"Aw, come on, man. You know we'd keep riding. My half-brother was the crazy one and your brother killed him," Rhey said, standing against the bars. Behind him, Hixon mumbled something no one understood.

"You'll be lucky if you get any further than

a hanging."

Rhey swallowed and retreated from the bars.

Holt made a fresh pot of coffee and put a short log into the cast-iron stove to help chase away the edge of cold that had settled in the office. He poured himself a cup and sat behind the marshal's desk. He drank a little of the hot brew and pulled his medicine stone from his pocket, fingered it, and laid the small rock on the desk. It had helped him get through some bad scrapes, he was certain. Even Silka believed.

Hannah was sleeping in and wasn't due until the afternoon, so he would be alone until then. Hopefully, the town would remain quiet, recovering from yesterday's activities.

Beside his chair, Tag was sleeping.

Holt's own lack of sleep was catching up with him. He was unable to get the new schoolteacher out of his mind. It was silly, he kept telling himself, but that didn't seem to matter. His mind relived seeing her and wishing he had gone over and at least introduced himself. What a fool.

A knock on the jail door broke his strange musings. He pulled one of his revolvers from his shoulder holsters and cocked it. Tag raised his head and growled.

"Come in," he said without looking up, and cocked the gun. "With your hands empty."

Into the small room stepped Claire Baldwin. She was stunning in a blue-and-white herringbone suit with large blue buttons and a short cape. A large blue hat set off her blond hair and matched her eyes. Seeing the gun, she was startled.

"Oh, I'm sorry, Sheriff. I didn't mean to scare you."

"You didn't. It comes with the badge." Holt chuckled, uncocked the gun, and returned the Russian Smith & Wesson to its holster.

"Maybe this isn't a good time," she said and smiled tentatively. "I don't believe we've had the opportunity to meet."

Holt stood, almost losing his balance. "Uh, h-how are you, Miss Baldwin? Please come in. P-please."

She walked into the office, to the desk, holding out her hand. "I wish that you would call me Claire."

Tag approached her; his tail, wagging.

"Y-yes, ma'am . . . uh, Claire. I'm Holt Corrigan."

"Everyone knows who you are, Holt Corrigan. You and your brothers are known all around this region." She leaned down and

411

patted the dog.

Holt realized he was staring at her and finally asked, "Would you like some coffee? I just made it." His smile was genuine. "If you keep giving Tag attention like that, he'll never go away."

"Coffee sounds great. May I sit down?" She looked up and met his eyes. "Tag, is it? He's a fine fellow. Reminds me of the dog I had growing up."

Holt shook his head. "Where are my manners? Of course, please sit down." He rushed around the desk and held a chair for her. He went to the cabinet and retrieved a coffee cup, then grabbed the coffeepot from the cast-iron stove.

"Would you like sugar . . . Claire? I'm sorry to tell you that we don't have any cream."

"One teaspoon. Please." She rested her large handbag on the floor beside her chair.

As he was returning to the desk, she asked him about the medicine stone lying there. "What is this, Holt? I feel like I've seen it somewhere before. May I hold it?"

"Sure. It's just an old rock I came across."

"I don't think so. It looks magical to me."

He handed her the cup, told her it was quite hot, and explained the stone's significance. It surprised him that he told her, the words just jumping from his mouth. And that began a conversation that lasted for over an hour with both sharing highlights of their respective childhoods. She had grown up in Indiana and played with Indian children of the Upper Kispoko band of the Shawnee tribe. She was certain that an old shaman had owned a stone identical to Holt's. As they talked, her eyes danced with his and time was forgotten.

She told him about her reluctance to come to Wilkon after hearing about Agon Bordner and his plans to control the region. When she heard the Corrigan brothers had defeated the outlaw king, she changed her mind. He told her they were still dealing with the last of the gang and motioned toward the cells.

A heavy knock was followed by a stocky blacksmith rushing inside.

"Holt! Holt! Oh, excuse me, ma'am," the blacksmith said, waving his arms.

"That's quite all right. Is something the matter?" Holt asked, trying to hide being annoyed at the interruption.

"Rider coming up the street," the townsman said, catching his breath. "He's yelling that Judge Pence has been murdered. Found his body a mile outside of town."

Holt rose and went toward the rifle rack.

Claudia reached down for her heavy purse.

"I've got to go." He winced.

"Of course. I understand. I want to continue this conversation, so I will wait to hear of your return."

He raced out the door to his already saddled horse, mounted, and rode off with Tag running beside them. Just down the street a bit, he turned in his saddle and looked back at her.

She was standing in front of the marshal's office, waving at him.

ABOUT THE AUTHOR

Cotton Smith's novels bring an exciting picture of the human spirit making its way through life-changing trials, driving through physical and emotional barriers, and resurrecting itself from defeat. His stories of the West are praised for historical accuracy, unexpected plot twists, and memorable characters. They are also enjoyed for their insightful descriptions of life of that era — and for their rousing adventure. *Dallas Morning News* said, "This western writer has a keener fidelity to history than any of his predecessors." *Publishers Weekly* said, "Smith knows cattle drives and cowboy lore."